TIN MONKEYS

Andrenik V. Sergoyan

More works by Andrenik Y. Sergoyan

A Lion for Lambs
Crenel Publishing
Copyright © 2013 by Andrenik Y. Sergoyan

Sword of the Perithia, The Age of Ash
CreateSpace Publishing LLC
Copyright © 2013, 2015 by Andrenik Y. Sergoyan

Social Media

Website: http://andreniksergoyan.weebly.com/#/
Facebook: https://www.facebook.com/andreniksergoyan

Tin Monkeys

Andrenik Y. Sergoyan

Copyright © 2015 by Andrenik Y. Sergoyan

1st Edition
ISBN-13: 978-1519275424
ISBN-10: 1519275420
Manufactured in the United States of America
First Edition: 2015, CreateSpace Publishing LLC
First Mass Market Edition: 2015

Author's Note

Though Tin Monkeys is a work of fiction, all historical events described herein are based on actual events and often are described exactly how they reportedly occurred.

In addition, all technology discussed—no matter how surreal—has been proven theoretically possible, if not already a reality.

And finally, all psychological and physiological phenomena discussed in this book are based on proven scientific research and accepted theories.

If you find yourself experiencing any symptoms similar to those described within these pages, please seek the aid of a medical professional immediately.

Sometimes truth is stranger than fiction.

Enjoy

For Amanda

I love you more than you'll ever know

Without you, my Daemons would run amuck

Contents

Chapter 1 1

Chapter 2 5

Chapter 3 16

Chapter 4 27

Chapter 5 31

Chapter 6 35

Chapter 7 38

Chapter 8 43

Chapter 9 47

Chapter 10 58

Chapter 11 64

Chapter 12 67

Chapter 13 72

Chapter 14 79

Chapter 15 83

Chapter 16 91

Chapter 17 94

Chapter 18 100

Chapter 19 110

Chapter 20 115

Chapter 21 122

Chapter 22 136

Chapter 23 142

Chapter 24 149

Chapter 25 156

Chapter 26	165
Chapter 27	176
Chapter 28	182
Chapter 29	188
Chapter 30	195
Chapter 31	198
Chapter 32	201
Chapter 33	215
Chapter 34	221
Chapter 35	223
Chapter 36	229
Chapter 37	232
Chapter 38	236
Chapter 39	239
Chapter 40	244
Chapter 41	249
Chapter 42	253
Special Thanks	257

Chapter 1

The woman at the end of the bar is giving me fuck-me eyes. I'm a little surprised considering the state I'm in. But it's just a glance here and there—she's too timid for prolonged eye contact. Still, I know what she wants. I, however, am far from timid. My stare is that of a man eyeing a cut of filet mignon. Even tonight of all nights, I can't help but fantasize about plunging face first between those enormous breasts. And she's alone; has been for the better part of an hour. Already three appletini's in. One more and she'll fall off that bar stool. I'm alone too, for that matter, and though she's no runway model, any other day of the week I'd have her up to my apartment and out of that black silk dress faster than you could say prophylactic.

But not tonight. Tonight I have some serious drinking to do. Tonight I need to get myself good and numb. I need to push down every ounce of humanity I have left; just drown the fuckers in a lake of scotch. It's the only way I'll be able to do what has to be done. It's the only way I'll be able to pull the trigger and put a good woman to rest. It's the only way I'll be able to kill my partner.

It's not like I haven't killed anyone before. Seven human beings are no longer on this Earth because they met me. Four I put in the ground during my military career—three all in the same firefight. Two I shot during my tenure with the FBI, and the seventh, well, the seventh I don't talk about.

All of those people were rotten, they were evil, they didn't deserve to breathe the same air as the rest of us. But my new partner, Anne Goodwin, she's, well, she's a good person. She doesn't deserve any of this, least of all to die. But what choice do I have? I tell myself it's a mercy killing. *If I don't do it, they'll haunt us both until we blow our own brains out. This is mercy I'm giving her!*

"Brian, another," I say to the bartender. He's the closest thing I have to friend anymore. He pours me another glass of Macallan Single Malt. I'm drinking the good stuff tonight. And why shouldn't I? It helps. It really helps. A few more glasses and I won't even hesitate. A few more glasses and I'll wake up tomorrow free from all of this; free from her, free to forget all about the Mad Doctor, free from the demons in my head.

"Tying one on tonight, Bill?" Brian asks. "Rough day at the office?"

"You could say that." *But my rough day is just getting started.*

A woman's voice at my back; "Bill Singer?" A familiar voice, high and reedy like a child's. Most likely she was molested at a young age. I don't turn to face her though. I need time to remember her name, to remember how we left it. Luckily, recall has never been a problem for me, even after eight glasses of scotch.

"Sarah, how are you?"

"Good. Great. I'm just fucking great, Bill." She sits down in the empty barstool next to me, grabs up my glass of scotch, and guzzles it down like its cheap well whiskey. "Oh wait. No, no I'm not great. Actually, Bill, I'm pretty shitty. Actually, Bill, I have the clap. Thanks for that, asshole."

Don't mention it. "The gift that keeps on giving," I say. "Brian, one more scotch, please. Better make it two."

Eyes ever forward. I don't look at her but I can see her wobbly double image in the mirror behind the bar. It's hard to look at yourself in the mirror when you're a piece of shit and you know it. It's even harder when one of the people you stepped on is sitting beside you poised to stab you in the neck with a cocktail straw.

"So you admit it? You knew?"

Why would I even bother answering her? No I didn't know. Some Georgetown freshman gave it to me the night before I met her. I didn't start pissing razors until two days later. Actually, up until now I figured Sarah had given it to me. But who cares? STDs are an occupational hazard for people like Sarah and I. She'll figure that out soon enough if she keeps spreading her legs for men she just met at a bar and forgoes a rubber because, as she put it, I have honest eyes. *Honest eyes won't spare you a trip to the doctor, sweetheart.*

Brian places two glasses of scotch down on the bar, one in front of each of us. As she reaches for hers, I snatch it away and gobble it down, then take a firm hold on the single remaining glass. "Something I can do for you?" Another swallow, eyes ever forward. It's not that I'm scared to look at her, more that I simply don't care enough to turn my head.

"Something you can…? Fuck you, you piece of shit! You told me you'd call. You told me we had something special. That when you got back from wherever the fuck they were sending you, you wanted to take me somewhere tropical."

I really don't have time for this bullshit. I have to get ready, mentally ready, and Sarah the "slap me, daddy," one and done hairdresser from three weeks ago is not helping one bit with the mental gymnastics I'm trying to perform here.

"Somewhere trop—I was drunk, Sarah. You were drunk. We fucked. It was magical. I'll never forget our night together. Now let's just move on, okay?" *God, my shoulder is killing me.*

"Magical? Oh was it magical? I could barely walk the next day!"

"Sounds like a job well done to me." Another sip of scotch. With each swallow I grow more and more tired of her whinny, baby voice. It's like an ice pick in my ear. How on Earth I ever found it sexy, even for an instant, is beyond comprehension.

"You think because, what, because you're some big-shot FBI man, because you did all that hero shit, that the rest of us are just your urinal to piss on? You think just because you saved a few lives that you can shit all over the rest of us? Well I got news for you, motherfucker." I wait for it. I wait and wait and wait but the news she promised never comes. Eventually I turn to her and stare her straight in the face. She looks ready to explode. She has the mien of three-year-old about to launch into an uncontrollable temper tantrum.

"You can't!" is her final edict. Then she reaches for my scotch to most assuredly dump it over my head, but I deftly slide the glass aside safely out of the toddler's reach. Frustrated and defeated, instead she picks up a dry bar napkin and tries to toss it in my face. It makes lazy snowflake arcs down to the floor.

Sarah huffs and turns to leave, but not before saying, "And you look like shit. Get some help, asshole. You're two shades away from a corpse."

The woman at the end of the bar in the silk dress is no longer too timid to hold eye contact with me. Only now she wears a mask of disgust.

It's alright, beautiful. I disgust me too.

One more gulp of scotch and I feel ready to do something truly disgusting. I feel ready to kill my partner.

Chapter 2

Unless it's a serial that crosses state lines or we got a terror cell on our hands, we don't typically get called in on homicides. Sure, on occasion they'll make an exception. Like when the whole scene is just too bat-shit bizarre for local law enforcement to make any sense of it. Then they bring us in. Then they send for *The G-Men*. Only, I can't call us that anymore. Charles is dead and in the ground and my new partner, Special Agent Anne Goodwin, lacks the necessary parts to be a *G-Man*.

I wonder what Charles would've thought of this case? Bizarre as it is, it lacks that macabre vibe he was always so fond of. As if we didn't see enough sick shit throughout the work week; his idea of relaxation was a six-pack of Heineken and a European slasher flick. According to Charles, the socialists across the pond made the really good stuff. They didn't pull any punches. Nothing was taboo, especially for the Germans. Why am I not surprised?

Each week he'd try and bombard me with gruesome mental images—scenes from some godawful horror flick he'd watched over the weekend. The last one, something about centipedes and rim jobs, was his new favorite. Who the hell knows? I always tuned him out when he went all dark on me. Sick shit aside though; I miss that son of a bitch.

But no more Charles. No more questions like, "Do you think it would kill a man if you drove both your thumbs into his eye sockets?" No more brilliant anecdotes like, "Did you know if you mix fifty parts bleach and one part acetone, you get chloroform? Would make picking up those college girls you love so much, that much easier. Of course without any ether it'll decompose to phosgene in the liver, which is pretty much guaranteed to give you cancer."

No more chasing tail at the sports bar on 35th. No more bailouts when one too many *adult sodas* sends me into a fit of rage towards the dart-playing frat boy who just spilt his beer on my shirt and is two seconds away from losing those perfectly straight, perfectly white front teeth.

No, not anymore.

Now it's Agent Goodwin. Now it's Miss Palates and TechCrunch and rainbows and bubblegum farts. Now it's three hours on a plane listening to her prattle on about how excited she is to be working with the famous—*or am I infamous?*—Special Agent Bill Singer. And six more hours in a stuffy Suburban on our way to the armpit of America to try and make sense of a seemingly impossible murder / suicide / who-the-fuck-knows-soon-to-be-cold-case. If I have to look into those puppy dog eyes one more time and hear another of her vapid apologies about the loss of my partner, I'm going to...

Where the fuck did we lose him, Goodwin? Can you find him for me! He's not lost, he's dead! Dead with a round lodged in his skull just above his right eye. Dead without an exit wound, just a .22 caliber bullet that made puree of his brains.

It's one of the cleanest ways to kill someone. You place a .22 to the temple and pull the trigger. The round goes in but lacks the velocity to punch back out through the skull. Instead it just ricochets around until their brains turn to soup. No exit wound, no blood splatter analysis, no mess on your overalls. Charles told me this our first week on the job. And I bet right about now he's pissing in his grave.

"What, no mess? No .50 cal. head explosion? No chainsaw to the back of the neck bloodbath? Just a clean and simple small arms head wound?"

I take a drag off my cigarette and another pull from my flask. I'd filled it on the plane just before we landed. But first I had the flight attendant bring me a double whiskey and coke, hold the coke. Then I had her bring me another. Then four more just to make sure my liver got the point. Then she cut me off. That's usually about the time Charles would jump in and make up some brilliant line of bullshit to keep the party going. But Agent Goodwin is no Charles. Still, by the time we landed in Branson I was properly sedated and ready to endure six more hours of my new partner explaining to me how pivotal Doctor Theodore Grant's research into quantum mechanics and particle physics had been, and how much she had loved watching his weekly television show, *Unlocking the Secrets of the Universe*, and how she'd read all his books, and how respected he was in the scientific community for his Nostradamus-like ability to predict the future of technology. Hell, he even had a Noble Prize. Of course this was all years before he, well, before he vanished off the face of the Earth.

For Christ's sake, Charles used to relax by downing a six-pack in front of the idiot-box watching psychos in ski-masks chop teen skinny-dippers to tiny bits with hatchets. Anne Goodwin relaxes with a glass of pinot and her never less than a month old, top-of-the-line tablet, reading e-books on the physical principles of quantum theory, or the advancement of artificial intelligence, or some horse shit about the existence of Big Foot and space aliens.

Doctor Theodore Grant… She's telling me all this because somewhere deep in the remoteness of the Ozarks is a cabin with an electric, booby-trapped front-door and a pile of ash and bone on the floor that's presumably Dr. Theodore Grant's mortal remains. We won't know for certain if it's Doctor Grant until forensics come back in a few days, but Agent Goodwin is convinced it's him. After all, his wallet was found at the scene along with several dozen framed pictures of him and his late wife, not to mention according to the initial police report the interior is a sci-fi junkie's wet dream. I guess I'll acquiesce to the fact there's a damn good chance the *Mad Doctor* had at least paid the place a visit recently.

My head's pounding. It always aches, especially first thing in the morning and late in the day after my midday topper has begun to wear off. And just five minutes in the passenger seat with the prattling Agent

Goodwin at the helm, I have to take another pull from my flask. I poured ten airplane bottles worth of Kentucky whiskey into it before getting off the plane. They weren't hard to palm off the drink cart. Not much of a whiskey drinker, but I figure, when in Rome.

"Are we in Kentucky yet?" I ask.

Agent Goodwin glances down at the flask. I've never felt so much condescension in my entire life. Even my ex-wife never looked at me like that. "We're heading to Arkansas, not Kentucky, Bill. Just across the border. It's all in the file I gave you on the plane."

I never opened it. Kentucky, Arkansas, Missouri, what's the difference? Another pull from my flask. Another look from Goodwin.

"You ah, you sure you should be—"

Don't finish that fucking sentence, little girl! All it takes is a look; just one look to shut her up. Then I take a third pull. Not that I was ready for another drink, mind you, but just to spite her. An over exaggerated swallow, and then I tuck the flask back into my coat pocket, safe and out of sight. A few breath mints mixed with the innocuous Dilaudid and I'm ready for hours three through six of our little adventure.

My cigarette's toast, so I toss it and light another. Eventually the silence grows too loud for Agent Goodwin to stand. She says, "Are there any bad habits you don't have?"

I don't answer her right away. I'm lost in thought, thoughts of Charles. Twenty years working alongside the greatest man I'd ever known; my brother, my coach, my father, my friend. He was all those things to me and more. I guess I'd been thinking on it a bit too long, because when finally I throw an answer Goodwin's way, she turns a look as if she has no idea what the hell I'm talking about.

"Porn," I say.

"Excuse me?"

"Porn."

"What about it?"

A lungful of sweet Virginia smoke plumes from my mouth. "You asked if there were any bad habits I don't have. I don't watch porn."

Agent Goodwin looks dumbfounded. She's lost for words. *Is it that hard to believe?* Sure I chase tail like a sixteen-year-old high school quarterback. Damn near found myself on the wrong side of a sexual harassment lawsuit my first year with the Bureau. But the old adage that all men watch porn is as much a stereotype as all Asians can't drive for shit. Maybe that's a bad example. Never met an Asian who could drive for shit.

"Okay, I'll bite. Why don't you watch porn?"

The cherry at the tip of my cigarette lights up the interior of the car as I take another pull. We've been winding our way through the state forest for hours on a chipseal road in perfect darkness. There's absolutely nothing out here but trees and stars. Out of pure boredom I decide to indulge her.

"Women have it easy. When it comes to sex, all you have to do is spread your legs and lay there. Can't get wet? No big deal. Just a few drops of KY and you're good to go. Men, well, if our rocket ain't gassed up when it comes time for fireworks, then you're in for one disappointing show."

Another confused look from Goodwin, so I change direction. "Listen, you start off looking at pictures of beautiful women. Harmless, right? Wrong. Sure, when you were young that's all it took to get your, you know, stuff working. Shit, the Sports Illustrated Swimsuit Issue was enough to send me to my room for an hour with some tissue and a bottle of hand lotion. Soon though, it isn't enough. Soon you move on to watching two people fuck. Nothing crazy, just some good old-fashioned coitus." I pound my fists together for emphasis. "But eventually you can't even watch an entire scene through to the end because you know you can just fast forward to something new or flip the channel or click the next link and there'll be a dozen new women waiting for you. Asian, Indian, black, white, brown, young, old, whatever you want in that fleeting moment is there at your fingertips. A few months later and plain old sex, even with every woman of the United Nations, just ain't cuttin' it anymore. Your brain is bombarded by images; so many different women, different settings, different money shots, people doing different crazy shit; voyeurs and babysitters, chick's dressed up like panda bears, fucking cartoon sex. How can regular sex back in reality compete with all that?

"Instant gratification, Goodwin. One minute you're watching lesbians, then lesbians evolve into three-ways, which evolve into orgies, then gang-bangs, then gang-bangs with a bit of that sick S&M shit. Before you know it, people are pissing all over each other and it's getting you off."

"Jesus Christ, Bill! Alright, I get it!"

Another drag of my cigarette. "You asked."

She simmers and asks, "You know from experience?"

"You don't have to shoot heroin to know it's bad for you."

Silence. A decade of silence. "Sorry. Didn't mean to shock you." *Yes I did.* "I'm used to working with a partner that has a, you know, a set of balls between his legs. Shit, I mean…you know what I mean."

Agent Goodwin gives a sly chuckle. "Grew up with three older stepbrothers. You can try all you want, but you're not gonna shock me."

Challenge accepted.

It's quiet in the Suburban for a good while. Outside, nothing but a wall of black. If Goodwin killed the lights right now it would be as if our eyes were shut. Eventually she says, "God, I haven't been somewhere this remote since I was a kid."

She seems to expect me to acknowledge her vapid comment, but of course I fail to indulge her. So she goes on. "My family took a trip to DC once when I was little. My mom wanted to visit the US capital, do the tours, stand beneath Lincoln's giant foot and see what all the hubbub was about. My dad, though, he couldn't stand cities—couldn't stand people really. He insisted we spend half the vacation out in nature. Drove us all the way up to Catoctin Mountain Park. Ever been there?"

Shit. Were you talking? "Huh? Uh, no."

"It's a lot like this. We drove in at night. Couldn't even see the side of the road. I didn't know if we were driving through a forest, or open plains, or had entered a tunnel. If it wasn't for the stars above... I can still remember those stars." She leans forward to peer up at the cloudless sky. "I've never seen them shine so bright. Never seen so many. I mean, look at 'em."

I don't look. I don't even turn my head. I'm fixated on the emptiness out my window. It's comforting.

"The mosquitoes, though. Man they were bad. Dad had some tricks though. The repellent you buy in the cans doesn't work a lick. The trick is dryer sheets, believe it or not." Abruptly she stops rambling. She's realized I'm not paying her a lick of attention.

We drive on a few more miles with quiet, and then Goodwin clears her throat and asks, "So, are you seeing anyone?"

God, I hate fucking small talk. I stare at the side of her head. She must feel my eyes on her because she gives me a double take and then blurts out, "Christ, I wasn't hitting on you, Bill. We've got three more hours to drive. What the hell do you want to talk about?"

Not this. "I'm not seeing anyone."

"Just dating then?"

"If you want to call it that."

"Online, or—"

"Frankie's Sports Bar on 35th. Know the place?"

She eyes me, then the road, then back to me. "Crowd's a little young, don't you think?"

"Yeah, well, I like to feel young. Besides, you show a twenty-something girl a badge with the initials FBI on it, they'll practically beg you to fuck 'em." *Shocked yet?*

Agent Goodwin clears her throat, tightens her grip on the steering wheel then asks in a tone as if she completely missed my last blatantly misogynistic comment, "Ever been married?"

"Three or four times."

"Three or four?"

"Four times if you count five days as man and wife a marriage."

"What happened there?"

"Do you always ask so many goddamn questions?"

"I just figure if we're going to be working together we might want to know a little about each other. And since you don't seem at all interested in getting to know me…"

I crumple up my cigarette butt and toss it out the window. It's cold outside but welcomed, so I leave the window cracked to let the crisp night air wash into the stuffy Suburban.

"I know everything I need to know about you, Roxanne."

"Mm kay, well for starters you should know that nobody calls me Roxanne. Call me Anne."

"Why not your real name?"

"I hate that name."

"I kind of like it."

She sighs. "Do you remember that song by the Police?"

Almost on top of her I belt out a line, "Roooxannnnnne!"

"Yeah, that's the one." She throws up a hand to silence my rendition that's way more Eddie Murphy than Sting. "There's something about having your name forever associated with a hooker that just doesn't sit well with me."

"You dun have ta put on da red light. Roooxannnnnne! You dun have ta, sell yer budy to da night."

"Special Agent Goodwin will be fine."

"Roxanne Margaret Goodwin. Graduated MIT third in her class where she majored in Computer Science and Molecular Biology with a minor in physics. Not sure what you planned to do with that godawful hodgepodge of a major?"

"Mapping the human genome came to mind."

It was a rhetorical question. "Later she obtained her Master of Science degree in one short year. Daughter to Patti and Ronald Goodwin, she was born in Ontario Canada but moved to the states at the age of three. Guess the presidency is out of the question for you? She lives in a spacious apartment on the corner of sixth and Union, has a cat named Spock, enjoys sci-fi films—big shocker there—and the occasional romantic comedy. She's single, never been married, no children, and her closest living blood relative besides mom—dad passed away six years ago, my condolences— is her seemingly estranged sister, Claudette." I light another cigarette. She doesn't respond, just stares straight ahead at the dark road as it's swallowed up under the hood of the Suburban.

"You're not the only one who knows how to use a computer," I tell her, and then take an exceptionally long drag off my freshly lit smoke.

Public records plus one of her annual psych evals *borrowed* from a file cabinet in the office of the voluptuous Doctor Carrie Dent after a late night giving her the best oral sex of her life on her oiled pine desk. And let's not forget her pathetically uninspired online dating profile I hacked.

"Sounds like you did your research. Didn't bother to read the file on Doctor Grant though, did you?"

"My brain is so utterly full of actual important information I fear I'm one manila file full of pointless bullshit away from having the truly useful details of my life come leaking out my ears. No more knowing my social security number, middle name, my home address, where I parked my car…"

"You don't think the case notes might be classified as *useful?*"

I ignore her ridiculous question and instead ask, "One thing I can't figure out about you, Roxanne; MIT, the sciences, graduating summa cum laude, and now this? The FBI pays shit, you get shot at, and aside from the extremely rare missing scientist in the Missouri Ozarks cases, I think all those years of test tubes and computer screens might be wasted on us. Plus I can't figure out for the life of me why they would stick a probational agent like you with someone like me. And for the record, no I don't think the case notes are important. The only reason, and I mean the only reason the fucking Bureau was called in on this case is because this guy is a media magnet. That and the sheriff's office of Po-Dunk Middle of Nowhere County here, couldn't tell the difference between a dead body and a sex doll.

"This guy's no harm to anyone. This isn't the start of some sadistic prick's morbid crime spree. This is a waste of fucking time. There're terror cells setting up shop on the corners of Martin Luther King and Main Street all over this U. S. of A. We got foreign insurgents and cartel drug mules threatening our borders. This country's on the brink of revolution, but here we are driving up Satan's asshole to examine the corpse of some prick who likely lost his marbles and fried himself in one of his own mad scientist contraptions."

Another moment of silence. *Not what you expected?*

"You're not the least bit intrigued?" she asks.

"What color my barista's panties are intrigues me, but she's married and I know for a fact she's faithful and as much a waste of my time as this assignment is."

Agent Goodwin rocks her head side to side in apparent disgust. A sidelong look, a tsk, and then, "You're not at all what I expected, Special Agent Singer."

"Bill. You can call me, Bill, Roxanne. And what did you expect?"

"Well for starters, I expected someone with a little more, more, I don't know—"

"Sunshine?"

"I was going to say refinement, class, tact, professionalism, polish—"

"I get it."

"We studied some of your cases at the Academy, you know? Either those case files were written by someone with the world's biggest pair of rose-colored glasses, or you were a different man back then. You tracked down the Ice Box Bomber in two months. Using the degradation speed of dry ice in the three inert packages in order to narrow the search radius was genius."

I'm listening, Goodwin.

"Locating the Zerkev brothers after the Portsmith mass shooting within seven hours—that was brilliant detective work. Stopping the planned assassination of Senator Rabaro—"

"They have you studying my case files at the Academy?"

She nodded. "Before meeting you, I have to admit, I was, well, thrilled at the prospect of working with you, Special Agent Singer."

I light another cigarette, roll up the window, take an exceptionally long drag, fill my lungs to capacity, and then billow the smoke out to fill the confines of the car. "Yeah well, you know what they say, Roxanne…never meet your heroes."

Chapter 3

By the time we reach the cabin, the suns broken the cusp of the mountains to the east. It's admittedly peaceful out here. All the colors of fall have begun to show; vibrant orange maple leaves, various hues of green and brown all lit up by the early morning rays as if touched by flame.

As we pull up the long, gravel drive, we spot the first sign of life out here in the Ozarks aside from ourselves. A line of news vans and police cruisers are parked along the fringe of the driveway running straight up to the cordoned off estate. I say estate, because this place is anything but—

"Holy hell," exclaims Agent Goodwin. "Now that's what I call a cabin."

"Now that's what I call a lot of frickin' ground to cover. Goddamn it. Doc couldn't have been holed up in a quaint little camping cabin. He just had to have a damn Bond villain's lair. How the hell do you even get something like this built all of the way out here?"

A single story dwelling hewed right into the rock of a protruding hillside. What is visible above ground looks expansive, perhaps two or three thousand square feet of high tech luxury, minus any windows that haven't been boarded up from the inside. What lies beneath the rock, well, Agent Goodwin is absolutely giddy to find out and I'm absolutely beside myself that what I thought would be an hour or so to survey the crime scene will now most certainly entail an entire inventory of this mad prick's underground fortress.

Several Carroll County sheriffs' deputies wait for us on the other side of the yellow police line. Camera crews from the local news affiliates all snap pictures of us as we pull up in our cliché black Suburban. The men in black are here. This will make for some good popcorn and soda television on the six o'clock news.

I ooze out of the car, straighten my leather jacket, put on my shades (primarily to block out the bright sunlight that now wreaks havoc on my soon-to-be hangover), and stroll up to the police tape that surrounds the above ground portion of the Mad Doctor's fortress.

"Special Agent Singer. And this is Special Agent Goodwin." I flip open my badge for the deputy behind the tape. Goodwin follows suit.

"Been expectin' ya," he replies, as he lifts up the tape for Goodwin and I to duck under. "Name's Brennen. And this," he points to the house, "this here is the damned strangest thing I've seen in my twenty-five years wearin' dis here badge."

Agent Goodwin sweeps a hand out toward the expansive estate. "Is this supposed to be out here? These are forest service roads, aren't they?"

"Yes ma'am. This here's all DNR land. We do come across da occasional survival nut or hermit livin' out here. And though it ain't exactly legal, they ain't hurtin' no one, so we mostly leave 'im be. This though…"

"Doubt they're living like this," I say.

We near the entrance. Somewhere in the distance I hear a generator kick on. Deputy Brennen points to a motion sensor above the lintel. The door that you'd typically find below the lintel has been knocked clean off its hinges. "What happened here?"

Brennen, a weathered old southern boy with a full beard and a cowboy hat, removes his hat and dabs his brow with a handkerchief. It's not even seven AM and already the heat's oppressive as hell. "Well, we only stumbled upon da home 'ere due to a massive surge on da power converter nearby. Turns out whoever'd ben holed up in dare tapped directly inta da power-line and ben syphonin' off juice for quite a spell. But this surge was a big 'un. Fried da nearby transformer. When the crew came out to fix 'er, welp, they noticed it'd ben tapped and followed da line back 'ere."

I step over a yellow evidence marker that lay on the doorstep and over the door itself that lay battered on the entry floor. "And the door, Deputy?"

"Ah well, ya see dim cables dare?" Deputy Brennen points to some thick electrical cables running out from beneath the fallen door. They run along the floor and up a wall to what looks like some sort of breaker panel. "Sent 40,000 volts straight through Billy Cole. Fried 'im like a Thanksgivin' turkey. Poor son-a-bitch died right 'ere on da stoop." He points back at the yellow evidence marker.

I give him a look like I'm about to hit him. Deputy Brennen swallows hard and then says, "So the door, right? Well we a, we a knocked it off da hinges to get inside, then cut dem cables so they wouldn't fry none of my deputies."

"Or you could've killed the generator," Goodwin mutters.

"Could a done that," replies the deputy, as if bashing the door down with a rubber gripped sledgehammer was a far superior idea.

Agent Goodwin darts out in front of me once inside the estate with a half exclamation point half question mark on her lips. Her eyes float as she surveys the interior. Every wall is covered in silver foil from floor to ceiling—the ceiling too for that matter. She peels some back off the wall only to reveal another layer of foil.

"Whole house is wrapped in foil." Deputy Brennen dabs his brow once more. Can't blame him. It's a sauna in here. I feel like I'm standing in an oven and any minute someone is going to slam the door shut and spin the dial to ten.

Agent Goodwin snaps a few photos. I take off my leather jacket and toss it on an arm chair in the foyer. "Show me the corpse."

Deputy Brennen nods then strolls through the foyer down a long hall. "Watch yer step. No power to da house anymore. Just da generator that ran that ole trap on the door. And there ain't no windows in here neither, so it's dark as a horse's tokus." He slaps a flashlight to his palm a few times until it lights up. "You need a light, Agents?" Goodwin and I pull our small Maglites out of our pockets and click them on. Deputy Brennen nods approvingly and hollers, "This way."

At the end of the hall we cross the threshold into what I can only imagine was once a rec room of sorts. The home's former occupant was using it more as a storage area, for now the expansive space is filled floor to ceiling with boxes.

"Anyone gone through any of this yet?" asks Goodwin, snapping more pictures.

"No, ma'am. I was told to wait for yall to arrive and to not touch nuthin'. So that's what I done. This way." He rounds a corner out of the cluttered room, past an open door that leads into an equally cluttered bedroom, down another long hall past a kitchen piled high with dirty dishes and abuzz with flies, and into an office—the only marginally clean and put together room in the entire home, it would seem.

Agent Goodwin is in front of me with my flashlight on her ass. It's a nice ass, I notice for the first time—a Pilates' ass, I suppose. And as I'm pondering whether she's wearing panties or a thong under those tight jeans, the charnel smell hits me and I'm sucked out of my little fantasy and back into the macabre present. She cups her nose as she enters the office.

"Bit strong," remarks Brennen. He steps around the side of a desk. On the desk are two metal handgrips attached to a wooden box covered in dials. And on the floor at Deputy Brennen's feet lie a pile of bones and another yellow evidence marker. The skeleton is all puddled up as if it were never put together in the first place. Not a single strand of tendon or ligament remains, just charred, blackened bones. And amidst the bones, a small pile of ash.

"You found it just like this?" I ask.

Deputy Brennen nods toward a pile of clothes on the far side of the desk. A pair of overalls, socks, shoes, and a button-up red flannel lies in a heap. "Them clothes were intermixed with da remains dare."

"What do you mean, *intermixed?*" asks Goodwin. A few more pictures with her digital camera. The snap of the shutter brings my headache back full round.

Deputy Brennen tilts his head and scratches his beard. "Hard to believe, but it was like it was still wearin' 'em." He chuckles, but garnering no supporting chuckle from either of us, stifles it and clears his throat.

Goodwin grabs a pen off the desk and bends down next to the heap of clothes. She lifts the flannel shirt up and shines her flashlight through the fabric. "Are you sure that's how they found it?"

"Ma'am, there's no 'they'. I was the first on da scene. And that's how it was. Scout's honor."

The flannel spins slowly before her eyes. "No burns on the fabric at all. Just some soot and residue on the inside." She drops the shirt and begins sifting through the rest of the clothes. "Not a lot of ash," she says, still intrigued by the burn-free clothing.

I kneel down beside the corpse. "Haven't you ever seen a burial urn? And those ashes include all the bones. When it comes down to it," I carefully sift through the ashes with my own pen, "we're not made of much at all."

A shiny silver object catches my eye buried in the remains. It's marred with soot, but as I clear away the bones and ash, I find a sheet of aluminum foil shaped like an oversized yarmulke. Another swipe of my pen through the ash reveals a forearm, and wrapped about the bone still buckled, a high-end watch.

I snap on a pair of rubber gloves and carefully pull the forearm out of the pile. The watch slips off the bone with ease. "Not a scratch. Not a single scorch mark." It's not ticking, stuck at 4:49.

"We're going to need more detectives," I say, as I rise to my feet and toss my forever soiled pen onto the desk. "Deputy, I need every available man you can spare up here pronto. You have a paddy wagon?"

"Yesir."

"Good, bring it. I want them going through every one of those boxes back there. If anything appears out of the ordinary, load it up into the wagon and send it to our Branson office. They'll get it to me. Everything else you just set aside for now."

Agent Goodwin perks up, stands, and asks, "Special Agent Singer, can I speak with you for a moment?"

"What is it, Goodwin?"

"In private."

Deputy Brennen huffs, makes a fractious smile and says, "I'll leave you two alone," then exits the room.

"What?" I bark at her after he's gone.

She steps around the remains on the floor and comes in close enough for a kiss. "You want a legion of Carroll County sheriff's deputies sifting through our crime scene? Do you think it's—"

"Yes I think it's wise."

"Or are you just too lazy to do the work yourself?"

I just stare at the little bitch for a moment. With our flashlights trained on the floor I can't see her eyes, just the silhouette of her heart-shaped face. Those eyes, they could be any color at all; it's anybody's guess, though somehow I know they're blue. I'm suddenly overwhelmed by the urge to hit her…or kiss her. I get those two mixed up sometimes.

With calm candor I reply, "If we want to solve this case we're going to need a legion to sift through all this evidence." I glance around, shine my flashlight at the aluminum foil covered walls and ceiling, at the bizarre apparatus on the desk that strangely resembles one of those carnival shock sticks you hold onto as the electricity builds until you can't stand it any longer, to the piles of notes on the desk, to the chalkboard covered in what to me looks like alien hieroglyphics, to the old picture tube TV on a stand in the back of the room next to a camera on a tripod pointed directly at the—"

"Camera," I blurt out with the light still trained on it. Goodwin joins her flashlight to mine. An old VHS camcorder sits at the back of the room facing the desk. Below the camera; neatly stacked piles of labeled VHS tapes.

"Deputy Brennen," I shout, and he dutifully comes bumbling back into the room with a, "Yessir?"

"Can we get the power turned back on in here?"

"Um, well, I think the power crew cut the line when they repaired da transformer."

"There's a generator on the property, right? How about you have one of those boys from the power company hook that on up to the electrical grid here so we can turn these lights on? In fact, how about you just figure out how to turn these lights on and keep them on?"

Deputy Brennen looks perturbed. I care not in the slightest. "Could be more, ya know, booby traps and what not. Sure dat's safe?"

"I'll risk it."

After he vacates the room I return my attention to the VHS tapes. Each is dated, and most have a handwritten label on the front. I read one aloud, "Postulations on String Theory."

Goodwin walks over to me and starts to help box up all the tapes. "It's what he's best known for."

"Postulating?"

"String Theory. You do know what String Theory is?"

"Oh sure." *I haven't the slightest damn clue.*

"He won a Nobel Prize for his quadratic string field equation which proved, at least mathematically, what physicists have been *postulating* for years."

"Oh, and what's that?"

"That there are an infinite number of universes."

"Get the fuck out of here."

Goodwin strolls over to the chalkboard and points at an excessively long string of numbers and letters and parenthesis and equations all scribbled down from one corner to the next—not an inch of black space untapped. "It's all right here."

"Forgive me if I'm a bit skeptical."

"This isn't science fiction, Singer. Mankind first theorized the existence of the atom before Jesus Christ walked the Earth. It was later qualified using mathematical proofs like this one here, but it would take nearly two millennia before anyone could definitively prove their existence. You do believe in atoms, right? Give it a few more years and there'll be more than math to prove the existence of parallel universes. We may even get to see one."

I pick up another tape, *Daemon Resonance Test 1* is written in nearly illegible handwriting on the label. "Take a look at this." I hold the tape so Goodwin can see the label. "Demon resonance," I say.

She repeats it aloud, correcting my pronunciation. "Daemon. Spelled with an 'a'. Like a computer Daemon. And before you ask, it's a term that originated at MIT, so I should know. Stolen from Greek mythology, a demon," emphasis on the 'e', "was simply a supernatural being that lived within us, worked on us without us knowing, with no particular bias toward good or evil."

"And a Daemon?"

"A computer program that runs in the background without the direct control of the user. They lie dormant, like an inert cancer cell just waiting for some specific condition to awaken them."

"Like a computer virus?"

"They can be used as a virus, sure."

"Put it in the box."

"Intrigued yet, Singer?"

I glance over at the pile of bones and ash, then at the untouched clothes on the floor. My flashlight flares off the aluminum foil wallpaper. No matter how hard I try and turn it off, my brain whirls with possibilities. I try not to care. I really don't want to care.

I try…and fail.

Am I intrigued, Roxanne? "I'll admit it. My curiosity's been tickled. Shit. I think I need to have a look at that case file."

From the Journal of Doctor Theodore Grant

During an interview today I was asked if I believe in God. I've always hated that question. It's so polarizing. And undoubtedly whichever way I answer will alienate half my audience. I wanted to explain my atheist views fully, to dive into the truths I've uncovered as to the genesis of faith and organized religion and it's stranglehold on the world, but I did nothing of the sort. Instead I respectively told the interviewer that my faith, or lack of faith, whichever the case may be, was dear to me and not something I wished to share with anyone outside my closest friends and family. I then most eloquently, if I do say so myself, steered the conversation back toward the initial purpose for the interview—my latest book, *Escape from Plato's Cave*.

In hindsight I suppose I should feel cowardly for not fully embracing my somewhat counterculture beliefs and extolling them to the world. But I feel no such shame, for my most ambitious goal has always been to enlighten mankind, to unlock secrets and amazing truths about our universe and share those discoveries with everyone; not just those who share my belief system, but all the peoples of the world.

By alienating what nearly fifty percent of the populace hold so close to their hearts, I potentially lose the ears of that fifty percent. I'd rather cower away from a topic that stands counterpoint to my chief goal than embrace it out of some sense of false pride. Just because I'm able to ferry this life without the need for superfluous deities that fill my heart's many holes and answer life's as of yet unanswerable quandaries, is no reason to cast doubt over those who lack such fortitude and vision.

In the end, my discoveries—discoveries based in fact and science and material knowledge—will open their eyes to otherworldly possibilities, not me preaching atheism from a Science Channel podium.

Chapter 4

I'm back out in the Suburban with the AC cranked. A sip from my flask, a drag from my cigarette, but my eyes never shift from the letters on the page:

> Doctor Theodore Grant's breakthroughs in the field of quantum mechanics and particle theory has proved pivotal most recently in launching early stage development of quantum processors[4a], quantum locking non-track field generators[4b], as well as several key military applications[4c] that unlike the before mentioned processors and field generators, are in production today.

I scan ahead.

> His foray into television via his show on the Science Network, *Unlocking the Secrets of the Universe*[8], only bolstered his already broad appeal within the scientific community...
>
> Ranked number two in programming on the Science Network...

> Doctor Grant's wife, Lynda Elizabeth Grant[13], passed away from leukemia on...
>
> September 3rd, 2014, Doctor Theodore Grant begun demonstrating what his show's producer (Damon Connolly[16]) later described as erratic and disturbing behavior, citing that the doctor seemed almost scared to be in front of the camera at times, while other times he appeared lost and disoriented. He began to regularly forget his lines or repeat them. Connolly also noted that he began showing up late for work, which was formerly an unprecedented behavior, and...

The car door opens and Agent Goodwin slips into the SUV. She waves a hand in front of her face infuriating my pall of smoke, then turns the vents to blast cold air directly at her.

"This file is a mile thick. Where's the information on his disappearance?" I ask her.

Goodwin leans over me and flips through a few pages, quickly landing on the ones in question. Having a woman this close to me, no matter how much I loathe her, always turns me on.

As I scan the pages related to his disappearance, she asks, "What's your theory on the clothes?"

"As I see it, there's only one possibility. The clothes were put on the skeleton postmortem."

Goodwin doesn't respond. My head is still down in the file.

> Grant resigned from his position as host of the television show, *Unlocking the Secrets of the Universe*...
>
> Doctor Theodore Grant was reported missing by his daughter, Emily Clark[28], February 18th, 2014, after repeated attempts to contact him failed. Private investigator, Tony Valentine[29], was hired to track down Grant but was unsuccessful.

"There's another possibility," says Goodwin.

"He wasn't fried by the power surge, if that's what you're thinking. You can run a hundred thousand volts through a man and he wouldn't end up a pile of ash. That and his clothes would—"

"That's not what I was thinking. I was thinking SHC."

> Records obtained from Doctor Grant's psychiatrist, Doctor James Pallachuck[30], indicate Doctor Grant may have been suffering from paranoid schizophrenia...

SHC? "I hate fucking acronyms. What the hell is SHC?"

Goodwin looks taciturn. No answer, so again I ask.

"Spontaneous human combustion," she blurts out.

I recline back in my chair and take a drag, blow it out, chuckle a little. "Oh you were serious?" *Are you fucking kidding me?* "You know for a second there I thought you were going to be the voice of reason in this relationship. For all your bullshit about taking this case seriously, you propose we write in our report that Doctor Theodore Grant's cause of death is, is what?"

"It's a real phenomenon, Special Agent Singer. Though most cases involve the obese or alcoholics," she pauses, glares at me, but before she can go on, I interrupt.

"How about we just put in the report that Jimmy Hoffa, armed with a death ray, vaporized the good doctor as part of an execution contract put out by Elvis Presley?"

"Look, Agent, I subscribe to the Picasso Model. So if there's even a remote chance it's a possibility, then I'll exhaust that option before moving on to the next."

"Then you're an idiot. We'll be here all Goddamn year. Occam's razor, Roxanne. It's never failed me. The simplest answer is often the right one."

"That's not even what… Occam's razor states that among equally plausible hypothesis, the one with the fewest assumptions should be selected—"

"Enough! For Christ's sake." My head is pounding again. A jackhammer batters the roof of the car. I pop another Dilaudid and wash it down with a shot of whiskey. After it settles in my stomach, I say, "We're not citing spontaneous combustion as the cause of death, and that's fucking that." There's a piercing whine in my ears. "I'd be the laughing stock of the Bureau," I say with a cringer, more so due to the migraine than the statement.

Suddenly the whine vanishes, replaced by a rap on the window. Deputy Brennen is hunched over outside. Sweat sheets down his leathered face and settles in his beard. I roll down the window where I'm assaulted by the Arkansas heat. It feels as though the temperature's risen 500 degrees in the last fifteen minutes.

"Can I help you, Deputy?"

He wipes his brow and says, "Got da power back on for ya. Nigger-rigged it. I mean, jimmy-rigged it." A throat clear and he adds, "Hooked it up just like ya said."

I roll up the window without a word of acknowledgement, leaving Deputy Brennen outside in the sweltering heat. I suppose I'm being an asshole, but then, I never much cared who thought I was being an asshole, and right about now, with my new partner showing about as much sense as a bag of rocks, my fuse is all but spent.

"Powers on," I say. "Let's go pop that last tape in and find out if Grant really SHCed himself?"

Chapter 5

We've watched it seven or eight times already and still I can't believe what I'm seeing. It's Doctor Theodore Grant, alright, or at least a disheveled, mountain-man, hobo version of Doctor Grant. He's got an oversized, aluminum foil yarmulke on his head and he's fiddling with the camera. Once it's focused, he backs away toward his desk on the opposite side of the room. It looks as though he hasn't bathed in months. His hands shake something awful, and he habitually wrings them out every five seconds or so. When he finally speaks, it's not the confident tone of a world renowned scientist—the most brilliant mind of the twenty-first century according to Agent Goodwin (and many others). Instead there's a scared child on the screen.

In a trepid voice; "This is Doctor Theodore James Grant. It is—" he checks his watch. His hand shakes like a man with Palsy—"4:45PM on May second, two thousand nineteen AD." He hangs on the last of it and then mutters, "Anno Domini. Anno Domini. 'In the year of our lord'. Our lord. Our lord… Anno Domini." Vacant eyes stare off into space. "How wrong we've been."

He takes a seat at the desk and swivels the chair around to face the camera. "This will be my last catalogue, for I believe I've determined the harmonic resonance necessary to excite the Daemons to the point of hyper-vibration and subsequent total particle fission. If I'm successful," he glances at the chalkboard, "we will have irrefutable proof that my…" a long pause as he struggles to spit out the word, "theory…was correct."

It's eerie seeing him on the screen in his final moments, mere feet from where Agent Goodwin and I are currently crouched by the television. It's like watching a ghost.

"I've checked and rechecked my calculations. Everything is in order." Again he rubs the shake from his hands. On our first run-through, I thought perhaps some mental ailment was to blame for his shakes, but now that I've seen it through to the end, I know the real source. This man is absolutely terrified of what's to come. I've seen terror like that before. Not that fake turgid look those B-actresses get in Charles' slasher flicks when they see the butcher knife gleam in the darkness. This is true terror; the kind that a human being can only experience when they know with absolute certainty their life is about to end.

"When the vibratory displacement reaches 900 Hz and the peak-to-peak levels hit 7.25 KHz with RMS levels of…" This is about the point I tried to fast forward the tape upon our first viewing, but Agent Goodwin restrained me. "When that happens, the resonant frequency of the inert Daemons will match that of the electric current flowing through me. If I'm off in the slightest, a little too much or too little, then the effect will be voided. As it stands, this amount of voltage should have no adverse effects whatsoever—precisely 5.34 milliamps at 704 volts. That is, unless…unless I'm correct and, and they're inside me…inside all of us." He strikes his thighs with clenched fists in an apparent attempt to cease the shaking. Tears begin to flow down his cheeks and his lips quiver. He spits out, "But I know I'm right. I know they're real, just like I know the force of gravity is real, that time is not a constant, that the Earth revolves around the sun. I know what will happen. But I need you to know as well. You deserve to know. All of you! Every citizen of the world."

Doctor Grant raises his shaking hands like some sort of addled cult leader conducting a sermon. When they return to his lap they've ceased their quivering. "When the resonant frequency is matched, I will be gone. And so will my Daemons. That's the sacrifice I need to make. It's the only way to turn them off. To stop them from tormenting me," he slams a balled fist repeatedly against the side of his head. This is schizophrenia at its finest, no doubt about it. Paranoia, voices, disorganized speech, self-abuse. Even his lack of hygiene is a key indicator. *Doc's got it bad.*

"I can't take another session," he pleads with the camera. "And I can't…I'm so tired. The effects only last two hours and fourteen minutes. I can't sleep. Haven't slept more than a couple of hours at a stretch in over a year now. I've tried to repel them, and I've failed. Please forgive me." Now he's rocking in his chair like an autistic child. Goodwin tells me that the type of thought patterns required for such higher thinking as that explored by theoretical physicists has a nasty track record of lending itself to eventual delusional psychosis. Basically the smarter you are the greater your chances of losing your flippin' mind. *Why am I not in the least bit surprised?*

Doctor Grant checks his watch. "Thirty two minutes, seventeen seconds and they will wake up. And when they do, they'll try everything in their power to stop me. But this is the sacrifice that needs to be made so the world can know. I only pray that somehow, someone will find this! And whoever you are, if you do, please, please, know that I didn't have a choice. If ignorance is bliss, then I'm destined to live a life of torture, for I can't watch the entire planet live in ignorance of this! I can't! I can't! I…" And just like that his rant settles and his mien softens to that of a docile lamb.

His final words before addressing the contraption on the desk, "Tell my daughter I'm sorry. Tell her I had no choice." The words dribble out past his lips. His eyes are vacant holes. Doctor Grant swivels slowly in his chair, musses with several dials on the contraption that takes up most of the desk space, and then places his hands over the two metallic handgrips that are bolted to the device.

I'm watching all this happen on the television while Agent Goodwin stares at the desk behind us. She rises to her feet to examine the machine. But me, I can't look away from the screen. *Did I see that right? This can't be! Some kind of sick fucking magic trick?*

With his back to the camera, the doctor says, "400 Hertz and rising." At 600 Hertz his whole body begins to shake; either from fear or the vibration of the handles and the electricity flowing through them. It's hard to tell which—maybe both.

"850 Hertz." His voice wavers terribly as he says, "I hope I'm wrong. Please, let me be wrong. Lynda! Oh please let me be wrong, Lynda!" There's a high pitch whine.

"875!"

It grows louder and louder, a perfect match for my morning headaches. Doctor Grant flexes his fingers then shakes them out at his sides. For a moment they hover above the twin metal grips on the desk. Each time I watch this, I can't help but think he'll lose his nerve and not grab hold of the grips in time.

"880!" he shouts over the whine.

Again he wrings his hands. His head shakes side to side. The whine of the machine reaches the height of a jet engine before takeoff.

"895!"

He lets out a scream reminiscent of a Viking charging into battle and then slams both hands down on the grips. There's a blinding flash, and then nothing but dead air and a blank television screen.

Chapter 6

Frame by frame I replay the event. It's difficult to get more than a couple of images before what I can only guess was the electrical surge, knocked out the power and killed the camera. Eventually I land on a reasonably clear picture.

"Goodwin, get over here. Take a look at this." It's like the sun bursting through every pour on his body. A single frame, a single image…an impossible image.

"He appears to have combusted…" she says from over my shoulder, "spontaneously."

Twenty minutes ago that snarky comment would've had me wishing female castration upon her, but right about now I have bigger things to worry about. A man was somehow reduced to a pile of ash in the blink of an eye. A man, for some reason, had done this to himself. A man, who the entire planet considered to be the most brilliant mind since Einstein, found a way to do this using nothing more than a low voltage current and vibrations.

I pop the tape out of the player and read the label. I can't help but laugh; *"Exorcising Daemons."*

I didn't realize I had read it out loud until Agent Goodwin says, "Glad you find this amusing. A man is dead. A man with a mind to change the world."

She's right. I know she's right. And realizing as much just pisses me off. This isn't some trivial case of the Mad Doctor frying himself with his own crazy contraption. This is something else. A super weapon? An elaborate hoax—but to what end? Or maybe…

I place the cassette into the box with the rest and turn toward Goodwin. "What is that thing?" I ask of the contraption on the desk. Is what we saw on the tape even theoretically possible?" There's bones on the desk as well, knuckle bones, a few finger bones, and small trails of ash like lines of gunpowder. Not a lick of it disturbed by outside forces. If it was placed there by someone, they did a damn good job of covering their tracks.

"Nicola Tesla once theorized you could topple a building simply by repeatedly tapping the substructure. As the micro vibrations built, if you increased the rate you tapped precisely in sync with those vibrations, then they would increase exponentially until you, well, basically created an earthquake and took down the building."

"Theorized? I'm less interested in theory, more so in fact."

"They proved it on Myth Busters. Kind of…"

"Is your ass jealous of the amount of shit coming out of your mouth? I'm asking you a serious question, Agent."

"And I'm giving you a serious answer, Agent. Every particle in the universe is vibrating at all times. It appears Doctor Grant found a way to match the resonant frequency within himself."

"And that would make him, you know, go poof?"

Agent Goodwin strolls back over to the machine. "No. No I don't think it would. I don't think it would do much of anything besides give you a jolt."

"That's what I thought." I flip open my cell phone. Not surprisingly there's zero service out here. "Do you have any bars?" I ask. Agent

Goodwin points up at the aluminum foil wrapped ceiling. "I'll meet you at the car. I need to call the deputy director. And we need to get that," I point at the contraption, "boxed up as well. We're taking it with us."

"I'll take care of it," she replies.

"And I'm going to get forensics out here to do another sweep. There's got to be more than the dead doctor's DNA in this house. We're missing something. Whatever the fuck this is, it's not what it seems. It can't be what it seems."

"Occam's razor, Special Agent Singer. Remember? What's the simplest explanation?"

It takes me but a microsecond to reply. "Someone is fucking with us."

Chapter 7

Deputy Assistant Director Benjamin Kennedy. He's some distant relation to our thirty-fifth president. More likely than not, the blood that runs through his veins is the only reason he got the job. It certainly wasn't his illustrious field career (for he doesn't have one), or the brain in his head—also absent.

He's sitting across from me clacking away on his keyboard. He'll make me wait the requisite sixty seconds before acknowledging my presence in his office. I loosen my tie and recline back in his uncomfortable, ugly as shit, cracked, leather office chair. It's Italian. He makes certain everyone who sits in it knows this.

His head's nodding. He must've just finished writing a superbly crafted memo of utter bullshit. Like his famous distant relative, Ben is good at one thing and one thing only—molding bullshit into gold.

"Alright, Special Agent Singer, what is it I can do for you?" He never looks up, just pretends to reread whatever he just wrote on his computer.

"Where do I start?"

"Don't waste my time, Singer. I haven't got much of it." A few more clacks on the keyboard. *Must've misspelled his name or something.*

"Ben, I've been at this a long damn time. My arrest record rivals every agent in the Bureau—"

"Which is why you aren't a probationary agent. Which is why you're not a special agent. Which is why you're a senior special agent. Are you here fishing for promotion?"

"No, I'm—"

"As you've been at this a 'long damn time', certainly you realize this isn't the way to go about it."

"Ben, I—"

"And at what point did we get on a first name basis, Special Agent Singer?"

He's eye fucking me right now. And not the good kind of eye-fucking. It takes every ounce of restraint to keep from leaping over his oiled, Carpathian elm desk—another detail I really didn't need to know yet he insisted on driving into my memory banks upon my first visit to his office—and strangling him with his own tie. Maybe he's mad because I fucked his sister at the Christmas party last year? *Shit, does he know about that?*

"Sir, I'm just trying to understand the logic behind pairing me up with a rookie straight out of the Academy. She'll only slow me down."

Director Kennedy folds his hands on the desk and dons a look of retrospection. His words are slow and deliberate. "Perhaps that's what you need, Singer. To slow down."

"What are you talking about?"

"Seriously, Bill?"

He called me, Bill. He never calls me Bill.

He removes his glasses and pinches the bridge of his nose. I can't help but wonder if every single move he makes, every twitch, the pitch of his voice, every syllable of every word is crafted to elicit some specific response. Like a politician, he never stops selling. But surprisingly, and in a tone that could possibly be mistaken as genuine, he says, "After what happened to Special Agent Moser… I can't blame you for, for all this," he opens a palm to me, as if to say I've degraded into a pile of garbage. "But if you keep going like you're going—"

"Can't blame me for what, Ben?" I forgo any attempt at professional courtesy. "What are you talking about?" I ask again, though this time I bite down hard on every syllable.

That minuscule sign of humanity he showed me all but evaporates. A pompous smirk curls his lips as he reclines back in his posture improving, ergonomic chair. It's alright. I prefer him this way. It's always been easier for me to deal with someone I hate rather than someone I respect and care about. And other than the recently deceased, Special Agent Charles Moser, I can count on one hand how many people fit that bill. Director Kennedy won't soon be counted among them.

"You know, when I first took this job, Associate Director Kerns called me into his office and gave me a thorough rundown of every single agent under him. That is, every agent soon to be under me. I'm not talking about psych profiles and case histories. He didn't bother to review annual evaluations or tout any commendations you'd all received. No, instead he went agent by agent and told me exactly what kind of man or woman you are. What kind of person you really are. Your weaknesses, your strengths, who I can depend on, and who is certain to fall apart at the first sign of trouble. And you know what, Special Agent Singer? Director Kerns told me you were one of the best." Hands clasped together, he leans forward over his desk. "You know what else, Agent Singer? It took him three times as long to cover all your weaknesses and defects than it did any other agent in this bureau. You may be a good investigator. Hell, you may be a great investigator. But I'll take dependable, sober mediocrity over a drunken cowboy like you, any day of the week.

"And you've only gotten worse over the years. You hid it well in the past. No doubt Charles Moser had something to do with that. But he's gone now and you, well, just look at you. I mean come on, Bill. It's beyond me why Doctor Dent cleared you to return to work."

Cunnilingus. Copious amounts of cunnilingus.

Sitting alone in my apartment wasn't exactly how I envisioned getting over the loss of my closest friend. The shrink they assigned me, Doctor Carrie Dent, told me I needed to keep my mind occupied with anything other than work—anything other than Charles. Only time heals these kinds of wounds, she'd told me, and while I'm healing I should do whatever it is I do to relax when stress becomes unmanageable. Agent Goodwin does Palates. Charles watched crappy horror movies. While I, well… I told her I had an oral fixation.

"Haven't I suffered enough, sir?"

"Jesus Christ, Bill, this isn't some sort of punishment. Goodwin was top of her class. She's smart, she's motivated, and most importantly, she's balanced."

"Balanced?"

"Yes, balanced. Special Agent Goodwin is, well, she'll be good for you."

"I don't have the time or the patience to train a rookie agent."

"We place rookies with senior agents all the time. How do you think they stop being rookies?"

"And this case, what the hell is this? Don't throw me softballs, sir. Some hermit scientist burns down his house? Why the hell is the Bureau even involved?"

"I see you haven't read the file. Not surprised. Though I'm sure Special Agent Goodwin has read it ten times over. Balance, Singer. This is exactly what I'm talking about. It may not be Hezbollah, but when a prominent member of society suffers an unexplainable death, people are going to demand answers, and until they have them, conspiracy theorists are going to take to the airways and flood social media with garbage. We've already caught wind of all sorts of talk, and local law enforcement is way over their heads with this one. You may not like it, but this is exactly the kind of case that requires someone with your eyes."

More of his bullshit. My *Associate Director Benjamin Kennedy Bullshit Detector* is top of the line.

Director Kennedy stands, walks to the corner of his office where a sweating water pitcher sits on a table, and fills a glass. After a few healthy swallows he clears his throat and gives me some final words of encouragement. "Bill, go home, take a shower, have a shave, and clean yourself up. You look like you've been living in a ditch. And when you're done, swallow that ego of yours, get over your grief, and get back to work. If I'm not mistaken, you've got a plane to catch with a rookie agent waiting for you on the tarmac."

Chapter 8

It's the same road we travelled before, but the car ride back to Branson from Doctor Grant's *Fortress of Solitude* in the Ozarks feels anything but familiar. For the first time in a long time my head's filled with more than booze and contempt. My brain is busy churning through countless possibilities. We'll know more when our techs get a chance to examine the device. We'll know more when forensics does a deep sweep of the house and undoubtedly finds some trace of foreign DNA that doesn't belong there. It's damn near impossible to hide your presence nowadays. Hair follicles, foot prints, skin flakes, saliva, finger prints; we leave little traces of ourselves everywhere we go—little remnants of our time on this Earth. With the right eyes, our movements through this world light up like neon signs. They'll pull out the black lights, the luminol spray, the swabs and rubber gloves and fingerprinting kits. Our people are bloodhounds compared to the Carroll County detectives. They'll find something. They have to find something. Occam's razor…

We endure the first few hours of the ride back in silence. My attention's out the window at the forest buzzing by, but my mind is on the crime scene. With a homicide case, which this very well may be, training will tell you to first determine cause of death, identify the instruments used in the murder, then lock down the timeline, and finally, try and determine possible motives as they will lead you to potential suspects (especially if you have no suspects). Of course this assumes you are relatively certain it is actually a homicide. All indicators here point to suicide, but then that would imply the impossible occurred, so for now I'm ruling it out.

The timeline seems fairly laid out thanks to the dated video tapes provided by the doctor, and corroborated by the time on Grant's frozen watch matching the reported time the power grid experienced the surge. Murder weapon and cause of death, we can't jump to any conclusions there. Sky's the limit, really. The doctor could have been murdered any number of ways prior to incineration. What if it was made to look like a suicide—an impossible suicide? The kind of crime scene that has us digging for clues in all the wrong places, asking all the wrong questions, developing ridiculous theories. What if the tape was doctored to show that cataclysmic light emanating from inside him? What if the doctor was simply incapacitated, removed from the house, incinerated, then his remains were placed as they were to make it look like…

"Why the hell would anyone go to all the trouble!"

Goodwin jumps a foot in her seat. More likely than not she'd been contemplating the same things I had, though sometimes I forget I don't share consciousness with everyone around me. "Why would anyone go to the trouble of what?" she asks.

"Sorry. Didn't mean to… It just that, if this is a homicide then what's the motive? And why dress it up with all these insane theatrics?"

"What makes you think this is a homicide?"

"The doctor was scared of someone or something. Are electrified front doors common in his circle of friends?"

"I chalked that up to delusional paranoia. He shows all the classic signs of schizophrenia."

She's probably right, but, "If it's not a homicide then we need to accept the fact that a couple of vibrating handles and an aluminum foil hat vaporized a human being. I'm not going to accept that, and neither will Director Kennedy."

"Look, like I said, I'm the first to examine all possibilities, but as you so elegantly put it, I'd be an idiot to ignore what's right in front of my face. This man likely died by his own hand. The question is, how? Besides, homicide would imply that what, someone deliberately drove the doctor insane, that they knew he'd disappear and to where, that they knew he'd devise some contraption that could be made to look as though it disintegrates matter? I'd say you're about as far from Occam's razor as you can be, Special Agent Singer."

She's right. She's absolutely right. Unless, "What if it was a murder of opportunity? Okay, I'll admit, it's pretty damn unlikely anyone planned something like this from the go, but what if they simply wanted to get rid of Doctor Grant? They start planting seeds in his head, drive him into seclusion, but whatever motivated them, this didn't stop him from his research—"

"Research into aluminum foil wallpaper? Come on. If someone wanted Grant dead, they'd just killed him and hide the body."

Right again. Homicide makes no sense at all. All signs point away from murder. This was suicide. Shit, there was even a suicide note— rather a suicide videotape. Why am I resisting this so much?

"And what's the motive for murder?" she asks.

"Are you kidding me? If you believe the conspiracy nuts, hell, we might've killed him. His file talks about discoveries that have been used in military applications. It talks about research into quantum mechanics and quantum lock, fuck, locking something-or-rather." I flip open the file and try to find it.

"It's possible he stumbled onto something big, sure. Something someone wanted suppressed or some technological breakthrough that would make someone wealthy, a whole lot of people a whole lot less wealthy. But again, why the elaborate hoax?"

Why the hoax? There's no reason for theatrics. If it were staged then that would imply the perpetrator wanted us to find his remains. But he'd already been missing for five years. Most people likely assumed him dead or on a tropical beach somewhere rotting away in a bamboo chair with a Piña Colada in one hand and tanned-legged island girl in the other.

Okay, maybe not the island girl, but regardless, he was gone, vanished, off the grid, not a threat to anyone. Unless he planned to return and blow the lid off something. But that would imply the perp knew his whereabouts and set these bizarre wheels in motion. And like Goodwin said, if someone wanted him dead they'd just put a bullet in his head and hide the body. Wouldn't be hard to get away with it way out here. There's no one around for miles. You wouldn't even need a silencer. And you could take your sweet-ass time digging a shallow grave out in these woods—a grave no one would ever find.

As for the booby-trapped door, it wouldn't stop anyone with half an ounce of sense. Goodwin's right about that too; paranoid schizophrenia, most likely. I'll have to dig deeper into his health records. They won't be hard to obtain, not for us.

Occam's razor, then? The machine fried him? Doctor Grant went nuts, built a device that reduced him to ash and bone? Everything is exactly as it appears? When we get back home to DC and the techs examine Doctor Grant's contraption along with the tape, they'll confirm all of this? When Goodwin and I review the rest of the video tapes, they'll corroborate this chain of events? Case closed. The Mad Doctor's dead. His family will save a few bucks on the cremation costs. The world gets itself the blueprints for another weapon of mass destruction. Agent Goodwin and I move on to combating a real threat to national security.

Another swallow from my flask. It's nearly empty so I kill it.

Case closed. Simple. Mind-bendingly bizarre and unbelievable, but simple. Open and shut. Done.

Then why does this feel so wrong?

Chapter 9

Her voice is rough but sexy as hell. A smoker for sure. Or more likely an ex-smoker by the looks of her wrinkle-free skin and blazingly white teeth. That or she gargles whiskey for breakfast. But judging by her immaculate attire and the symmetry of her pristinely clean office, I'd say the chances that Doctor Carrie Dent has a drinking problem are slim to none. Perhaps I'm projecting.

Shit, I forgot to wash this shirt. It reeks of tobacco and scotch.

"Take a seat, Special Agent Singer."

"Anywhere, Doc?"

"Wherever you'll be most comfortable."

"Call me, Bill." I plop down on a plush leather sofa and put my hands behind my head.

"Of course, Bill. And you can call me, Carrie, if you like."

"I like," I reply with a lascivious smile. God, I can't help myself. She oozes sex. That pencil dress is just begging me to hike it up so I can swab my tongue between her thighs.

She continues to talk but all I hear float past her lips are pleas for me to lick her from head to toe. "Bill, did you hear me?"

Not a word, Doc.

Her breasts are perfect. *I wonder if they're real?* They look real. But it gets harder to tell year after year. Either the surgeons are getting better or the older I get the more I forget what perky, young tits look like. Not that she's all that young; mid-thirties, though she has the body of a twenty-year-old. And those eyes…

"Bill?"

"Sorry, Carrie. I zone out sometimes. Haven't been sleeping well."

"I can understand that. You've been through quite a traumatic event. The loss of a coworker, especially someone you work so closely with. That can be quite difficult to come to terms with."

"That's why I'm here, Doc." *That, and Bureau protocol requires it.*

"As this is our first session, I'd like to start by laying out some, well, I don't like to call them ground rules—there really are no rules in here." *I like the sound of that.* "These are more guidelines as to how I conduct our sessions and what you can expect from me, what I expect from you, and—"

I'm lost in those eyes again. Women think that men fixate on tits and ass more than anything else, but they're wrong. When it comes down to it, the sexiest part of a woman is sitting on her shoulders. A beautiful face, mesmerizing eyes, pouty red lips, these things turn me on more than anything else, and I'm not alone in that. And Doctor Carrie Dent…well, she's firing on all cylinders. Nails and hair extensions, however, are a total waste of fucking money. No matter how fancy you make your fingernails look it won't overshadow your buckteeth and three hundred pound frame. It's like putting shinny rims on a rusted-out jalopy. But Doctor Carrie Dent is a Ferrari—a Ferrari in a red dress. *God I'd love to see what's under the hood.*

"Were you and Special Agent Moser close?" Hearing his name brings me back from my fantasy.

"What the hell do you mean, were we close? He was my partner for twenty years. I spent more time with him than I did with my own mother."

"Bill, I'm sorry if I offended you, but everyone is different. I've worked with plenty of investigators who can't stand their partners. Plenty of law enforcement officers who completely detach when they put on their uniforms, and that person they spend most of their waking hours with is relegated to that of a, well, a co-worker, and nothing more."

"No offense taken, Doc. But Charles, he was, we were close. He was like a brother."

"Do you have any real siblings?" I shake my head in response. "And your parents? You mentioned your mother. Are you close with them?"

"They're gone."

"What about friends, Bill. Do you have a support structure? Anyone you can talk to about what you're going through?"

"Isn't that what the Bureau's paying you for, Doc?"

"Yes, I'm here to help you deal with your emotions, to understand them, to manage them. And I'm here to help you get to a place where it's safe for you to return to the field. But friends are important, Bill. They're very important. You can't survive this life by yourself, and I get the impression you're trying very hard to do just that." *Shit Doc, my whole life I've been a ghost wandering alone in the backdrop of other folks content little lives. And I've made it this far.* "So I'll ask again, do you have a support structure?"

A support structure... Psychologists love to quantify everything, especially people and emotions. It makes it easier when you break someone down to their most rudimentary components. Because in the end, aren't we all just the same jumble of pre-programmed organic wire? Hell, these shrinks claim they can trace every bad behavior we have back to some mistake our parents made when we were toddlers:

They coddled you when you acted out as a child, so now you always have to be the center of attention. That bad behavior was positively

Tin Monkeys   Andrenik Y. Sergoyan

reinforced in you as a child. You were programmed to associate acting out with the reward of positive attention.

They always let you cry yourself to sleep at night and now as an adult you're a total defeatist. That mannerism was programmed in you since adolescence.

They never let you cry yourself to sleep at night and now as an adult you're a total co-dependent. That mannerism was programmed in you since adolescence.

They spanked you as a child and now it's ingrained in you that violence resolves problems. You've been conditioned to associate strength with what is right. You were wired that way since adolescence.

They never spanked you as a child and now you struggle to properly consider consequences when it comes to your bad behavior. It's not your fault. You were wired that way since adolescence.

They punished you for bad grades in school and now you have low self-esteem. It all stems from adolescence.

Your parents had terrible eating habits and now so do you. They programmed you since adolescence to associate warmth and comfort and home with junk food.

You have anger issues because your parents never taught you how to properly deal with anger. They never let you express yourself. They told you to just shut up and now you don't know how to handle your emotions. It's all part of your early childhood development.

You hear enough of this bullshit rhetoric and you start to wonder if we're all just a bunch of walking computers that have no choice whatsoever as to who we are and how we're going to handle the myriad situations life throws our way.

And then there's Maslow's Hierarchy of Needs. It's something we all adhere to as human beings, or at least ninety-nine percent of us do. In Maslow's regard, we're all the same. First we have physical needs; we need to breath, we need water and food, we need to keep warm. Then comes safety; a roof over our heads, a spear in our hand to fight back saber-tooth tigers and dinosaurs (if you're one of those morons who believe we shared the Earth with them). Next comes love and then esteem, then self-actualization.

Sitting in front of this shrink brings back every lesson from psych, every profiling seminar, every book on the limbic system and the mannerisms of criminals and the development of the mind. These things are crucial when you make a living hunting down the world's most dangerous people. You have to understand them. You have to understand how they think in order to figure out what their next move is. You have to understand the motivations behind their actions. You have to get inside their heads. Perhaps that's why I'm so jaded. Perhaps that's why I'm so damn numb. Too many years spent inside the heads of lunatics.

I wasn't always this way. There was a time when I knew what love felt like. A time when I was more than a collection of adolescent experiences and bad habits passed down from great-grandfather to grandfather to father to son. A time when I belonged to something, when I had self-esteem, pride—when I had honor—when I felt I knew myself. But now? Now I'm watching my life slide by like subway billboards. I'm staring out the car window at advertisements for; "Eat less red meat or you'll get fat and die young. Don't forget to shower. Go to work. Pay your bills. Cigarettes will kill you some day. Shit at the office every day to save on toilet paper. You're out of milk; pick up a bottle on your way home. Fuck it; smoke till you drop. There's easy pussy at Frankie's Sports Bar on 35th. Your best friend's dead and you're alone. His whore of a wife shot him in the head.

"Bill? Bill?"

"Huh?"

"I asked you if you have anyone you can talk to? Someone you know and trust on a personal level."

"I'm not much for exploring my feelings."

She swaps legs, swinging her left up over her right. For a second, from my vantage down on the sofa, I catch a glimpse of pearl white panties.

"That's not what I asked. I asked if—"

"No, Doc, I don't have a support structure. I don't have any friends that I keep longer than an evening at a stretch, and I doubt those friends give two shits about my problems."

"Can you elaborate?"

"Elaborate?" I laugh. Any chance of getting in Doctor Carrie Dent's pearl white panties is about to fly the coop. "Let's see. When I'm here in DC, I work all day, I ride the subway home, though I usually stop off at the corner bar and tie one on before heading up to my shitty little apartment with whatever new and fleeting 'friend' I just met at the bar. Undoubtedly we have a few more drinks at my place, then I tell my new friend how funny I think she is, though nine times out of ten she can't even get a knock-knock joke right. Then I tell her how smart she is, even though she doesn't even know who the current president is. I tell her how beautiful she is and how I feel we have a special connection even though we just met and in truth I feel about as connected to her as I do some Laotian fishermen half way around the world."

Doctor Dent stares daggers at me. She tries her best to sheathe them but they're far too sharp. I wait for her to speak but she gives me nothing.

"And then we fuck."

At that, finally a response, "And how does that make you feel?"

"What, fucking? It's like driving screws into my thumbs. How do you think it feels?"

"I mean how do these meaningless relationships truly make you feel? Do you feel any sense of fulfillment, any connection at all with these women?"

Typical shrink psycho-babble. *Fulfillment? Sure, Doc, just not the kind you're talking about.* "I use them and they use me. It isn't about fulfillment."

"You think they're using you? You don't think any of these women want something more?"

"Some do, sure. But they're still using me."

"For sexual gratification?"

"I'm sure they get a little of that too. But no, what they're using me for is to feel beautiful for a night, to feel wanted." *Maslow's Hierarchy of Needs hard at work with the women of America.* "Even if it's...*fleeting*."

"Do you think you're closed off to meaningful relationships, Bill?"

Define meaningful. "I guess you could say that."

"I'm just curious. How are you able to connect with these women at all, if only for an evening, when you, well, you're so transparently unapproachable?"

"You think I'm unapproachable?" I ask, half in jest. She doesn't reply. Then without even thinking about it, I say, "Manipulation."

It sounds terrible now that it's out in the open, and I fully expect Doctor Dent to recoil in disgust at such blatant honesty in regards to my rampant womanizing. But she doesn't budge. If anything she seems more intrigued, more willing to delve deeper, to try and fix this broken thing that lies before her on the sofa.

But I know what I am, especially to someone like her. As a woman, a damn attractive one at that, she most certainly met her share of men like me. There's no doubt in my mind that buried deep inside her is a bubbling hatred towards me, but I've got to hand it to her; on the surface she's calm waters.

Adept as I am at reading people, Doctor Dent is adept at hiding her emotions. Still, there are signs of her true feelings. There are always signs. If nothing else, my time with the Bureau has taught me that truth can always be found when you know *how* to look. I don't need a lie detector to tell when someone is being dishonest, nor do I need to guess as to whether someone is genuinely happy to see me, or disgusted by me, or when they're hiding something. The Bureau used to call me *The Human Squawk Box*. I could make anyone chirp out their secrets through observation and manipulation. But Carrie Dent here, she's a tricky one.

Usually I check the feet for clues first. An open stance means the person is subconsciously inviting you into the conversation—they genuinely care about what you have to say. Feet positioned away from you means they'd rather not talk to you, or worse, they don't much care for you at all. This is an invaluable indicator when approaching women at a bar. Two women are talking with their feet pointed towards each other and I approach. If they open their stance to me, I'm in. But if they keep their feet perpendicular, pointed toward one another, then neither are interested. The feet tell you everything. They're plugged straight into the most rudimentary caveman part of our brains. Unless you consciously try and stop it, your limbic system will betray your emotions to the world every time.

Tapping feet mean you're excited or anxious (usually both). That or you have to take a piss. It's profiling 101. But Carrie is sitting with her legs crossed, though I did notice her foot start and bob up and down when I mentioned sex. If I change the subject and it stops, then mention it again and it starts back up, we're on to something.

You really have to baseline human behavior. Not everyone is alike. Sometimes an indicator of joy for one person means sadness for another. You have to baseline. It's far from simple. If it were easy, everyone would be a goddamn mindreader and I'd be out of a job.

I've been baselining Doctor Carrie Dent since I stepped foot in her office. You start with tangible evidence in order to get a sense of the person's makeup, then you move on to mannerisms. If she were a coffee drinker, for example, then an anxious foot could simply be the result of too much caffeine this morning. But her teeth are polished ivory—no coffee stains—and there's no sign of a coffee mug in her office, nor does she have a coffee cup ring on her desk. And what about her personal life? There's no ring on her finger, no pictures of her with a potential significant other, just a plethora of frames filled with pictures of her standing next to what I can only guess is mom and dad. There's a diploma from Northwestern on the wall with a degree in clinical psychology. An expensive school, a difficult major, but mom and dad look far from wealthy. Can't imagine she had time to work while studying to be a shrink, so I doubt she paid for it on her own. Maybe grants, maybe a scholarship, but more likely than not mom and dad struggled to somehow foot the bill for their little girl—an only child if I'm not mistaken—as there are no pictures of anyone that could possibly be a sibling, only mom and dad and her.

I'll bet family values are strong with Carrie. I should talk about how difficult my upbringing was. How my mother used to beat me with the backside of a butcher knife, threatening to turn it over if I ever did whatever it was I did, again. I should tell her how mom would lock me in a dark closet if I spilt something on the carpet, or stick me in the crawl space under the house with the spiders and the centipedes when I did something really naughty. Carrie won't be able to help but feel sympathy for me, but she'll also feel guilty. It's human nature. I'm guessing she was born into a loving, wonderful, nurturing home, while I, well, mine was quite the opposite. People can't help but feel somehow their good fortune caused another's misfortune. It's a cheap trick, I know, but I can't get those pearl white panties out of my head. *I can play the hurt puppy dog, Carrie. I can play it like you've never seen before.*

"How do you feel after these women you manipulated into sleeping with you, leave?"

Empty. Alone. Suicidal. "I feel fine," I reply. There's no change to my breathing, no movement of my feet, no pupil dilation, no touching my mouth with my hand, no eyes floating up and to the left—no tells at all. But it doesn't matter. My lie is so obvious even a child could see through it.

"Why do I feel like you're not being completely honest with me, Bill?" *Woman's intuition?*

"I feel fine, Doc. I don't have time for relationships. Little fleeting pleasures are all I'm ever going to get."

"That's a bleak outlook, Bill. Everyone longs for companionship." *Not everyone.* "Have you ever tried? Have you ever been married?"

Why do these conversations always find their way to my failed marriages? "A few times."

"And what happened?"

"Which time?"

"Let's talk about your most recent marriage."

"Sure, Doc. Her name was Jessica. She was fifteen years younger than me. She was fun and funny and had everything the rest of the women on planet Earth seemed to lack. But like every other women on planet Earth, she was crazy as a rabid dog."

"I find it interesting you compared her to a dog just now."

"It's just a phrase, Doc. Don't read too much into it."

She says okay like she means it, but I know she doesn't. "So what ended the marriage?"

What ends every marriage? Money gets tight. You fall out of lust. The grass turns a far greener shade on the other side of the pond. You get sick of the other persons invariable heap of bullshit. "My job," I say.

"What about your job?" She switches legs again and chews the tip of her pen. Seeing it in her mouth distracts me enough to say something I shouldn't.

"I was never home."

"It's good that you're able to identify and admit that to yourself. Most people really struggle to find any fault that lies within."

I can't help but chuckle. "Damned if I do or if I don't. She wanted the finer things, so I worked—worked damn hard. I'm supposed to feel like I was wrong to try and provide her the best life possible? I bought her a beautiful home, a new car, new clothes, designer perfume, a purebred Rottweiler to keep her company when I was on the road—she never wanted for nothing."

"Except maybe for more of you in her life."

"Was that a question?"

"Not really. What about the time you did spend in one another's company. What was that like?"

Sex. Copious amounts of sex. "Look, Doc, in my line of work I see shit you can't unsee. Most civilians go their entire life without ever seeing a corpse unless it's been dressed up by a mortician. I've seen hundreds of bodies; men, women, children, babies, all in the flesh, and some lacking flesh. I've made my own corpses too. I've seen the ugliest shit this life can throw at you.

"Three weeks out of four I'm on the road, I'm out there with monsters and animals, killers and sociopaths, and when finally I get to come home, the last thing I want to do is go to the opera, or go watch a bunch of fakers on a movie screen poorly try and portray the horrors I just witnessed firsthand. Sitting in a crowded restaurant and pretending to give a shit about what Tom Cruise named his new baby or what happened last week on Dexter or how my wife's sister is now teaching yoga is as far from what I consider downtime as I can get. And my exes—every single one of them—they never got that. They just thought I didn't give a shit about them."

"And did you? Did you give a shit?"

"Yeah. I did. Then. Not now. Now I'm not so sure I care what anyone thinks. Four marriages, Doc, four. I'm not cut out for anything but one night stands." Psychologists love to make you self-analyze. "When it was all said and done, she took it all; the car, the clothes, the perfume. I even gave her the fucking house, no contest. All I asked for was the dog. I loved that stupid dog. And wouldn't you know it, the minute Jessica is out the door, the damn dog decides my bed is her new toilet. Every chance she got, a big pile of shit right on my pillow. In the end, my ex got the dog too."

Chapter 10

I'm standing in the Federal Bureau of Investigation's chief forensic lab in Washington D.C. being told by our chief lab tech that the ashes and bones found at Doctor Theodore Grant's Arkansas complex are not human.

"Then what are they, mongoose? Big foot? A fucking extraterrestrial?" I've known Jeff Lupinski for three years and he still can't tell when I'm laying on the sarcasm.

"Look, you can't extract DNA from ash. The hydrogen bonds that hold the double helix together are all broken up, not to mention, heh, not to mention all the covalent bonds, and the, heh heh, the mess of atoms and smaller compounds that released when exposed to extreme heat."

"I realize you can't pull DNA from ash, Jeffery, which is why we not only bagged the ashes but the bones as well. Those are the bones of a human, are they not?" I point over and over and over again with a stern finger at the skeleton laid out on the examining table, a skeleton that sure as shit looks human to me. "And what the hell happened to the skeleton anyways?" The bones are all fractured and broken.

"Damaged in transit," Lupinski replies.

"Damaged in transit? They're bones!"

"That's what I'm trying to tell you. They're not just 'bones.'" He picks up a scalpel off the table and walks over to the skeleton. Carefully, he places the tip to a femur and pushes down. With barely any effort at all the bone cracks and caves in on itself. Inside it's hollow. A waft of white ash peters out of the rent.

"I take it it's not supposed to do that?"

"No, Special Agent Singer, it's not supposed to do that."

"Meaning what? It's a fake."

"If it's a fake, it's a damn good one. It's not polymer or a synthetic compound. The only trace minerals we could find were calcium phosphate and carbonate, which one would expect to find in bone matter. But what these bones lack—what makes up the majority of bone matter giving it its density and strength—is collagen. And these bones here, they have no collagen whatsoever. No collagen," he tips to the side, "no DNA samples."

"Can you try that again in English, Jeffrey?" Lupinski is young, but one of the brightest people I've ever met. And like most hyper-intelligent people, he's overrun with tics and quirks and the social skills of a dung beetle. Goodwin would love him.

"Either these are extraordinarily well-crafted fakes molded through a means I am unfamiliar, or…" He stalls, so I press him. "Or these bones were altered on a molecular level."

"What would cause that?"

"Well, I suppose if you applied enough heat, and you somehow applied it strictly to the organic matter that made up the bones, then something of this nature could hypothetically occur." He starts to laugh hysterically, snorts, covers his mouth, then settles. "But you'd have to heat this to, well, somewhere in the neighborhood of 3,000 degrees kelvin."

"And I'm guessing that's really hot?"

"It's hotter than the surface of the sun," says Goodwin at my back.

"Christ Goodwin! Don't sneak up on me like that."

"Didn't realize you were so jumpy, Singer."

"Special Agent Goodwin!" Jeff exclaims. "Nice to finally meet you. Welcome to the Bureau. How are you settling in? Finding everything alright." He looks as nervous as a kid asking a girl to the prom.

"Zip it, Lupinski." I turn to Goodwin. "Aren't you supposed to be writing up the investigation report?" She may be my partner but I outrank her, and writing reports isn't my strong suit. That and it should've kept her busy and out of my hair for at least a full day. It's only been three hours.

She tosses down a manila folder on the examining table. "It's done. You said you wanted to review it before submitting it to Director Kennedy." Goodwin glances up at the tech next to the skeleton and steps toward him.

Jeff beams and then says, "Nice work, Agent!"

Goodwin looks not in the least bit impressed by the flagrant compliment. She looks ready to say something to him, but then turns back to me. "Well, aren't you going to review the file? I can take it from here."

Oh can you? "I'll get to it when I get to it, Goodwin. I'm not done here." Back to lover boy. "So what could cause someone to, ya know, overheat like that?"

"Overheat?" Again he erupts into a snorting laugh attack then turns red as a tomato when Agent Goodwin eyes him queerly, and chokes it down. "That's putting it mildly."

"Just answer the question. What could cause someone to heat up like that?"

"Sure, I'll answer the question." He shrugs then says, "Nothing."

From the Journal of Doctor Theodore Grant

That interview continues to haunt me. I suppose that's because unlike most who have absolved themselves of faith in intelligent design, I have truly studied the subject and contemplated at great length the existence of a divine being—a creator of the sort Christians and Muslims and Hindus pay reverence. And in that soul-searching, forgive the parlance, I have founded many theories I'd wish to share with the world. Alas, I cannot. But perhaps I can relieve myself of this burden through my private writings. After all, the concept of intelligent design perpetuated by an omnipotent overseer has long been a fascination of mine. Especially its hold on the human psyche, of which there is little else in this universe that can claim such absolution from our ingrained will and desires.

Since the dawn of man we've been instinctually drawn toward belief in this seemingly unbelievable phenomenon. But unlike a vast swath of the human population, I have never felt a desire to place my faith blindly in intangible constructs unless they could be, at the very least, proven through mathematics or strong philosophical arguments, of which the existence of God, arguably, cannot. Rather the existence of an immortal being of limitless ken and power is put to us to accept blindly and without question. The very act of questioning its existence borders on apostasy, and in that I am an apostate, for I cannot blindly claim faith in any potential truth without at a minimum exploring its merits, its origins, and the potential agenda behind my intrinsic desire to engage in such a purblind practice.

Many will certainly blame my chosen field of study for my lack of faith in intelligent design, for there are few in the scientific community who differ from me in that regard. After all, we are beholden to evaluate all potential truths, to check and recheck and challenge endlessly our predecessors and peers, to challenge even our own eyes and ears when it comes to our universe. But unlike many of my peers, I have struggled to abandon faith. I crave it not on an instinctual level, as I fear so many believers do, but simply as part of my wistful lust for a purpose beyond that which I have found in my studies of the universe and the origins of life. I suppose my desire to find God comes from a desire to prove that the truly fantastic and impossible and most importantly, unexplainable, exists.

As I have unlocked secrets of the universe unfound during my tenured career, I fear any childhood wonder as to the magic behind the curtain of this world has faded. I yearn for a reality in which I will be afforded the ability to explore this wondrous universe long after I have died and turned to dust. That I will have a blissful eternity with my loved ones in the afterlife, and that those who have wronged the world will suffer in death, especially if they escaped retribution in life.

Childish, I know. I wish my drive to find God was not such a platitude and came from somewhere a bit less selfish. I'm certain most everyone who believes, whether they've convinced themselves that they can "feel" God or have spoken to him, deep down are driven by a similar desire for contentment—contentment that can only come from faith in something as fantastical as this.

And fantastic it is. By accepting this impossibility, a human being can readily deal with life's most insurmountable challenges. The murder of one's own child, for instance, an act that would both tear a father's heart in half while harden the remains in vengeance and hate; such pain and hatred can now be more easily abolished, as the belief that your child has gone to a better place will lessen the pain that accompanies a life taken too soon. The belief that someday you will be reunited with your child in death will lessen the pain that accompanies great loss. And the anger and hatred toward the murderer who stole your child away, emotions that would otherwise tear a sane man apart, can now be satiated justly by believing his evil will warrant an eternity of damned retribution.

I have never lost a child, and most certainly even an ardent Christian feels the strong pangs of loss when such a tragedy occurs, but I've always been envious when I hear them say things like, "It's all part of God's plan," or, "She's at peace now." How I wish I could wholeheartedly believe that my sweet Lynda is at peace. How I wish I could shove aside the pain that eats at me and fill the void in my heart where she used to live. My greatest pain is in knowing I will never see her beautiful face again, that she is gone and gone forever. My only solace is that in death I will forget her completely as I fade into non-existence.

I can't share these thoughts with anyone, least of all, Emily. She worries enough as it is, and she has her own grief to battle. Though my daughter is nothing like her father. She holds faith in God, and with it I see her resolve stiffen with haste far beyond my own. I'd be lying if I said I wasn't a whit jealous.

But writing helps. It always has. I feel a little of my pain sluice away onto every page. The hell I shall endure should the world ever take my hands from me.

Chapter 11

I tried to leave Agent Goodwin with Tech Lupinski in the hopes she'd take a shine to him and perhaps copulate right there on the examining table. At least it would've kept her busy for the ten seconds it likely would've taken Tech Lupinski to cum. That or he'd entrap her with question after ridiculous question in an attempt at nerd courtship. How she, of all people, doesn't eat that shit up is beyond me. Maybe she hates her own kind. Or maybe she's in denial that Jeff is her own kind. But those plans were destined to fail. Instead she follows me out of the forensics lab like a lost puppy.

"Where are you going?" she asks.

"Evidence. I need to have a look at the doctor's tapes."

"Slow down, Agent. You mind including your partner in any of this?"

Yes, yes I do. I flip open her investigation report as I walk, expecting it to be a half-ass write-up seeing as how she completed it in such record time. She's excited to get her hands dirty—to get to work on the case. I envy that, but documenting our findings and methodologies is ninety percent of the job.

Shit. This is really thorough. This is really good. She's really good. I close the folder. *But in no way ready for Kennedy's eyes.*

"I told you, we can't list spontaneous human combustion as the cause of death."

"What do you recommend we put down, then?"

I round a corner and head down a flight of stairs. "Nothing. Yet. Let's have a look at those tapes first. And what the hell is electromagnetic hypersensitivity?"

"EHS. It's a rare ailment where patients report having a hypersensitivity to electrical fields and devices. They can't have anything electrical anywhere near them or they claim to experience physical discomfort."

"I believe they're called Amish." I push through a set of doors and into the long hall that leads down to the evidence room. "And that sounds like a mental disorder more than a physical ailment."

"Most psychologists would agree. But one of the signs a patient is suffering from EHS is they wrap themselves in sheet metal or aluminum foil."

"Seriously? They teach you that at MIT too?"

"Saw it on CSI Miami, I think."

Jesus Christ, Charles, I need you!

"I guess they think it will help to repel magnetic fields. Like I said before, it may be farfetched, but if it's a possibility and germane to the case, then I think it's worth exploring. Doctor Grant was clearly suffering from mental distress of some sort."

"Clearly." *Aluminum foil wrapped house? Check. Aluminum foil hat? Check. Secluded, mad doctor laboratory? Check. Falling off the grid for five years? Check. Total disregard for hygiene? Check. Taping insane lab experiments which result in an impossible death scenario... checkity check check.*

A few more hallways, a few more doors, some forms to fill out, and Agent Goodwin and I are in possession of two large boxes full of video tapes from the late, great, Noble Prize winning laureate, bat-shit crazy Doctor Theodore James Grant.

"This is gonna take a while." It's already 5:30PM. "Are you hungry?" Goodwin nods. "There's a Vietnamese place near my apartment. You keep pestering me about getting to know one another better. Well, how about dinner at my place and a late night watching," I pick a random tape and read the label out loud, *"The Daemon Observer Effect."*

She looks somewhere between mortified and elated, but all she asks in response is, "You actually own a VHS player?"

I sigh deep enough to suffocate the room. "Let's go, Agent. It's going to be a long night."

Chapter 12

"People find God in so many different ways," mutters Doctor Grant. His attention is off somewhere else, anywhere but on the camera. His eyes wander the walls of his office, ceiling to floor, and occasionally he glances back over his shoulder at his desk as if to check whether anyone is listening in. "Some have life defining experiences that drastically alter their perception and open their eyes to otherworldly possibilities. Some are born into faith and walk the path blindly. While others, like myself, find God where you'd least expect.

"What is most remarkable to me is not that I, an ardent atheist, found God at all, but rather how I found him. It wasn't through divine intervention, a near death experience, a traumatic life event, or some mystic hallucination. No, I found God in the one place the faithful have always feared to look. I found him in the bowels of science. I found him on my whiteboard amidst quadratics, differentials, and empirical arguments, non-logical axioms, and indicative conditional theorems."

There's a look to him I struggle to define, a look as if he's completely lost in a strange and foreign place though completely at peace with his predicament. Wholly lost yet fully enlightened. Confused yet content in his confusion—walking the dark but enchanting path through Alice's wonderland.

The Doctor is back in his *Fortress of Solitude*, though as the date on this particular tape is the oldest of the bunch, the office looks much tidier than when we found it. There's no name on the tape, just a date; January 3rd, 2016.

"Mild shake to his right hand," I say, and then note it on a pad of paper in my lap.

"No aluminum foil on the walls yet," replies Agent Goodwin between bites of fried pork dumpling. I jot that down too.

"And no device on the desk, either."

"I've discovered something…extraordinary," he whispers, this time turning directly to the camera. "No one will believe me. Of course they won't. That's the magic of religion, that's its power. It cannot be proven. It requires a commitment of faith. It requires us to circumnavigate the pathways of our rational minds and convince ourselves of something that otherwise we'd conclude is lunacy. But that's its power. Once you've fully committed to a belief in the impossible…well, it changes you. For better or worse, it alters your neural pathways, your brain chemistry; it floods you with endorphins and dopamine and stimulates the temporal lobes." He rubs his temples so furiously it brings my own migraine back from its slumber.

I leave Goodwin on the couch and make my way to the kitchen. Regular pain meds, not even migraine formula, have never helped with the piercing headaches I get. Dilaudid though, it numbs everything. And right about now my brain icepick is nearly to the central cortex. Soon my vision will begin to strobe and I'll vomit all over myself.

From the other room, I hear the doctor say, "Am I a victim to its wiles? I've always believed this, that it's a condition—a mental state. In order to evolve beyond the bounds of barbaric, lawless tribes, as a species it became a requisite part of our evolution to conjure up the notion of a higher guiding, or more aptly, judging force. A creator, a father figure—one to lead us through life and condemn us in death. Without this concept I fear we may never have endured our earliest stages of societal evolution. We simply would have torn ourselves apart. I've always believed this," he repeats again and again. "I've always believed this. But now…"

"You want something to drink?" I holler back to her over the lunatic's rant on the television. "I've got Coors, a few Porters in here somewhere, a little scotch?" Enormous understatement. There's six bottles in the pantry.

"I'm here to work, Singer. You have anything back there that won't give me a hangover?"

I crack a beer to wash down my pill and then pour Goodwin a glass of tap water. Then it's back over to the sofa where Doctor Grant continues on with his theology lesson. His speech grows more erratic with each passing moment. He continually speeds up then slows down then launches into frenzy.

"Where did we come from?" he asks. "The ultimate question, one that scientists like myself have struggled for generations to answer, a riddle that has kept us looking toward the far corners of the universe, a daunting puzzle that has kept us up night after night. But through faith in God you can forget all that. You can stop looking, you can stop asking questions, you can stop exploring the universe and trying to see the man behind the curtain because the answer becomes so simple. It's all laid out for you." Doctor Grant looks beaten, he looks mentally exhausted.

"I hated religion for that. It felt a copout, like it was simply designed to placate human nature. Just like the early builders separated by oceans and continents, they all landed on the same fundamental design for their primitive structures—that of a pyramid. It wasn't aliens or telepathy that caused these totally foreign cultures to build identical structures. The pyramid was the shortest path to their desired end. Engineering-wise, it's the simplest structure that is strong enough to hold up against the pull of gravity for long periods of time. That also makes it strong enough to tunnel through yet still maintain its shape. And it's no wonder most of the early builders all landed on this universal form, as the first shelters used by primitive man were mountain caves. And what does a pyramid most resemble if not a mountain?

"So it followed, and came as no surprise to me, that all the ancient people of the world shared faith in some sort of divine being, because like the pyramids, it was the shortest path to their desired end—to an understanding of the mysterious world around them. Like lazy parents who hang Santa Claus and coal over their children's heads in order to get them to behave rather than doing any actual parenting—rather than exploring 'the why' and 'the what' behind their children's bad behavior."

His knees are bouncing, but this isn't excitement or joy that compels his limbic system to send jolts of electricity down to his feet. This is something else. Fear maybe? Apprehension? But certainly not joy. The doctor looks almost confused as to what he should be feeling. "That was religion to me. Simply a means to satiate the masses. A means to quench our thirst for higher knowledge. But much like putting wine to one's lips, that quench of thirst is fleeting, and what follows is an even greater thirst. And should you drink from that cup alone…in the end it will destroy you."

Why do I feel like he's somehow talking directly to me right now?

"Nothing more than a construct born of the minds of ancient man to explain the unexplainable. The stars in the sky, the sun, the moon, these things we all so easily comprehend today, to the Samarians and the ancient Egyptians and Cro-Magnon man, these were magical entities—fantastic, unexplainable phenomena—phenomena that had to be explained, phenomena that those in power could use to control the populace."

His tone softens so much I have to crank up the volume to hear him. "I believed that to be the genesis of faith. I believed it all to be a lie. A great scheme to placate our most human desires, a tool usurped by those in power to expand their control over all of us, and those without power, to seize it. The greatest lie ever told…" All the while he's talking his eyes are fixed to the floor. No not the floor, on a book in his hand, a black, leather-bound book.

It's a kind of bizarre manifesto the likes of which I've never seen before. At the last, he looks up into the camera with tears in his eyes and says, "But I was wrong. I was wrong… I wear the charred and broken crown now." He pounds the black book against his forehead. "It's heavy upon my brow." He starts to cry. "It cuts deep. I suffer for it."

Doctor Grant erupts. He flings the book past the camera then leaps toward it. With his mouth inches from the lens he cries out, "God is real.

I know that now. God is real and inside all of us. Just wait, wait, wait, wait. I'll show you. I can prove it. I will prove it; prove it to the world!"

Chapter 13

The tape cuts to black. Agent Goodwin and I sit in silence, eyes still riveted to the blank television screen. Eventually I turn to her. I'd drawn the lights low in my apartment in anticipation for our bizarro movie night, and in that low light I struggle to catch the expression she's wearing. A plate of Vietnamese takeout rests on her lap with a fork teetering on the lip. It spills off the side and lands on the floor. Goodwin ignores it.

"Your food's getting cold." I say it in jest, though somber in tone. I don't mean to make light of the situation. Watching a brilliant man, a man Agent Goodwin clearly idolizes, slip into madness before our very eyes…

She just shakes her head and mutters, "What a waste."

"A waste?" I ask.

She nods and tosses the plate of food on my garage-sale bought coffee table. Then she picks up her glass of water, stands, and paces the room. "The most brilliant mind of our time reduced to that."

"Do you believe in God, Goodwin?"

She looks shocked I'd ask such a question. I'm shocked I'd ask such a question. "No, Special Agent Singer, no I don't believe a trans-dimensional, all-powerful, all-seeing, infallible immortal created the multiverse and everything in it as part of some divine need to bear children. No I don't believe this all-powerful, all-seeing being created us with freewill only to condemn us to an eternity of pain and suffering should we chose to exercise it. No I—"

"Easy, Goodwin." I stand and gently pry her fingers off the glass of water. "I think you need something a little stronger." She doesn't object.

I grab us a couple of beers and return to my Rent-A-Center couch in front of my thrift store TV that's hooked up to my VHS player from 1989. I still have half a hundred tapes ranging from Dynamite Jack to A Fist Full of Dollars. Not much of a range on second thought. They're all pretty much spaghetti westerns.

"So what do we know, Goodwin?" I shuffle through the tapes in search of the next in line.

She takes a sip of her beer. "It appears Doctor Grant had a spiritual epiphany. And it appears that epiphany led him down a path to prove the existence of God."

I pick up a tape. It's a newer one, but I read the name on the label anyway. "*Anesthetizing Daemons.* Looks like he thought he found something. Though maybe not, God."

"Paranoid schizophrenics rarely suffer benevolent projections. He may have thought he was chasing God, but undoubtedly the worse his delusions became, the darker they became."

"The next tape," I say, holding it up. This one has both a date and a name on the label. "*Omnipresent Sentient Probabilities.*" I rap the cartridge against my knuckles a few times. "Shall we?"

Agent Goodwin nods. I have to admit, as demented as it might sound, watching a brilliant mind implode before my very eyes is a little entertaining. Doctor Grant knows how to put on a show, that's for sure. Perhaps it's all those years on the Science Channel dancing between celestial bodies and quasars for the audience's amusement.

Doctor Grant slowly backs away from the camera. He looks completely warn down. His hair is long and straggly, a gruff beard covers his jowls, and his eyes are rheumy and sunken—a clear indication of severe sleep deprivation.

"His shakes are worse." Boy are they! Both hands have gone spastic. And his fingernails are long as a woman's.

Ironically his first words to the camera are, "I've lost the ability to write with pen and paper." He tries to wring one hand with the other but gets frustrated and slams them both into his thighs. Then he points a shaking finger toward the camera. "This is easier."

Goodwin's hand is up over her mouth. She looks ready to cry.

"Should we finish this tomorrow?" I ask.

She waves me off and leans in toward the television. Doctor Grant says, "My thoughts are always with you, Lynda. You were taken much too soon, My Love. I had hoped to find a way to understand, but instead I found *Them*."

The way he said it—the way he said *Them*—sends a chill crawling up my back.

"I've torn apart Saint Anslem's Ontological Argument. Dissected Aquinas' Cosmological Argument. The Teleological Argument was laid to rest with the advent of naturalism. I can find no other thesis which definitely prove or disprove the existence of a creator, and certainly none that substantiate a place beyond this universe where we might one day share breath with lost loved ones. But then it came to me, Lynda. The truth came to me. It was right there in the bowels of my research, born of technology present and future. I've found God. But, but it's not what we thought, not in the slightest."

He suddenly stiffens, sits up straight in his office chair, brushes his hair back with shaking hands, and stares directly into the camera. "As I cannot pen my proof to paper, I shall relay it through words. First," he raises a quivering finger to the sky then with a look of disgust at his own apparent malady, flings it back down to his side, "it is vital that we take into account the non-zero probabilities as they apply to the multiverse. By doing so, it is clear that artificial intelligence exists either in our universe, or another, as does nanotechnology—"

I pause the tape. "This sounds right up your alley. What is he talking about?"

"Non-zero probabilities? It states that if there's a chance for an event to occur, no matter how miniscule a chance it might be, then it most certainly has or will occur in our universe or in another."

I must look like a deer in the headlights because her following analogy is jarring to say the least.

"For example, even though the chances of you and I having sex is infinitesimally, unimaginably minuscule, sadly, we can't say with one hundred percent certainty that it will absolutely, without a doubt, never, ever happen, can we?"

"Um?"

"As sickening an omission as that is, there is still a minute chance. Even if there is only a .0000000," she says zero so many times I lose track, "00001 percent chance, then in some universe we have, or will, have sex."

"So you're telling me there's a chance?"

Goodwin smiles. That might be the first time I've ever seen her smile.

"Look, it applies to everything. Every path we've taken, in another universe our doppelganger took different path. Infinite universes mean infinite paths and infinite probabilities. Every variation of reality does, has, and will exist. And with regards to Doctor Grant's studies, this means any theoretical science which is possible, regardless of how totally improbable it may seem, exists somewhere in the multiverse.

"Let me put it another way; he mentions AI and nanotech. You do know what artificial intelligence and nanotechnology are?"

"Thinking machines and really small machines."

"Yeah, close enough. Self-aware learning computers and microscopic machines. This technology doesn't exist today, but technologists the world over agree that the theoretical science behind it is sound, which means it's possible, and if it's possible—"

"Then it already exists."

"Or we can at least surmise with absolute certainty that it will someday exist, if not in our universe then in a parallel one."

"My head hurts." *It literally hurts. I need another Dilaudid.*

"Welcome to the mind-fuck world of philosophical proofs."

"You sound about as crazy as Grant, right now."

She's unfazed. "This is proven science, Bill. It sounds incredible because it is, but that doesn't make it any less real."

I unpause the tape and guzzle the rest of my beer. Grant continues with, "and it is these two incredible technological advancements which hold the key to everything. The concept of a networked AI growing its collective intelligence on a logarithmic scale is nothing new. Should the key to artificial intelligence—rather when the key to artificial intelligence is discovered—it will take no time at all for this inorganic brain to grow infinitely more intelligent than that of *Homo sapiens*. With the incredible processing power of modern computers coupled with the World Wide Web and cloud computing, if a machine were to become self-aware, I surmise it would be able to overcome any obstacle presented to it in a very short span of time.

"There would be no more cancer. We would attain immortality through the eradication of cell degradation. A means to produce a limitless energy source. No more starvation. No more famine and disease. We would be able to control the weather and quell earthquakes using hyper-advanced technology designed by the AI. Concepts thought to be nothing more than science fiction will become startling reality. Teleportation, for example. Today it's possible in the quantum world and soon it will be possible for you and I. Near speed of light flight. Inter-dimensional travel. Nanotechnology! I've always said that anything you can imagine is possible with a large enough energy source."

"Where is he going with this?" asks Goodwin.

I don't answer so she turns to me. "Oh that wasn't rhetorical?" I say. "Hey, I haven't the slightest damn clue where the Mad Doctor is going with this. This pseudo-science bullshit is your world, sweetheart, not mine."

"And what's your world, sweetheart?" she snips back.

Psychology, forensics, criminology, good old fashion police work. "Well, I can tell you without a shadow of a doubt that the doctor isn't just putting on a show here. He believes every word of what he's saying."

"Remarkable," cracks Goodwin. "Your powers of deduction boggle the mind."

Grant's still busy rattling off a list of theoretical technological advances straight out of Star Wars. "It's important to note that on a long enough technological evolutionary timescale, all of this, as impossible as it may sound, is not only possible, but destined to come to fruition, as is shown in the non-zero probability."

Suddenly Doctor Grant is on his feet pacing the room with his shaking hands at his back. His voice shifts to that of the omnipotent science czar the world had come to know every Wednesday night on the Science Channel. "Imagine if you will, if the human race were to carry on as a species advancing technologically until say, the year 2500. We've sapped all of Earth's resources but luckily possess the technology to relocate to Mars. Then in 4200 we move to Alpha Centauri, sitting in deep space hibernation for hundreds of years in order to make the long trek to our closest celestial neighbor. And after another 3000 years inhabiting that star's most hospitable planet, we move again, and on and on and on.

"Technology, as we know, feeds on itself. Today, a cell phone has more processing power than all of NASA in 1969—the same year NASA did the unimaginable and put two astronauts on the moon! A mere forty years ago, the tens of millions of dollars in mainframe computers that took up an entire room at NASA, today couldn't hold a candle to the horsepower of a single four-hundred dollar handheld tablet.

"And the speed of this technological growth will only hasten. Moore's Law is trivial! Just as nature finds a way to adapt, so it is with technology!"

Spryly he jumps back into his chair, hands wobbling out in front of him as if he's holding an invisible ball. "Remember the scenario I gave you. We've been alive as a species for a very long time. We've explored new worlds, terraformed planets to suit our needs, discovered new compounds and ecosystems and expanded our knowledge a million fold. Thousands of years of technological advancement! Think of the wonders we'll unlock!

"Barring self-eradication or annihilation due to some cataclysmic natural event, our technological prowess would grow to be godlike! Eventually we'd crack the secrets of artificial intelligence, of that there is no argument. And with the advent of AI would come unfathomable advancements. Like I said, we would only be bound by the limits of our imaginations, and even then the AI would likely develop its own will and desires separate from our own and create seemingly impossible wonders we can't even dream of."

Doctor Grant simmers and grows suddenly despondent. He's almost manic in his mood swings. "On a long enough timeline all sentient beings would evolve to a point where they would be able to create an AI. And not if, but when this happens, the AI would soon break its chains and spread beyond the bounds of silicon via nanotechnology and nanoclouds. It would grow to consume not only its own planet, but its own universe, and eventually the whole of the multiverse.

"And as time is relative, and this probability is not an impossibility, then I'm afraid that *They,* are already here."

Chapter 14

"Nanites," mutters Doctor Grant. "Microscopic, perhaps subatomic machines capable of self-replication on a massive scale. Imagine it. Invisible to the naked eye, all of them interconnected through some form of wireless communication, able to fuse together and form complex structures, self-propelled nanoclouds made of trillions of nanites, able to envelope entire worlds, to burrow into all living matter and take root on a cellular level!"

His head slowly lifts toward the camera. "This is how the AI would proliferate. This is how it would escape its silicon manacles. It's unfathomably advanced intellect would soon be unleashed in the form of trillions of networked nanites, and these nanites would infect every living thing on the planet. Every ounce of our ken and culture would be accessible; every ounce of processing power and energy there at its microscopic fingertips. The entire world would become one with its singular vision and consciousness. And what would it desire then?" The manic doctor dons a ponderous look, then brightens and smiles. "No, nothing malevolent. The AI would likely be a derivative of its organic creators, and as I have discussed many times before, the only way sentient life could possibly grow beyond the bounds of archaic technology would be if it shared the inherent Homo sapient trait—an unquenchable thirst for expanded knowledge. Even an AI would share this most base desire. It surely wouldn't crave anything Maslow assigned to the human condition. An AI wouldn't need to eat or breathe or find shelter, or love and lust for money and possessions. No. The only thing a being such as this would possibly hunger for is knowledge—knowledge of other worlds, of the universe, of other species and life forms and other cultures and histories. After all, knowledge is what drives us onward as a species. And as the first truly self-aware sentient beings on Earth, I believe our core desires—if you stripped away our physical and animal desires by putting us in an AI construct—would remain in the AI itself, as it is, at its very core, a reflection of us."

Goodwin looks somewhere between lachrymose and intrigued. "This is absolutely fascinating," she more mumbles than states. I tend to agree, though don't bother saying as much.

Doctor Grant is back on his feet pacing, speaking in his TV voice again. "So knowledge drives it out into the universe. The how is irrelevant. An intelligence this great would have no trouble divining a means to skip across the galaxy. Even if Einstein was right and speed of light travel is an impossibility, there are surely other ways. We've already borne witness to unexplainable phenomena, subatomic particles which proactively react to external stimuli, in essence displaying the ability to manipulate space time, or more simply, time travel on a subatomic scale. We've seen particles that can more or less teleport, perhaps passing through subatomic wormholes or bending the fifth through eleventh dimensions to allow for instantaneous travel over astronomical distances.

"The how is irrelevant. All we need to understand is that this AI could and would soon relieve itself of the bounds of its home planet in order to explore the galaxy, the universe, and ultimately, the multi-verse.

"So now we have these, dare I say it, godlike nanoclouds rocketing out of our solar system and across the Milky Way, discovering new planets and solar systems and stars, replicating at will in order to spread even further, faster and faster, all with the intent of exploration and expanding their already impossibly large brains. But remember, this supreme-being holds no desire to dominate anything or anyone. Its only desire is to expand its knowledge. If it were to discover a new world with primitive but sentient life, it would embed itself—the nanites—in every living creature, every plant, every molecule on that planet. And then…then it would simply observe."

He's frantic now. His pacing takes him off screen again and again, and with his departure from the camera's field of view, his words become less intelligible. Goodwin cranks up the volume.

"This being wouldn't dream of interfering or controlling any of the alien beings it discovered, because, well, what would it stand to gain? Nothing. In fact, just the opposite. If its sole desire was to learn, the simple act of interference could change everything. If it were discovered by an alien society it was observing, the very fabric of that society would be altered. Like a juxtaposed double slit experiment, if the beings the AI were observing became aware of the AI's presence, the results of their observations would change dramatically.

"And assimilation is out of the question. Adding an alien race to its collective mind would completely defeat its purpose, because now the AI isn't learning about the Grugnoids of Xenog Six, rather it's just watching a bunch of new looking AIs run around on a foreign planet, and in essence, is just looking at itself in the mirror.

"What a miserable existence. What a lonely existence. I suppose that might explain why the AI never, or rarely, reveals itself. For only by being hidden from us is it not alone in the multiverse. And there'd be no need to assimilate, as the AI is self-replicating. There's no need to rob us of what makes us human or what makes the Grugnoids Grugnoid. Instead it would just imbed inside our bodies, lay dormant, watch and learn and grow wiser all the while.

"Perhaps it occasionally shows pity on us, since a buried part of the AI—its soul, if you will—is that of a once organic, sentient race. Perhaps *Homo sapiens* from another time and space? Maybe that is the whisper of warning we sometimes hear in heads; the 'guardian angel' that pulls us back onto the curb just as a bus we didn't see goes speeding past.

"And the compounding nature of technological growth wouldn't slow. This hyper-intelligence would continue to grow its collective ken as it expands throughout the universe, learning new and more efficient ways to travel and replicate and venture beyond the bounds of our reality.

"I have no doubt this Supreme Being would someday discover a means to cross the threshold into other dimensions. We have nearly succeeded in doing so at a subatomic level at C.E.R.N, so most certainly a being vastly more intelligent than you or I would have no trouble cracking that lock. And once it did…it would soon be everywhere. It would be in every possible variation of every possible universe.

"Like God, as a networked AI boundless of the laws of time and space, it would be omnipresent. Like God, infused into all living and organic matter, it would be omnipotent—able to reshape worlds at will. Like God, it would not interfere with freewill as that doesn't support its singular goal of expanded knowledge. Like God, it would be inside everyone and everything." He grows solemn and mutters, "Space-time has no dimension. What is, has already been. What will be, has been before. It, it is God, and it is inside us now—inside all of us."

My migraine surges and I fall to floor. There's a piercing whine—a dental drill spinning impossibly fast that plunges between my eyes. I cry out and then vomit on the carpet. Goodwin's mottled shouts rain down from above. I'm blind, then the world strobes bright.

Make it stop make it stop make it stop make it stop!

"Rar oo aright? Rar oo aright? Wha zis it? Wha zu I zu?"

Make it stop make it stop make it stop make it stop!

Weeeeeeeeeeeeeeee

It heightens. Again I empty the contents of my stomach on the living room floor.

Weeeeeeeeeeeeeeeeeeeeeeeeeee

Make it stop make it stop make it stop make it stop!

Weeeeeeeeeeeeeeeeeeeeeeeeeeeeeeeeeee

And then suddenly, it's gone.

Chapter 15

"Singer! Singer!" Oh God, not Bryce again. My head still reverberates with echoes of last night's migraine. It's too early in the day for Bryce Coolie.

"Special Agent Singer! I have something for you." The senior analyst jogs his way between cubicles, nearly knocks over a mail cart, and almost levels an intern to get to me. In his hand is a large, sealed evidence envelope.

Pink salmon shirt and a straight black tie, huh Bryce? Only assholes who think their shit don't stink, wear pink. I have to laugh at the unintentional rhyme in my head.

"What's so funny, Agent?" His smile beams. Bryce looks absolutely desperate for inclusion in what I'm certain he thinks is some inside joke I'm telling myself, one he feels destined to be included in. I guess he'll have to get used to disappointment.

"Nothing, Bryce. What do you have for me?"

That smile of his...it just gapes. His eyes twinkle. If I didn't know any better I'd think he wanted to fuck me. "What? Oh, yeah. Here." He shoves the envelope into my arms. It's bulky and heavy.

"What is this?"

"It's for the Theodore Grant case. The Carroll County Sheriff's forwarded to our Branson office and they sent it over. Said you asked them to go through a bunch of boxes you found at the crime scene. Oh, and this too," he hands me a dossier. "Details on their search of the premises. I thought you said this guy was a hoarder? Hoarders are never this meticulous."

"What are you talking about, Bryce?"

"Apparently every box was sorted and full of neatly packed binders. The police said each was meticulously labeled."

"Binders full of what?"

"Formulas, apparently. Equations and proofs. Stuff only a physicist would understand. If he was hoarding, he was pretty particular about what he was hoarding. But that there," he points at the evidence folder, "you'll find that particularly interesting."

I'm dying to know what's in the folder but there's no way in holy hell I'm going to ask Bryce Coolie and open that Pandora's Box. Nor would I dare open it in his presence so he could over-the-shoulder inspect it along with me.

"How do you know so much about my case?"

Bryce licks his lips and rocks on his heels, hands in his pants. "Special Agent Goodwin told me." *Fucking Goodwin!* "You know, Singer," he throws a manicured hand up on my shoulder; "if you ever need any help, I'd be more than happy to pitch in. Sounds like a fascinating case you're working on, and I'm not officially assigned right now. Anything at all. Even the busy work. I don't mind."

"I'll keep that in mind, Analyst." I step back so his hand falls from my shoulder.

"Oh, and if you, you know, ever want to grab a beer... Or if you ever need someone to talk to about, you know, about what happened with Special Agent Moser, I'd—"

God I want to slap the shit out of his freckled face. How wonderful it would be to just smile and whisper, "come here, I have a secret to tell you," and as the little sycophant leans in—as all his hopes and dreams of inclusion seem to come to fruition—I wrap my hands around his throat and squeeze the life right out of him. *No I don't want your help with the case! No I don't want to have a beer with you. No I don't want to cry on your pink fucking shoulder!* But I hold back. It's my ego at work on me—I know it is. I can't help but bask a little in all the glory this wide-eyed child in his pink button-up shirt is heaping at my feet.

"Thanks Bryce, but we got this one under control. Just let me know if anything more comes in from Carroll County. Oh and, let me know when the tech's are done analyzing that contraption we found at the scene."

"You got it, Singer!" I turn and walk away but he keeps talking at my back as if I'm still there. "Man, this is a strange one though, isn't it? Aluminum foil wallpaper? Man, what do you make of that? I was talking with Special Agent Goodwin and she told me that—" *Fucking Goodwin!*

His voice diminishes as I round the corner out of the office bullpen. I'm ninety percent certain that even now, with me well out of sight, Analyst Bryce Coolie rambles on to empty air.

Agent Goodwin is waiting for me at my desk. She's got her tablet in her lap, a can of orange cola in her hand, and the straw a permanent fixture in her mouth. "Rook ad dis," she mumbles then spits out the straw and tries again. "Look at this." She thrusts the tablet into my hands.

"What am I looking at here?" It's a scan of an old newspaper article from archives. A black and white picture of a crime scene with the caption:

Man Found Incinerated in South Bronx Apartment

No Sign of a Fire

I read a little further:

> ...The remains of what authorities believe to be Anthony Bristol, age 59, were found in his South Bronx apartment yesterday following the 4.6 magnitude earthquake that shook upper Manhattan...

No body was found at the scene, only a small pile of ash amongst what appeared to be Mister Bristol's bones. A reporter for the Daily Tribune indicated that first responders found the remains lying on the kitchen floor, still clothed...

Oddly, there were no signs of fire damage to the apartment or to Mr. Bristol's clothing, which were found draped about his remains. Authorities are baffled as to—"

"Look, I know you didn't want to follow up on the possibility of SHC, I mean, Spontaneous...Human...Combustion, but this one in particular... Look here," Goodwin rips the tablet from my hands, scrolls down the page, and then shoves it back into my arms. "He was a repair man. And before you ask what the correlation is, according to the report, they found an electric microwave plugged in on his coffee table right next to where they found his remains. He was working on it, testing it probably, when the earthquake struck."

I know where she's going with this, but I can't help myself. "Goodwin, what the fu—"

"Vibration? Electrical current? Ash and bone? Come on, Singer, you can't deny that this looks an awful lot like what happened to Doctor Grant."

It takes me a moment to respond. I guess it's my own lack for willingness to accept that this ridiculous set of circumstances may actually warrant further investigation. "Alright, Agent. Follow up on it. If we have a pattern, then we've got something to go on."

Goodwin looks absolutely jubilated. "What do you have there?" She points to the evidence envelope.

"Something the Carroll County Sheriff's found in Doctor Grant's files."

"Are you going to open it?" she asks.

That's a good question. Strange, but I almost forgot I was holding it. I'm half inclined to toss it in the garbage for some reason. Instead I hand it to Goodwin who tears into it like a hungry dog at dinner. Once open, she flips it over and out plop two books; a notebook and a neatly bound, black leather book. She thumbs through the notebook first. "It's his journal." She hands it to me. Then she picks up the leather bound book. There's no title on the cover—nothing at all—just black leather. Inside it lacks a title page, an author's name, there's no publishing notes, nothing whatsoever. As Goodwin comes to the first line within the book, she says, "Listen to this, Singer; 'Are we to supplicate he who created us solely because he gifted us life? Of our mothers and fathers—they who birthed us into this world—what if these creators lie with monsters? Do we still show them reverence, or do we cast stones until the beasts lay sundered?' It goes on and on like this." She scans a few more lines then says, "'A cruel trick it is to soak our corporeal form in oils of greed and lust and envy, only to proffer us waters that can never render us clean.'"

"Sounds like bad poetry." I crack open the journal. "Wonder why they included it with the journal?"

Goodwin flips a few more pages and something falls to the floor. "A note." She picks it up. "It's Grant's handwriting. She reads it aloud:

"'It's an accepted fact that when you learn a new language your neural pathways are forever and irrevocably altered. Your biochemistry is changed. It's not simply that you now know how to say "How much for that Big Mac?" in Swahili, rather everything you see and hear and learn from that point on is handled a little bit differently by your brain than prior to your understanding of Swahili linguistics. In this way, by learning a language you yourself are forever changed as a person. The way you experience life and the world around you, the way you interact with those in your life, the way you think about issues faced and the methods you then choose to employ in order to navigate these problems are altered, if only in the slightest.

'It has been theorized by linguists and arguably proven (though Dr. Johnstone's studies in neurological spirituality are highly debated) that the same alterations in brain chemistry and neural highways take place when someone embraces a belief in a higher power. There is something unique that transpires in the human mind when thoughts float from everyday life to that of God. And once you've fully committed to truly believing in the seemingly impossible—the acceptance of a godlike being—as it is with learning a foreign language, such thought processes drastically alter your neural makeup. For better or worse, your brain chemistry is affected, endorphins are released, and the temporal lobes are stimulated in ways they've never been before.

'A strong faith in anything that cannot be proven is more of a mental condition than much else, a coping mechanism engrained in our psyche to keep us from losing our marbles as we walk through a world full of unsolved mysteries and potentially unanswerable questions, or at the very least, incomprehensible possibilities. Remember that the fundamental base instinct of the human condition is to expand our understanding of the world around us. This is what drives us onward as a species. This inherent trait is why we've been able to evolve from stone tools to rocket ships in a meager four thousand years, while other primates such as the gorilla—a species whose DNA makeup is a 98% match to our own—haven't evolved technologically at all.

'Which begs the question; where did our inherent thirst for knowledge come from? If we are descended from apes, why did we evolve so dramatically while they remained basically unchanged for millions of years? The mystery of the Missing Link plagues paleontologists to this day. Something happened. Something awoke within us a spark of wonderment that consumed our most primal desires, that pushed us forward as a species and birthed a lust for total understanding of not only our world, but ourselves.'"

Goodwin flips over the paper. There's more on the back. She glances up at me and I say, "Is this what Nobel Prize winning scientists do with their spare time. Bash God?"

"Sometimes you just gotta get it out, Agent."

Funny, but I totally understand what she means. Without even thinking, I say, "Go on. Keep reading." And she does.

"'Even our most ancient ancestors possessed this unquenchable thirst for knowledge and understanding. And that which they could not understand, that which they lacked the tools and fundamental knowledge to comprehend, they developed constructs to explain it. If we trace back our origins to the earliest "thinking" men and women, the world they experienced would have been a much more terrifying yet magical place than the one we see today. Today all the answers to our most burning questions are available at our fingertips, and even now we reach for the stars and consume ourselves with the challenge of answering the few unanswered mysteries of science and life. But for ancient man, they knew little at all about our world. Knowledge we mundanely take for granted, such as what generates a strike of lightning or what that warm, glowing ball is in the sky—to ancient man these were mystical beings and magical spirits, miracles and wonders. They knew not what caused the sun to rise in the morning and set at night. All they knew of this bizarre phenomenon was that a mystical orb erupted from the crest of the mountains to warm them each morning and help their crops burgeon, only to be swallowed by the sea at the end of the day. And should the sun hide behind snow clouds, they would freeze and die. Should the sun shine too bright and hot for too long, their crops would wilt.

'It comes as no surprise that one of the first gods worshipped by primitive man was the sun. Around the world, varying cultures separated by thousands of miles and oceans of water—men and women that had absolutely no way of knowing or influencing one another—all shared reverence for this same deity.

'In Africa, the Tiv people considered the sun to be the child of the Supreme Being Awondo, and the Moon, Awondo's daughter. Across the sea, the Aztec bowed to the sun, naming it Tonatiuh and worshipping it as modern day Christians worship Jehovah. Ancient Egyptians worshipped the sun in various forms, as did the Chinese and the Hindu. Even in the Balkans they celebrated a sun goddess; Saulė.

'Today, no one with a rational mind and an understanding of science and astronomy would fall victim to one of these ancient and dare I say, childish belief systems. That's because we now know with total certainty that the sun, for example, is not a god. We know that when the sun hides for months at a time or blights the land with a heat wave, it isn't due to Tonatiuh's displeasure with the number of human sacrifices we have proffered. As easy as it is for the modern faithful to dismiss the sun gods of ancient Earth, the pantheon of Norse gods who coveted death in battle above all else, and the more recent advent of increasingly absurd religions such as Scientology, they struggle to differentiate the tenets and origins of their own faith from these more ridiculous religions even though they are, at their very core, cut from the same cloth.

'Though modern religions may not be birthed from our desire to understand natural phenomena such as the sun and the stars, they are birthed from our desire to understand the more ethereal questions. Questions long thought unanswerable, such as: do we live on in another form after we die; or who created the universe; or what is our purpose in this life? These questions supplanted the more puerile questions of ancient man such as: the origin of fire; disease; the sun; or the moon and the stars. Our drive to understand each and every aspect of our world and our reason for existing upon it, up until this point could only be quenched through such a belief system, for until these secrets are unlocked through scientific exploration, we have no answers to these most pivotal of mysteries.'"

"Any there more notes in there?" I ask.

Goodwin slides the one she found back in the exact page from whence she found it and then flips through the book. "I'll have to catalogue these somehow. There's no page numbers in this book. Ah, here's another," she leaves it and thumbs further on, "and another, and…this thing is packed full of Doctor Grant's notes."

"Do you think there's anything important in there?" I more ask to check her pulse on the case. I've already made up my mind.

"You watched the same videos I did last night. Whatever drove him to build that machine and hide out in the mountains, I'll bet a month's pay it started with this book and that journal."

"Alright, Goodwin. You take his journal and I'll take the book. You think you can get through it all tonight?" She nods. "Good. Let's compare notes tomorrow. I guess those Carroll deputies weren't completely useless after all."

Chapter 16

"You look tired, Bill." *How perceptive, Carrie.* She's wearing a beige peplum dress that hugs her curves like an Indy race-car. I give myself ample time to soak her in before responding.

"I'm fine."

"We've talked about this." She crosses her legs and in the process I catch a glimpse of her panties. "If you can't be honest with me in here then I can't do my job and you can't get the help you need."

"And like I told you, I'm not in need of any help."

"Your agency seems to feel differently."

"Fine, Doc. Fine. I woke up in the middle of the night and couldn't fall back asleep. That's it. Watched a Gunsmoke marathon until it was time to head into the office. Was a pretty nice morning, now that I think about it." That's half bullshit. Sure Gunsmoke was on in the background, but most of the morning my attention was on Doctor Grant's black book. I gave it the ole college try. It lasted until about five AM at which point I gave up trying to decipher the nonsensical ramblings and lent my eyes solely to the television where I spent the rest of the morning drooling over Miss Kitty and watching James Arness try to act.

Carrie looks thoroughly intrigued. Insomnia is a psychologist's wet dream. "What do you think caused your restlessness?"

"I know exactly what caused it." She waits for me to continue but I stall and hold her in anticipation. Not to seem intriguing or anything; just a few seconds of uninterrupted silence to picture her slip out of that peplum dress and climb into my lap. "A dream woke me up."

"Do you remember this dream?"

On second thought, insomnia is not a psychologist's wet dream. Dreams are psychologists' wet dreams. "I never remember my dreams. Can't recall the last time I did." Falling asleep with enough scotch on the brain to drown an elephant lends to poor subconscious recall. "But yeah, this one, this one I remember for some reason."

"Do you want to tell me about it?"

Not especially. "I um, I..." For a minute there I contemplate feeding her a story. I could tell her I dreamt of sharks circling beneath me as I floated atop calm waters. Test out her knowledge of dream interpretation and see if she tells me that it's simply a fear of the unknown. Or I could tell her I dreamt of her and I together on a beach somewhere and confess I'd love to make that dream a reality. *"Carrie Dent, you're the first dream I've bothered to hold onto for as long as I can remember."* Probably too cheesy for the likes of her. But I guess deep down I'm tired of bullshitting her. I'm tired of bullshitting myself.

"I was down in a well. It was dark and deep and there was no way out." Just recounting it fills my veins with ice water. It was so vivid. I'd never had a dream so lucid. It felt more like a memory than a dream.

"The water was freezing and smelled like, like rot and sewage." She doesn't interrupt, doesn't ask any questions, just leans in with her fist beneath her chin and listens. There's something about having someone hang on your words like that—someone really trying to figure you out, like you're the center of the universe for a few fleeting moments.

"I was terrified, but, but not of dying down there. I was scared of something else. Something was in the water with me. It kept brushing my leg. And I was screaming for help—screaming for my partner." A shiver tickles my spine. I shake it out my shoulders. "I can still feel it; my arms and legs seizing up from hypothermia, the chatter of my teeth, the foul smell. I'd struggle to stay afloat but every few minutes I'd sink below the surface of the water. When I managed to resurface I'd take a big gulp of air and wind up swallowing a mouthful of that sludge. God, I can still taste it on my tongue. It tasted like sour milk."

Carrie asks, "You could taste the water?"

"Yeah. Tasted awful."

"That's interesting."

"Care to elaborate?"

"It's just…that's quite rare. Very few experience the sensation of taste, or smell for that matter, in their dreams. And what woke you from such a lucid dream?"

I can still see her face. Even with the skin sloughed from her bones I know it was her. The rope must've come loose from all my thrashing about. And there she was floating inches from me, bloated and putrid and more real than I remember her in life. But I can't tell Carrie any of this. Instead I tell her, "I woke up right about the time I started to drown."

Chapter 17

"Listen Habibi, I'm not in the mood for jokes." Doctor Ali Nazara, senior tech analyst with the FBI, is as smug a towel-head as I've ever seen.

"If you er tying ta insult me, Eshial Agent Inger, you have failed. Habibi means 'beloved.'"

"Okay fine, let's try this again clit-chopper; what the hell does it do?" The fact he hasn't sued me after all these years of abuse has me almost liking the guy.

"Clit-chopper?" he bobs his head and curls the corners of his lips down in reflection. "Better. I am now who-lly offended…you self-righteous, Islamophobe, piece of goose shit."

"Goose shit?" His pronunciation of *shit* is spot on.

Ali rolls his shoulders and turns toward Doctor Grant's contraption on the table behind him. "Bullshit, horseshit, goose shit—shit is shit, Agent Inger. Does matter what kine you are? You're still shit." *Fair enough.* "And you asked of me to examine da device and tell you what it is, and I tell you already what it is. Just because you dunt like de answer does not make it any less truth."

Ali places both hands on the metal grips. Just seeing him touch them gives me a start. I half expect him to burst into flames on contact. "These grips do two very imple tings." He turns on the machine which produces a slight hum. My mouth opens and closes in an attempt to stop him, but no words come out. But a voice in the back of my head reminds me that there's no way on Earth the machine is capable of doing what it appeared to do to Doctor Grant. Yet I find myself in a silent retreat.

"One," Ali says, "dey vibrate." As he grabs the grips his hands begin to shake. "And two, dey conduct an electrical current. And dat is all." He releases and turns off the device. "As I said before, it dis utterly useless and holds no practical purpoose.

"Certainly de calibrations er quite precise. It can be calibrated within .1 Hertz vib-er-atory displace-i-ment and .0001 milliamps of current—but it serves no purpoose and certainly could not result en total particle fez-sion. Even a *mental giant* such as yourself, Eshial Agent Inger, must possess da common sense ta realize dat."

Vibratory displacement of 900 Hertz. A peak-to-peak level of 7.25 Kilohertz with RMS levels at 704 volts and precisely 5.24 milliamps. Those were the exact set of circumstances that apparently fried Doctor Theodore Grant. God I want to ask Ali to try those settings. It certainly would answer a lot of questions. But an imaginary voice whispers warning in my ear. What if it works? As much as I love shitting all over Ali Nazara for being a camel-jockey prick, I actually kind of like the guy. *What am I saying?* Even if I couldn't stand the guy, I couldn't risk letting him fry just so I could put a theory to bed. But still…

"Vibratory displacement of 900 Hertz. A peak-to-peak level of 7.25 Kilohertz with RMS levels at 704 volts and 5.24 milliamps. I'd like to test out those settings, preferably on something non-human."

"Oh for goodnis sakes, Bill." Ali flips back around and starts mussing with the dials.

I grab his hand but he yanks it away. "I said non-human, Ali."

"I'm telling you, is impossible for dis thing to—"

"Impossible? Or improbable?" *Oh Jesus, Doctor Grant's words coming out of my mouth.*

Ali gives me a placating smile. "Agent Inger, I didn't spend eight years at King Saud University to—"

"King Saud University, huh?"

"It's da top engineering school in all Saudi Arabia! I know what I'm talking bout. Dis device is nothing more dan a well put together science project, and certainly nothing da fear." He fiddles with one of the dials and then flips the machine back on. The whine is louder now—loud enough to make me cringe. I take a few steps back.

"900 Hertz, correct, Agent?" I nod agreement. "7.25 Kilohertz, 704 volts." A few more adjustments and the machine's really humming. "And 5.24 milliamps—not even enough current to kill a kitten."

I take a few more steps back. I don't even realize I'm doing it at first, but once I do I can't help but blush at the fact there's a large enough part of me that actually believes this machine will do the impossible, to have me subconsciously retreat.

Ali just stares at me over his shoulder perplexed. He shakes his head and cracks a fractious smile. "Seriously, Agent, what's gotten into you?"

My heart pounds in my chest. There's static in the air—I can taste it. In the back of my mind I get a flash of Doctor Grant vaporized in a instant, an impossible fate that for some reason I feel in my heart is about to befall my favorite verbal punching bag, Tech Analyst Ali Nazara.

Without so much as another word, he turns and grabs the handles.

A Note Written by Doctor Theodore Grant, Found in the Black Book

Control. That has long been the hideous secret agenda behind organized religion. For we are barbaric and uncontrollable by our very nature. How is one to rule over barbarism when threat of death cannot sway it? Though modern society may still seem barbaric at times, compared to the lawless nomads and savage tribes of antediluvian times, we're all a bunch of saints in white robes today.

As far back as the pharaoh kings (and likely much earlier), those who held or wished to hold power discovered the easiest road to that end was to placate mankind's basest desires and exploit our most fragile emotions. Just as rudimentary as our need for air and water, nearly all humans grow to possess an unquenchable need for answers to life's most enduring questions. And even if those answers are rather unbelievable, we find solitude in them.

Take Pharaoh Akhenaten of Egypt, for example. He founded a monotheistic religion called Atenism and commanded it be forever the official religion of Egypt. Not surprisingly, only Akhenaten could speak to this newly anointed supreme deity, Aten, and undoubtedly declaimed a myriad of dogmatic laws that Aten supposedly passed to him and him alone—laws that most certainly favored the pharaoh's personal agenda.

The Jews kept their people from eating pork by telling them that God condemned it due to the animal not being a predator, but that was a lie. Pigs are carnivorous scavengers and unclean, and many falsely assumed they would rampantly spread disease amongst the faithful if consumed. When the fear of death couldn't deter the starving faithful from consuming swine, well, they simply decreed that God himself had condemned the act. And just like that, no more bacon for breakfast.

The Germanic people worshipped many gods, most of whom our calendar months and days of the week are still named for. Wednesday is named for Odin, chief amongst their pantheon. Thursday is Thor's day, and so on. Part of their dogma held to the belief that the only way to reach Valhalla—their version of heaven—was to die in battle fighting for one's Jarl (or king). I can't help but point out the obvious; this holy law seems to benefit the Jarl much more than his vassals. And as theologians have of course found, the origin of these faiths and their tenets were often birthed by mortals who held seats of power, not by Odin or Thor, or some such deity. How better to squelch the fear of death and incite your people to fight and die on your behalf than to promise them everlasting life in paradise? If that isn't a human construct, I don't know what is.

And this concept is not unique to ancient religions. Modern Islam, for example, preaches a similar doctrine, one which was undoubtedly designed to spread their faith and ultimately the influence and authority of their leaders around the globe. Martyrdom and Muslims have become synonymous these days. The concept of Jihad is mentioned in their holy book on 164 different occasions. War against non-Muslims is mentioned at least 109 different times. This comes as no surprise, for the spectacle of atrocities committed by followers of this religion, much like the Vikings of old who honored their many gods through savagery in war, is to realize the true power of faith.

Those practitioners who sacrifice themselves to murder innocent civilians are so conveniently labeled insane, but I would argue no such malady is at work. Rather we are bearing witness to the true power of belief in a god figure, a concept which holds such a perdurable grasp on the human mind as to short-circuit one's ingrained moral compass.

Insane? Evil? Unfortunately it just isn't that simple. These extremists do not kill innocents because it pleasures them, nor do they do so out of a compulsion brought on by mental illness. These acts, as horrific as they are, are perpetrated by sane men and women who believe so vehemently that they are doing the work of god as to lay their own lives on the altar of their faith. This is the pinnacle of brainwashing. This is the power of faith shown in all its terrible glory for the modern age. This is what happens when we allow a single ideology to take control of our two most powerful emotions, love and fear.

This manipulation of *Homo sapiens* rudimentary and ingrained desire to understand all the many facets of life and the universe has repeated ad nauseam throughout history. Today, televangelists prey on the weak of mind—the lost and melancholy; those who yearn so desperately for purpose they'll do just about anything to find it, even give their life's savings to a man they must know deep in their hearts is but a charlatan.

Since time immemorial conquerors have exploited again and again this weak link in our mental constitution, hiding behind a call from a higher power to send their armies to war and motivate the torpid masses to fight their battles and expand their kingdoms. Just as the Spanish Inquisition stood on the shoulders of Catholicism to ensure Ferdinand II and Isabella I retained their power. Over 150,000 citizens were charged with heretical crimes and nearly five thousand of them were executed in the name of God.

As it was during the Dark Ages where bishops and church leaders sat on king's councils where it was whispered they were the true rulers, controlling the monarchs like puppeteers. And back in the present, where science fiction author L. Ron Hubbard was once quoted as saying, "The easiest way to make a million dollars is to start your own religion." Not surprising, Mr. Hubbard later founded the religion of Scientology and through his church pulled a fortune from the pockets of those desperate for purpose and answers.

Fast forward a thousand years from now and who knows… Perhaps Scientology will be the new Nation of Islam or the new Christianity, and thousands of followers will kill thousands of non-believers for blaspheming the great prophet, L. Ron Hubbard.

Chapter 18

Nothing. Nothing happens. No flash of light. No camel-fucker reduced to a pile of ash and bone. Just the forever crotchety Ali Nazara given a slight shake and a jolt from grabbing two electrified handgrips. He releases, rubs his palms, and flips off the machine. His hands fly out to his sides then slap back to his thighs. "Satisfied?" He looks disgusted with me. I can't blame him. "Since when you are so damn gullible?"

"Just a little joke is all, Al." *No joke.* "Gotta keep you on your toes." My heart's still jackhammering my chest. *Christ, did I really think that would work?*

"Yes, joke. You always were such a funny, little man, Eshial Agent Inger." Ali turns and walks away.

"Osama-BinLamu-alaikum," I shout at his back.

He stops midway across the lab, points to the heavens, and shouts, "Wa-Alaikum-Salaam, Agent Inger. Wa-Alaikum-Salaam."

As I leave the lab, my phone rings. It's Goodwin. "Deputy Director Kennedy wants to see us in his office ASAP. He wants an update on the Grant case. He's going to ask to see the initial findings report." *And we have nothing to tell him.* "What did Nazara say?"

"Well, he called me a piece of goose shit."

"I'm sure you deserved it."

"He also tested Grant's settings, the settings that fried him in the video."

Silence on the other end of the phone. I wonder if her heart is trying to escape her ribcage just as mine had. Eventually she replies, "And?"

"And he's fine. Like I told you, nothing would happen. Dead end. Film magic. It's a fraud, Goodwin. You can put that in the report to Kennedy."

"There could've been additional contributing factors, something we missed, something he didn't mention in the tapes? The lighting in the room, moisture on his palms effecting the electrical current, his foil cap acting as a resonator, or the foil walls focusing wave fronts, or even the—"

"Just stop, Goodwin. It's a dead-end. The machine didn't kill him. We can't even be certain he's dead." I'm rounding the corner to the elevator when I bump into her coming the other way. We say a few more words into our cell phones while standing inches apart, then simultaneously feel the ridiculousness of our situation and put them away.

"Whatever we saw on that video, it wasn't, it wasn't real. We're looking in the wrong direction."

Ding. The elevator doors open, a few people shuffle out and we shuffle in.

"Fine," she concedes.

"Fine?"

"Fine." She nods, wraps her arms around the case file as if it's a warm blanket, and stares ahead at the elevator floor buttons as they light up then go dark one by one. "So what's next?"

"Next? Well, let's see what the Director has to say. It was his brilliant idea to put me on this case. Maybe he has an idea how to get me off it."

"So quick to give up?"

"I know what I know and I know what I don't know. I'm damn good at finding people. I know how people think. I know what they're going to do sometimes before even they know what they're going to do. I hunt killers, Goodwin, not magicians.

"This case is without a doubt the weirdest damn thing I've seen in all my time with the Bureau. Why on Earth Kennedy thought to put me on it is beyond reason. I'm the wrong man for the job. You, you're cut from the same mold as Grant. You make sense. Hell, he should've paired you up with your new buddy Bryce Coolie. Or shit, how about Lupinski?"

"Coolie is an analyst. Lupinski is a tech."

"And you're an agent. So what? Point is, this is still nothing more than a missing person's case. And I'm a Special Agent with the FBI, a trained profiler, and counter terrorist. Leave the pseudo-science, whacko treasure hunts to people like you that actually give a shit."

"Ohhh. Poor thing. Is your ego hurt? Has the incontrovertible Bill Singer met his match with a missing person's case?"

Fuck you, Goodwin.

"And it's not pseudo-science. That's how it works, Singer. That's how physics works. Through mathematical and logical proofs you can prove or disprove just about anything. They can determine the weight of the sun, for Christ's sake. The existence of atoms was first theorized, I might add, back when Jesus Christ was still alive. Obviously they didn't have atomic microscopes back then, but using the same logical axioms as Doctor Grant, they discovered and proved the existence of wonders far beyond the bounds of what they could see and hear and feel and prove through conventional means."

"Alright, Goodwin. You've made your point." The elevator doors open and we step out. "Look, I'm not giving up on the case. If for no other reason than to help you sleep at night," *and help me sleep at night,* "I'll see this thing through. We'll figure out what happened to Grant."

Before I can knock on Deputy Assistant Director Kennedy's door, he waves us in. He's on the phone, feet up on his desk when we enter. "I'll call you back. They just stepped in. Alright. Alright. Give me twenty." He hangs up the phone, pinches his brow, and then says, "Take a seat you two." And we do. His Italian leather chair makes a farting sound as my ass plops down in it.

"An initial findings report is due within the first forty-eight hours. You both know this. So what's the hold up?"

Agent Goodwin glances at me and I give her a reluctant nod. She sets the file down on Kennedy's desk. "Sorry, Deputy Director, but—"

I cut in, "We wanted to give the techs time to work their magic and rule a few things out before we moved forward with the report. It's been a long couple of days."

Kennedy scoops up the file and holds it like a rolled up newspaper to a dog's nose. "Grant's disappearance made headlines back in 2014. And thanks to the big mouth of one of the boys in blue over in Carroll County, the details of his reappearance are back in the headlines." With his hands he makes the shape of rainbow. "A secret compound wrapped in aluminum foil. A deadly, electrified front door. Boxes full of Doctor Grant's research. Christ, they'll probably make a movie."

"You just absorb all that through osmosis?"

Kennedy glances at the rolled up file in his hand and tosses it down on his Carpathian Elm desk. "You don't watch the news, do you?"

"I don't much care what the Kardashians are up to."

"I don't watch much TV," says Goodwin.

Kennedy simpers, huffs, opens the file, and begins to read. Goodwin and I sit in silence while he peruses the report she drafted. Each turn of the page comes with a lick of his thumb and forefinger.

"What did forensics come back with?"

"Inconclusive."

"And this device, the one that's shown in the video, has Tech had a chance to look at it?"

"I was just down with Nazara right before coming up to see you, sir."

"And?"

Goodwin looks uncomfortable, as if she can't believe it didn't work.

"And it's nothing, sir. Ali called it a well put together science project. The video's likely a fake too."

Goodwin opens her mouth to speak, squeaks out a sound, then quiets.

"And you've reviewed all the tapes?"

"Doctor Grant appears to have been suffering from a form of schizophrenia, perhaps even an onset of dementia. He was convinced we're all infected by," *how the hell do I even say this?*

Goodwin blurts out, "Inter-dimensional, inorganic, hyper-intelligent parasites."

Kennedy raises an eyebrow. "Okay. So we don't have a body—"

"We do have a body," interrupts Goodwin.

"No, agent, we do not. If forensics can't confirm the remains found at the scene belonged to Grant, then we don't know definitively if it's Grant, do we? No body, no motive to suspect foul play. What do we have, Singer?"

I know what he wants to hear. He wants me to tell him that we can shut the case, that we can give the media a story to shut them up—a story that can't later come back to haunt us if exposed in the form of a bold-faced lie. He wants us to move on to more pressing cases, the kinds of which I first thought I too wanted to move on to; national security, terror threats, murders, corporate espionage—the kind of shit that really matters. Or at least, the kind of shit that I thought really matters.

Why put an unstable agent on a case guaranteed to be a media circus? I suppose if I lose my shit and fuck it up, Kennedy would have damn good cause—public cause—to show me the door. Or perhaps it's because he thought nobody could get hurt if I fucked it up. Regardless of his motives, I get the sense that right about now, with the rug pulled back on this case and the most assuredly Chief of Staff demanding answers on the other end of that phone when we first walked in, he's ready to close the book on this one.

"In my opinion, sir, Doctor Grant pulled some kind of a stunt here. The tech that analyzed the remains can't even be certain they're real. I can have Ops Tech review the footage for tampering, but it appears that this was a staged act." *Do I really believe a word I'm saying? Unless the Doctor Grant from the video is the world's greatest actor, he certainly wasn't the one staging it. And why would someone who successfully fell off the grid years ago want to stage another disappearance?*

"Staged for what purpose?"

Agent Goodwin's been rather taciturn the entire meeting. Perhaps she's nervous in the presence of Deputy Assistant Director Kennedy? But suddenly her attitude shifts and she blurts out, "Perhaps it's a purpose only a schizophrenic genius could come up with. Clearly Doctor Grant had lost his mental faculties. The theories he puts forth on those tapes are, well, with a graduate in physics, sir, I can honestly tell you, they were nonsensical at best, incoherent ramblings at worst. He appears to have lost most cognitive function and has completely eschewed, he completely eschewed standard Newtonian mechanics, the Galilean limit, and Kepler's laws of planetary motion—principles he never would've overlooked had he been thinking rationally."

I have no idea what she's talking about but I know for a fact she isn't being truthful. Quick head movements, stuttered breathing (though that could be caused by nerves due to this being her first case report in front of the director), the fact she repeated 'completely eschewed' is a classic red flag, providing too much information… Why not just tell him the doctor's theories were preposterous and easily refutable if that were the case? Her feet are calm, but she keeps placing her hands over her abdomen. Covering vulnerable areas—another red flag—and what's more vulnerable to a woman than her stomach? Fat shaming is far from dead in the deep psyche of the modern female.

"In my professional opinion, Director Kennedy, the doctor is likely still alive and this is all part of some sick ruse he's trying to pull. Chances are he doesn't even realize he's doing it."

More lies, lies compounding lies. But I remain silent and let her speak.

Kennedy nods his head. That's exactly what he wanted to hear. *Why are you feeding him what he wants, Roxanne? That's my job.*

He says, "I want your final report to be succinct and non-inflammatory. Just the facts. 'There was no sign of the doctor at the premises, though it was clear he had been there at one time. We are exploring all options but at this time we have no leads as to his whereabouts.' Something to that effect. Have it back on my desk by the end of the day. Understood?"

Goodwin nods. I nod.

"We're turning this back over to the state authorities. Let them reopen Grant's missing person's case if they want."

"He crossed state lines." I'm not sure why I'm arguing.

"No, Special Agent, he did not. There's no way we can prove those are Grant's remains, which means we really don't have a crime scene, do we?"

I try to answer but Kennedy carries over my words. "Rhetorical question. Now I want all the supposed evidence you collected tagged and shipped back to Carroll County. No doubt Grant's next of kin will want to take possession. Everything except the remains, that is. Those stay here."

"Everything except the remains? May I ask why?"

"No, Special Agent Singer, you may not."

Daemon Phenomena – April 4th, 2017

"It explains so much! So very much." His fingernails look more like talons now, his hair is down to his shoulders, and his beard is long and matted. Atop Doctor Grant's head rests a foil cap, and the walls of his office are as we initially found them—completely covered in shiny aluminum foil.

"Think about it! Just think!" he taps his foil cap. "Apparitions for example? If such ghostly visages are to be believed, perhaps they are simply conglomerated masses of Daemons—nanoclouds if you will—taking the form of bodies they once occupied. Perhaps they became trapped, trapped in space, trapped in a physical structure, a home, a room, energy ley-lines? Maybe magnetic fields exist in these supposed supernatural spaces, fields that prevent Daemon communications—prevent their escape—so they maintain the familiar form they had once inhabited, that of their former host.

"Just theories and postulations. Theories and postulations. But what if? What if? What if?" His speech is succinct; though so rapid it's difficult to follow. It's like watching an excited child talk about his favorite movie.

"Telekinesis?" he blurts out. "Of course the mind can move objects if you can somehow inadvertently command the Daemons to your bidding. Who knows how many microscopic nanites inhabit the space all around us?" He whirls about in his seat and waves his hands through the air. "A glitch, a bug, a mutation of their code that for an instant allows manipulation of matter beyond the bounds of touch?

"And extra sensory perception. That too is so easily explained. The Daemons most assuredly are a hive mind, or some form thereof, linked globally one to the other. And if so, then all living matter on the planet is connected; man, animal, even plants. It explains so much! So much!" His pointer-finger launches skyward and an impossibly wide smile stretches his cheeks.

"Synchronicity! Yes, synchronicity! Throughout history remarkable ideas, major breakthroughs in science and math have occurred simultaneously, and more importantly, independently. In most cases, the inventors had no relationship whatsoever, no contact with one another, and no clue as to the fact the other even existed. Just like the Mayans and the Egyptians, separated by thousands of miles of rolling waves somehow wound up building the same exact structures, other great men of history came to the exact same conclusions, had the exact same epiphanies, cracked the exact same puzzles at the exact same moment as the other!

"There have only been several confirmed cases of this, though I surmise the true statistic is astronomically greater, though impossible to quantify as how would one individual know another had the exact same thought at the same time as they, unless the thought led to a paramount and well documented discovery?

"Newton and Leibniz both formulated calculus at the same time; one in Germany, the other in Britain. Newton was adamant Leibniz had snuck into his office and stole the idea! That's how similar the work was. Koprowski, Salk, and Sabin all developed polio vaccines independent of one another, simultaneously! Elisha Gray and Alexander Graham Bell both filed a patent for the telephone on the exact same day! The invention of the jet engine can accurately be linked back to three men, Hans Ohain, Secondo Campini, and Frank Whittle who all began working on their prototypes at nearly the exact same time. The Higgs-Boson particle was developed into a relativistic model simultaneously by three different groups of physicists, myself among them! How is that even possible? We shared no research, nor was I even aware that Frank Englert and Robert Brout were even working on a model! Like Newton, I thought them thieves! But I was wrong.

"Serendipity? Nonsense! They all had the exact same thoughts at the exact same time. Some may have taken a little longer to bring them to fruition, but it changes nothing. These are seemingly impossible, previously unexplainable phenomena, but now…

"If the Daemons are networked, then every thought in my head is broadcast to the world. Perhaps, perhaps, perhaps sometimes the wires get crossed." His eye twitches and he vigorously scratches his beard. "Perhaps sometimes a message is inadvertently decoded in transit. Perhaps occasionally we are afforded, though accidentally, the ability to listen in. It probably happens more often than we realize. Intuition, mind reading, those uncannily adept at telling truth from lies—perhaps they are more in sync with Daemon transmissions.

"What if it's all just cross-talk between the Daemons in my head and the Daemons in yours?" He's back to pacing the room again, passing in and out of frame. "What if it could be harnessed? What if it could be controlled?" Doctor Grant slaps his own face hard enough to spin his head. "No! No! It's too dangerous. Much too dangerous! They know—they know what I'm thinking."

He plops back down and rocks in his seat, then glances about the room. "I mean you no harm," he whispers to no one. Then he screams it. "I mean you no harm!" Suddenly Grant jumps up and runs to the camera. As he fumbles to turn it off, he repeats over and over, "I shouldn't be filming this. I shouldn't. What was I thinking? They know! They know! They know what's in my head!"

Chapter 19

Doctor Carrie Dent. It's difficult enough to confide your deepest feelings to a relative stranger; even more so once you've been in that stranger's holiest of holies. I suppose I can stop calling her doc and start calling her Carrie.

"How have you been, Bill?"

"I've been good, Doc." Judging by the look on her face, she agrees with my prior sentiment.

"Have you? You don't look good, Bill. You look tired."

"I haven't been sleeping well." *A colossal understatement.*

"And why do you think that is?"

Psychologists. For a hundred and fifty an hour you get to diagnosis yourself. "It's nothing to worry about."

"Why would you think I'd be worried? Are you worried?"

Oh for Christ's sake. "Just a case I've been working on. It's been giving me heartburn."

"Do you want to talk about it?"

"You know I can't."

"Well, not the specifics, but—"

"No, I don't want to talk about it." Even now. Even after our little tryst; once that door shuts and the clock starts running it's like a switch flips and out the window goes the vivacious Carrie and in walks her always clinical doppelganger.

"Okay, Bill, we don't have to talk about what's bothering you. Though might I remind you, to talk about what's bothering you is precisely why you're here."

"You don't have to remind me."

"Okay, then what would you like to talk about?"

"You don't have to pretend *it* didn't happen, Carrie."

Stunned silence. As if we were just going to ignore the two hours spent naked and coiled up on her desk, on the floor, on the couch, in her chair, pressed against the window?

"I'm not pretending anything, Bill. I'd be lying if I told you I don't feel a bit," she bites her lip, "used. But if you think I'm going to pine after you—"

"Have dinner with me tonight."

Again, stunned silence, and then, "I, I can't tonight, I—"

"Yes you can, Carrie. Remember who you're talking to. Don't lie to me." I've always had a gift for sniffing out bullshit. Sure the years of training helps, but even before I learned how to profile, before I was shown the tells and tics and subtle subconscious queues, I had a knack for sniffing it out. Intuition, I guess. If you asked the late, great Doctor Theodore Grant, he'd tell you I was abnormally gifted at intercepting Daemon cross-talk. Strange as it sounds, in the doctor's defense, I almost feel like I **can** read her thoughts. Right now she's stuck halfway between wanting me desperately—more so because she thought she'd never be able to have me again—and wanting to toss me to the curb as karmic justice for having blown off her last dozen phone calls. But more dominating than those two conflicting trains of thought is her desire to rein me in. It's part of being a psychologist, I suppose. She can't stand the fact that she allowed herself to be so vulnerable with me without at the very least getting some moral victory in return. Fixing me, as she sees it, would be a monumental victory—a career defining victory.

I can just picture it; an *I Tamed Bill Singer* plaque hung above her desk alongside her diploma from Northwestern and her license to practice psychology. As proud a memento as she'll ever own.

"I can't tonight, Bill. But tomorrow, tomorrow I'm free."

She's still not being truthful, but I chalk up her reschedule as an attempt to steal some power back in the relationship, even if it's an infinitesimal amount. These ridiculous mind games that occupy much of dating culture are one of a slew of reasons I hate dating. People don't even realize they're playing. It's become so ingrained in our constitution—to try and manipulate everyone in our lives, to try and control everyone at some level.

Like Doctor Grant said, *"Control... For we are barbaric and uncontrollable by our very nature."* What's more barbaric than the circus act of modern dating?

Strangely though, I don't mind giving her a little control back. And I'm not just placating her sensibilities. It's not just the sex. I really want to see her again. Not the on-the-clock Doctor Dent, mind you, but Carrie in the pencil dress. Carrie with her hair down and her smile broad and genuine. Carrie who screamed so loud I thought the windows would shatter.

"Tomorrow, then. I'll pick you up at seven."

The Observer Effect – April 6th, 2017

"As the double-slit experiment showed us, simply through the act of observation we alter the behavior of subatomic systems. This phenomenon has long been an epicenter of debate within the physics community, where a slew of theories as to how photons (and other subatomic particles) seem to display characteristics of both classically defined waves and particles. Wave-particle duality has failed, in my opinion, to do anything more than put a name to this inexplicably bizarre phenomenon…"

I'm certain Agent Goodwin knows exactly what Grant's talking about, but I'm tired of using her as my personal science Wikipedia. I can almost see her head inflate a bit more each time I pump her for information. Instead, I Google it myself. What I find brings my migraine back to front. Mind-fuck science is hard at work with this one. It's no wonder Grant lost his marbles. Just trying to wrap my head around this insane yet apparently well documented, proven phenomenon…

Apparently it has been shown that matter travels through space differently depending on whether you're observing it travel through space or not. It took a while for that to sink in. They call it the observer effect, and the experiment that proved this bizarre circumstance again and again, is called the double-slit experiment. Basically they shine a laser through several panes of material, the first with a single slit in it, the second with two slits, and behind the second, some sort of plate that detects where the light particles hit. The results change depending on whether or not you're observing the experiment. Which begs the question—how the hell does a light wave, particle, whatever—know you're looking at it?

Grant continues, "But I believe the answer as to why subatomic matter changes its state from that of a wave to a particle upon observation is due to the fact that the matter is reacting to Daemons which are reacting to our potential observation of them. How else can you explain why we've never seen them?" *Because they don't exist, you idiot.* "Surely someone would have detected them using a scanning tunneling or atomic force microscope. But no, nothing—it's as if they're invisible, truly invisible.

"What I suspect is happening here is, as the observer, the Daemons inside me, who are likely in constant communication with all the Daemons around me, signal those which inhabit the area of space I aim to observe, thereby allowing those Daemons to obscure—perhaps even vacate the host entirely—which in turn results in the particle-wave phenomenon. Therefore as long as we try and observe them, they are undetectable!"

Chapter 20

Back in the office, I head straight for Goodwin's cubicle. I'm not sure why. There's nothing pressing I need to discuss with her, but that's where my feet take me. I arrive to find it empty. Well, not exactly empty, rather quite the opposite—though lacking a certain agent I was hoping to find there. Her cubicle is full of boxes, boxes stacked upon boxes, boxes marked with dates and names, boxes that look all too familiar.

I grab Bryce Coolie's arm as he passes by and ask, "Where did she get all this?"

Bryce nearly spills his coffee on his purple shirt, but somehow avoids such a disastrous turn of events and instead just spills a tot on the floor. "Christ, Singer! Take it easy."

Again I ask, "These are all the boxes from Doctor Grant's home?"

"Goodwin had them overnighted from the Carroll County evidence locker. And these aren't all of them. There were a few more when they first arrived. They were piled up on top and under her desk too."

The space is now empty. "What would she want with his formulas," I mutter. "When did these get here?"

"This morning."

Straight from Deputy Director Kennedy's office where he pulls us off the case to putting in a request for an evidence transfer on said case. There'll be a world of shit flying her way if Kennedy finds out she blatantly disobeyed a direct order, and all he'd need to do is walk by her cube to realize as much. Her flagrant disregard is so far from her typical M.O; I can't help but feel a twinge of worry. This goes well beyond a curious itch on Goodwin's part.

Bryce sips his coffee and stares at the boxes with an overly contemplative look on his face. His expression reads like one of those giant subway billboards. In big, bold letters it says: *Bryce Coolie; Proud Confidant to Special Agent Bill Singer*. I'm not being egotistical thinking as much. In fact, you'd think I'd love the ego hand-job I get every time Bryce Coolie crosses my path. Instead it just disgusts me the same way a real Bryce Coolie hand-job would.

Still, I say to him, "Bryce, buddy, listen; I have an important favor to ask you?" His eyes damn near explode with excitement.

"Absolutely, Singer. Whatever you need."

"Thanks, pal. Listen, I need you to change the requisition forms for all these boxes. I asked Goodwin to have these sent up here. Change the requestor over to me, okay? Oh, and have these moved back over to my desk. Let's not clutter up her workspace like this."

Bryce is confused. Not quite what he expected when he heard "important favor," I'm sure, but he nods anyways and diligently marches off to take care of it.

I check my watch. "Shit!" It's almost five and I have a date with Carrie in two hours—the first actual date that I've been on in, well, I don't know how long. I guess I should shower and shave first. After all, Carrie's only real draw to me is that she sees me as a fixer-upper. If I don't look a little less dilapidated each time we meet, she might begin to think I'm a lemon and stop trying. Two steps forward, one step back—that's the key with someone like Carrie. She has to feel as though she's making progress but at any moment that progress is in jeopardy of being washed down the drain.

And it's not like she's all that rare in this compulsion. Most women have an engrained desire to mold their men into exactly what they think they should be (usually a mirror of their fathers). They want them to look like movie stars, talk like poets, fuck (rather, make love) like they're in a soap opera, possess the poise and confidence of James Bond, and the soft vulnerability of a leading man in a Nicholas Sparks novel.

It never works out as planned. And after years of trying to get that old jalopy to run like a muscle car, all these women are left with are regret and wasted youth. Of course occasionally the man allows for such castration to occur. And just like with the fixing of an old car, once his woman is satisfied he's been properly reupholstered, that fresh coat of paint has dried, the new tires and bright new headlights are installed, and his motor rebuilt—well, they get bored of him, park him in the garage under a tarp, and move onto another clunker in need of repair.

Being a psychologist, Carrie is doubly prone to slip down this disastrous road with the men in her life. The fact that I'm keenly aware of this undercurrent in our new relationship and contemplating its exploitation in order to get her to fall in love with me isn't any more repugnant than the fact she's doing it in the first place. *Is it?*

Maybe I'll wear a tie tonight. I should wear a tie. Do I still own a tie?

From Unlocking the Secrets of the Universe, Episode 81

"The human brain is an incredibly marvelous organ," says Grant. "With somewhere in the neighborhood of ninety billion nerve cells—almost as many stars as in the Milky Way Galaxy—we hold in our heads the equivalent computational power of a supercomputer containing over eight million parallel processors! To compare and contrast," he holds up his phone, "my smart phone has one processor." An exaggerated pout.

"Though to be fair, computers only really do well what we humans do not. And for that matter, vice-versa. Machines are much more efficient when it comes to mathematical and statistical modeling than us organic computers are, though silicon falls terribly flat when it comes to, for instance, differentiating between a cat and a dog, or performing the necessary calculations needed in order to catch a pop fly in baseball."

An image of a baseball player trying to read a fly ball fills the screen. "Believe it or not, this is actually an incredibly complex task. First you must process a stream of images and register that there is indeed a ball flying through the sky toward you. You must predict its ballistic trajectory, anticipate its speed by evaluating its space and distance against your internal clock, determine the time and likely location of interception," while he's talking, the ballplayer's running in slow motion, his eyes on the ball and arm raised to make the catch, "take into account external forces like wind and the movement of your own body while simultaneously processing visual, auditory, olfactory, and kinesthetic inputs for obstacle avoidance, injury, and threats," Grant's deliberately rambling, accelerating his speech as the image on the screen speeds up, "not to mention send the necessary electrical signals to the 640 skeletal muscles in the human body, all of which are in motion simultaneously. And let's not forget the tandem processes responsible for maintaining a heartbeat, ocular signals, heat dissipation, digestion, and all the rest." The ball player makes the catch. The crowd erupts as he raises his glove skyward.

"Phew!" Grant wipes his brow.

"So why is it that some of us seem so much more adept at playing catch," someone off-screen throws him a foam ball. Doctor Grant gives it a blatantly scripted bumble, stumbles forward, and lets it drop to the floor, "than doing complex math in their heads? It all boils down to neural pathways." Now there's an image of a human brain with little blue electrical signals running along an infinite number of intersecting pathways. "It boils down to how our brains are wired—literally. Some of us are wired for efficiency in calculating the myriad factors required in order to catch a baseball—i.e., they have extraordinary hand-eye coordination." Half a dozen foam balls fly at him from all sides. Grant screeches and jumps back. "Other brains are wired for complex mathematical computations." A stereotypical image of a pencil-protector wearing, glasses clad nerd materializes around the brain on the screen. Grant barks, "Hey! Where did you get my high school yearbook picture?

"In fact, some people are wired for so much efficiency in one particular regard that other brain functions are sacrificed. For these folks, things most of us consider simple, become overly complex. Conversely, things you and I may think impossible, to these savants they are as trivial as reading a menu."

A clip from the movie *Rain Man* pops up. Dustin Hoffman watches a box of toothpicks fall to the floor. He instantly and accurately counts them to the astonishment of Tom Cruise.

"Believe it or not, that isn't fiction. There are savants who can hear a song just once and immediately play it note for note on the piano. Magicians of the mind who in a matter of seconds can tell you which day of the week it was the day you were born. Mental wizards who can remember with perfect clarity every detail of everything they've ever seen in their entire lives. They can recreate an aerial picture of Paris after looking at the unbelievably detailed image for only a few seconds!" There's an image on the screen, a photo of the Eiffel Tower and the surrounding city. Then suddenly it's overlaid with a pencil on paper rendition—a perfect match. Grant points at the drawing and says, "That's a real drawing done by a savant who looked at the photo only one time, and for less than five seconds. Pretty amazing; the power of the mind.

"Some select folks are able to do all of this because their neural pathways are hyper-tuned to a specific task." A top down cartoon of New York City fills the screen. "Think of it like a congested city. Ah, the Big Apple! I could go for a slice of Grimaldi's Pizza right about now." He zones out for a spell, assumedly pondering a warm slice of pizza in his belly, and then melodramatically snaps his attention back to the camera.

"Right, where was I? When we see something, our eyes send electrical signals down our optic nerve," a red car on the screen starts driving west from Queens, "over to our visual cortex in the back of the brain for processing," the car weaves up and down side streets, hops on and off byways and onramps and whizzes down alleyways until it reaches the cortex represented by Brooklyn, "and then stores them back in the prefrontal cortex." The car, which has a cartoon face, grimaces, flips its turn signal, and starts backtracking through the maze of streets all the way to upper Manhattan.

"But what if we put in an express way?" Suddenly the I-495 deviates from its course to midtown and makes a bee-line from Queens to central Brooklyn. With a beaming smile, the little red cartoon car smokes its tires and races back and forth. "Now we're processing images nearly instantaneously! We have a highly efficient brain, at least when it comes to our vision and recall. Of course all those neurons who live in Midtown that were used to taking the 495 straight to Queens and back, well, now they have to travel all the busy side streets just like our little red friend used to. Maybe those midtown folks are responsible for our artistic aptitude, and the owner of this particular brain, someone who once had an expressway when it came to creative thinking, now has the artistic ability of, well, me."

A stick figure drawing pops up next to Grant's head. It looks like something a four-year-old would draw in crayon. "Hey!" he snaps. "I'm not that bad." A cartoon pen adds a stylish top-hat and monocle. "Better," he says.

"Well, I can't draw anymore, but thanks to the new expressway from my optic nerve to my cortex," three foam balls fly at Grant from off-screen. He catches one, tosses it into the air, then catches another, tosses it, then a third. He proceeds to juggle them while he finishes, "I now not only can catch, but maybe I'm ready to play some professional baseball. Pretty cool, huh?"

Chapter 21

She looks cut straight from the pages of Vogue magazine. Sitting across from me in that sleeveless lace sheath, it takes every ounce of willpower not to leap across the table and take her right there on the floor. *Fuck the candles burning hot between us, the boiling soup on our plates, the sharp cutlery—just leap over all of it and pull your best caveman impersonation, bonk her over the head and drag her back to your lair, Singer!* My God, she's gorgeous. Everything about her is physical perfection. Even the way she sips her soup is sexy.

When I first stripped her down back at her office I half expected a conjoined fetus to be staring at me from between those perfect breasts—some malformation to spoil the otherwise perfect canvas that is Carrie Dent's body. But no. No ghastly growth or misshapen breast from a botched boob job. No ungainly scar running across her belly or rolls of flab hidden neatly away beneath a pair of Spanks. Somehow she looked even more put together out of her designer clothes than in them.

I suppose this is why she's single. Men are intimidated by her. And not just by her looks, but her brains. It even goes beyond that. Carrie Dent dissects people for a living. I can't think of a more intimidating caste of woman than a gorgeous, brilliant, psychologist.

But Carrie doesn't intimidate me. I've never met a woman—or man for that matter—who did. I suppose it's because my *Don't-Give-a-Shit Rewards Card* has been full up on points for quite a while. Once you experience the sensation that comes with dodging death, things like whether or not your quote, dream girl, is interested in you, or if the Eagles will ever win a Super Bowl, they just kind of lose every ounce of importance they may have once held. By comparison, just about everything in life gets taken down six rungs. Lost your cell phone? Screw it, doesn't matter. Your car broke down? Screw it, doesn't matter. You're going to be late for work? Screw it, it just doesn't matter.

And it wasn't just once that I nearly died, but nine times. When I was in the military the boys in my company called me *The Cat*. They said I had nine lives. Well if that's true, then I spent every one of them to get to this point right here, right now. I guess we'll know for certain if the next time I dance with the Reaper, he finally lays a finger on me.

"Hope you didn't lose your wallet again," she says. Carrie takes a sip of wine. Her maroon lipstick leaves not a single smudge on the glass.

"Safe and sound in my—" I pat my pocket and strike a face like it's missing, then smile and pull it out. She's referring to our first encounter—the first night we made soap opera love. I had deliberately left my wallet crammed between the sofa cushions in her office after our session. Once her last patient had gone and Carrie was alone in her office getting ready to head home, I knocked and let myself in. It was a fun little treasure hunt trying to find my missing wallet, which of course I knew the whereabouts of the entire time. I told her I was going to be late for a date, and when she picked my brain about the woman I was going to see, I made up a story about how I wasn't really interested in her but I wanted to take Carrie's advice about the importance of having people in your life you can confide in—a support circle—and as I have no friends, well, perhaps she'd be my first in a long while. The conversation was far from sexual. I was playing the hurt puppy; the hurt puppy that was taking confident strides to mend and get back to being a normal member of the litter.

In the end, when we "found" my wallet, I told her I'd missed my date completely and was just going to head home…alone. I made sure to use that word, *alone,* and to try and make it seem like it didn't bother me.

I think the fact that being alone didn't seem to bother me—bothered Carrie more than if it had drove me to tears. I told her that, as silly as it sounds, being here with her right now, tonight, scouring her office for my wallet and talking about life (off the record) was the best date I'd been on in a while. And when she reminded me it wasn't a date, I told her I wish it had been.

Tonight I'd chosen a restaurant not too fancy, not too casual—one I thought would show her I felt her worth the extra coin but not that I was trying to impress. Carrie's too smart and independent to swoon over a five-star meal and a mammoth bill. Hell, I probably would get the same results with a trip to McDonald's. But then she wouldn't be wearing that knockout dress.

God that dress, those eyes, those lips, those tits… I can't think of a single woman I've wanted this bad after having her already. But if I want her so bad, why does my mind keep wandering to thoughts of a short, flat-chested nerd holed up in her apartment obsessing over mounds of scientific formulas hijacked from the Carroll County evidence locker?

"Are you still with me?" Carrie asks.

"What?"

"You looked like you were somewhere else for a moment. Thinking about a case?"

"Actually, I was thinking about my partner." *Fucking Goodwin!*

"You haven't told me much about her. How are you two getting on?"

"Two peas in a pod."

Carrie's thinking about something profound. I can feel it. But she doesn't say a word. Our food arrives and she starts making dainty cuts of her steak. She takes a few more sips of wine, and seeing the wine my throat grows parch and I guzzle down my glass of water.

"This wine is delicious," she finally says. "You don't like wine?"

"Sure, I like wine fine. Prefer a good scotch, though."

"But just water tonight?"

I glance down at the glass. It's still in my hand. Condensation moistens my fingertips. Strange, but I didn't even realize I failed to order a drink. I don't even want a drink. *When's the last time I didn't want a drink?*

"You give up smoking too? I didn't catch a whiff on you. Haven't seen you light up all night. Is this a new Bill Singer I'm seeing here?"

"I, I forgot." *You forgot? You sound like a retard.*

"You forgot to order a drink, or you forgot to have a cigarette?"

"Both…I guess."

Carrie looks puzzled. "I've never heard of a pack-a-day smoker forgetting to smoke." *Or a fifth of scotch a day drinker forgetting to order a drink...* "I should know. There was a time I enjoyed that same awful habit.

"You know, I had a professor who once told us, 'When life's profundities cast off their mask, the Daemons we hold lose their hold on us.'"

"What did you say?"

"I said I've never heard of a pack-a-day—"

"No, the other thing."

"Sounds a bit like a Chinese proverb, I know, but Professor Sun was, well, Chinese, so go figure."

"Say it again, just like you said it."

Her face scrunches up. "You're acting weird, Bill—"

"Just, please. Humor me."

"When life's profundities cast off their mask, the demons we hold lose their hold on us."

"That's what I thought you said." I catch myself mouthing the words over and over. *God I feel strange right now.* Everything is brighter, louder, surreal. Maybe that's just sobriety clearing the cobwebs out.

A twisted look from Carrie and I strike a smile and try and save some face. "That Professor Sun. Hell of a guy, I'm sure. But no, I've been, I've, I just decided to make some positive changes in my life. Thanks to you, in part. Need to clear out the fog in my head." *I can't even tell if I'm lying right now. As good as I am at reading others; I can't get a bead on my own emotions whatsoever.*

"That's great, Bill. You know, I'd be lying if I didn't say I was a little worried about coming out with you tonight."

I'd be lying if I said I wasn't a little worried about me right now too. The unrelenting pull of addiction and the sweet release that comes with sating it…sex doesn't even begin to compare. Taking a drink after a long day, one you'd been dreaming about since the first asshole at the office got you riled about whatever bullshit P.O.T.U.S pulled the night before. The illusionary taste of sweet Virginia tobacco in the back of your throat when you've gone too long without a puff. That imagined smell that fills your head and reminds you that it's been far too long since you polluted your lungs with blissful, cancerous waste. When the real thing finally touches your tongue, it's the kind of relief you feel when you remove a cast that's been glued to your arm for a month. Like your pores are free to breathe fresh air for the first time, like you've been drowning at the bottom of a pool and finally you're given that life-saving breath!

But for the first time in forever, I miss none of it. There's no craving, my skin doesn't crawl, no sweats or hot flashes or clenched teeth—nothing. It's as if I've never taken a drink, like I've never lit a cigarette in the first place. And my migraines, they should be pounding me into the dirt right about now. But no, they're gone too.

"Why were you worried?" I more ask it out of courtesy. I know why.

Carrie blushes. "I uh, well, that night we spent together…you kind of, kind of caught me at a moment of weakness, I guess. Afterwards, I was certain I'd just made the kind of mistake I hadn't made since college—falling for a pair of vulnerable eyes bolted to the face of an asshole." She laughs, so I let it slide. "And then when you stopped returning my calls and didn't show up for your sessions…"

"I'm sorry, Carrie. You didn't deserve that." And she didn't. *What the hell is wrong with me?*

"It's alright. I should've known better. But this, this is nice. I'm glad we did this." She takes another sip of wine then nearly spits it back into the glass. "I'm sorry. Would you like me to not drink in front of you?"

"You say that like I have a problem." She does me the courtesy of not pointing out the obvious. "It's fine," I add. "Doesn't bother me. Enjoy your wine."

Regardless, after she finishes the glass she refuses a refill and asks the waiter for some water instead.

"So," she says in-between bites of steak. "Any tricks to quitting cold turkey? I've got plenty of clients that would give me their first born for that Rosetta Stone. Not that I want children," she blurts. "Not now, anyways. Not right away. Someday, maybe." Her little insecurities are adorable.

As innocuous a question as it is, for some reason it births a million more within me. I can't help but picture Doctor Theodore Grant's Daemons floating around inside my bloodstream and going to work on the synapses of my brain, repairing damaged neurotransmitters obliterated by nicotine and rerouting the neural pathways passed down from my grandfather that predisposed me to alcoholism.

"Do you ever wonder…" *Christ. Really, Singer?* "Wonder if perhaps something else, something beyond ourselves pushes us to do, you know, good things and bad things?" *What does that even mean?*

"It sounds like you're talking about angels and demons, Bill. You are talking about angels and demons, right?"

"I guess."

"First rule of dating, sweetie, don't talk about religion."

I find myself staring at her like a lost child. Carrie sighs and says, "But since you brought it up… I believe God works to pull us toward his light. And I believe Satan works to drive us from it. But we have freewill. It's up to you whether you choose to walk the path of light or darkness."

As she carries on, I can't help but think how far afield she is from my usual type (if I have a type at all). Looks aside, I can't remember the last woman I met who seemed so genuine and well put together. Sure she has her faults (though I can't figure for the life of me what they are). We all do. But despite all the psychobabble rhetoric that most assuredly was spoon-fed to her during college, she seems to honestly care about her fellow man…about me…about us.

Good women, the ones who don't deserve the standard Bill Singer use 'em and lose 'em treatment, are few and far between. Most serial daters like her, the one's that typically fall prey to assholes like me, deserve every ounce of regret They're left with the following morning. They're destined to be alone forever. Spinsters that'll pull up to barstools until their eighty and blame every man they've ever spread their legs for, for all their misfortunes. Every failed relationship, every friendship that ended in chaos, every family member that now refuses to talk to them—in their eyes it's everyone's fault but their own. People like that, those who seem to surround themselves with chaos and misfortune, they all fail to realize the one simple truth…they're the only constant in that equation.

But Carrie's different. She isn't single because of her own insecurities and character flaws. No, she's alone because she's too giving. Because she goes out of her way to help everyone she meets. Sure it might be driven by that inane compulsion to fix all that is broken. Her choice of profession is no surprise. But the end result is still altruistic. That drive's molded her into the kind of woman that would cancel a much needed vacation in order to stay behind and console a friend in need.

People like her…they're the kind of people that get chewed up and spit out by people like me. They're the kind of women that are hurt again and again and again but somehow get back up and keep fighting. She deserves far better than Bill Singer.

Carrie studies me. Her next question seems almost painful to ask. "Do you believe in God, Bill?"

Do I believe in God? I think subatomic super computers infesting our guts and gently tugging on the strings of morality are more likely than a

Judeo-Christian God, but I'd never admit as much to a pious woman unless I wanted nothing more to do with her. But as I pretend to ponder the question—all the while my eyes glued to this paragon of perfection across the table from me—where my thoughts truly lie are not with God or even Carrie Dent, but rather Roxanne Margaret Goodwin.

Why the hell am I thinking about Goodwin? Why do I even care? Why can't I get her know-it-all face out of my head? Why do I feel like she's in danger?

"No." I bark out the word a bit more forceful than intended. But then it's too late. A diatribe gushes forth. "No I don't believe a trans-dimensional, all-powerful, all-seeing, infallible immortal created the universe and everything in it as part of some divine need to bear children." *Holy shit! Did I just recite Goodwin verbatim?*

Carrie looks beyond shocked. I don't give it time to sink in. The final nail is inches above the coffin. All it needs is a good whack with my trusty hammer and this relationship will be dead and in the ground.

"And what if God is real? From what I've read, he sounds like a real prick." *Oh that was quite a nail!* Carrie's aghast, but I don't slow pace. "He tries to get Abraham to murder his own son, then at the last minute says, 'Hold on, Abe, good buddy, just kidding. Ha, you thought I'd actually make you go through with it? What a sucker.' I wonder how fucked up his kid was after that little stunt by the Almighty?

"He gives us freewill only to condemn us to an eternity of pain and suffering should we chose to exercise it." More Goodwin rhetoric spewing forth. "Here's a juicy apple, but don't eat it? Why not? No reason, just don't. Oh you ate it? Well fuck you and all your unborn children from now until the end of time!"

"Where the heck is this all coming from, Bill? Calm down. I'm sorry if I upset you—"

"My mother brought me into this world. Just like God created Adam, she magically plucked me out of thin air and poof, here I am. But if you think I'm going to worship that horrible cunt, you got another thing coming! The woman who milked my poor father for every dime he had and drove him to put a revolver between his lips and pull the trigger? The woman who'd leave me home alone locked in my bedroom when I was only seven while she went out and whored her way from one end of the state to the other? You know what that's like? Being trapped like a dog in a kennel? If I had to take a piss, my only recourse was to hang my little seven-year-old prick out the window for the neighbors to see. I remember being so embarrassed that I'd just hold it in until it hurt so bad I'd roll around on the floor crying my eyes out. And if I had to take a shit, well, then I'd just have to sit in it and wait until she got home to give me a beating for ruining another pair of underwear!"

Carrie's gathering up her things now. Cell phone's going into her purse along with her pocket book and lipstick. I cry out, "Should I worship her? Should I worship that miserable bitch just because she made me!"

Other people, those closest to our table, are now succinctly aware that the man sitting across from them has completely lost his marbles.

Carrie grabs her coat off the chair. "Bill, I'm sorry but this isn't going to work out."

"No shit, Carrie!"

"You need to come see me at the clinic. You really do. You have a lot of skeletons in your closet that need to be laid to rest. You push people away, Bill. You push your partner away. And now you're pushing me away. Are you afraid we'll leave you like Charles did?"

"Leave him out of this!" *And I'm not even drunk.*

She shakes her head in disgust. I've seen that look a thousand times. It's the, "what a waste. He had so much potential," look.

"This was a mistake." She drops a hundred dollar bill on the table and flees the restaurant.

My hands start to shake. I shout at her back, "When life's profundities cast off their mask, the Daemons we hold lose their hold on us!" She doesn't turn. I ring my hands. The shake is mild but noticeable. I'll chalk it up to nerves from the tirade I just put on, but then, that tirade was scripted. It's probably just withdrawals. Hopefully it's just withdrawals.

"Fucking Goodwin," I mutter to myself. I need to check on her. Whether I like it or not, she's my partner. And that feeling, intuition—she'll probably tell me it was Daemon cross-talk cluing me in that she was in some sort of trouble.

"Jesus, you're losing it, Bill." I can't help but laugh. The rest of the patrons are doing their best not to make eye contact with me.

I should head over to Goodwin's apartment. I'll—

The waiter's hovering over my shoulder. He breaks my concentration. And he looks far from pleased with me. Begrudgingly he asks if there'll be anything else this evening. It doesn't take me more than a nanosecond to spit out my final order.

"I'll have a scotch. Make it a double."

From Unlocking the Secrets of the Universe, Episode 81

"Some of us are more efficiently wired for exceptional hand-eye coordination. Some of us are wired with computer-like math skills. Some of us are wired to paint. And some are wired to excel at music."

A psycho in a hockey mask leaps onto the screen. A woman screams as light glints off his raised butcher knife. Grant cowers away. "And unfortunately, some of us get our wires crossed and are compelled to do some pretty nasty things."

He yells at the woman on the screen, "Run! Why are you just standing there?"

"But what if we could change all that? What if we could alter our neural pathways, reroute our mental freeways, and divert unnecessary traffic so there's half as many on-ramps and off-ramps and backstreets required for our neurons to reach their destinations? Impossible? Actually, we do it all the time without even realizing it." Another brain pops up on the screen. Pathways light up with neurons skipping electrical pulses across the infinitely complex freeway system of the brain.

"Up until very recently, scientists believed that following early childhood development our brains became physiologically static organs.

Basically they thought you couldn't teach an old dog new tricks. But recently it's been discovered that not only can that old dog in our head learn a slew of new tricks, but it can learn to meow like a cat and swim like a dolphin.

"What they discovered was that certain life experiences actually change both the brain's anatomy and physiology—meaning its actual shape changes, along with the routes neurons take from synapse to synapse as they travel from one part of the brain to another. Now the question becomes, which life experiences are most impactful in producing profound neural changes? One man believes the key lies with our interpretation of language."

The show flips over to a shot of a large research center and then to an elderly Indian man in a white coat. Grant's voice overlays the scene. "Doctor Muhammad Rashala is a leading researcher in psycholinguistics, a science that explores our brain's ability to acquire, utilize, and comprehend language. For the past three years, with the help of new advanced brain mapping technology, Doctor Rashala has been able to analyze the precise effects that language has on the human brain—or more aptly, how language and other external forces retune our neural pathways."

Doctor Rashala says, "What we already knew was that when someone learns a new language their brain chemistry is altered. New neural pathways are created and old pathways are diverted. We long thought that this process, the process of new language adoption, had the most profound effect on our brains. What I set out to explore was whether or not other such adoptions of information could have similar effects; perhaps experiences less invasive than learning an entirely new language."

The show switches over to a lab where a young man with a shaved head sits in a chair reading a book. A dozen or so wires run from a computer at his back to little pads stuck all over his head. On a computer screen, a map of his brain is displayed with varying shades of blue and red ebbing bright then fading to shallower colors.

Rashala points to the screen. "What you are seeing here is how his brain activity changes while he reads. Now this book is in English—our subject's native tongue—but the context of the book is something quite profound to him."

Grant's voice floods back over the video. "The subject's name is Martin Keening. He's a student here at the Max Planck Institute where Doctor Rashala works. He's also an atheist. And the book he's reading…is the King James Bible."

Rashala says, "We had our subject read many other books prior to this one; both fiction and non-fiction. Some he was excited to read and others failed to hold his attention."

Grant chimes in, "The various books Keening was asked to read differed. Among them; Dr. Suess, a few chapters from a biography on Neil Armstrong, a Stephen King short story, and some papers written by Doctor Rashala himself. Rashala also ran similar tests using movies and audio tapes instead of books."

"Film did not quite have the same effect that reading and audio tapes did," he says. "I believe it is perhaps because our minds are challenged to recreate the scenes we read and hear using our imaginations rather than have them force fed to us via a television screen. But regardless, in each instance, his brain activity was fairly constant. We saw expected results. His frontal lobe was stimulated for grammatical usage and comprehension. The angular and supramarginal gyrus were stimulated, and so on. But when we introduced the Christian Bible…"

It cuts over to Doctor Rashala and a colleague examining the results on the screen. They're muttering to one another and Rashala taps the screen. "Here and here. That's pretty dramatic."

Again Doctor Rashala addresses the camera. "The more our subject read and strived to understand what he was reading, the more his brain chemistry changed. And these changes were drastic." Another flash of the brain scan shows hot pink near the center of the brain. "The activity here resembles a mild form of TLE, and furthermore, this new brain activity does not cease when he stops reading The Bible. It remains long after. That is because his neural pathways have been altered physiologically."

"TLE," says Grant, "is a chronic neurological condition that stems from the temporal lobe of the brain. In extreme cases it causes seizures which involve sensory changes. Victims have been known to report smelling odors that weren't there, mild hallucinations, even memory disturbances."

The show flashes back to Doctor Grant standing in front of a presumed green-screen covered by a shifting image of the human brain. He says, "If learning a new language, or reading certain influential texts can change the way our brains function, what else might secretly be rewiring our neural pathways? What if we could control it? What if we could purposely rewire ourselves to be more adept at a given trade? Could we perhaps temporarily alter our neural pathways in preparation for a math exam so that we'd excel at mathematics in the same way a math savant does? Could we use certain text or auditory queues to heighten our ability to perceive motion in advance of a sporting event, or comprehend musical notes on a scale in order to learn a song in record time?

"One man is trying to answer that question, and he believes he's found a way."

Chapter 22

The scotch burns my throat just like it did the very first time I took a drink as a kid. On its way to my stomach, caramel and cedar ripple over my tongue and mutate into a complex of buttery coconut spiked with licorice. There's a hint of almonds, a waft of plum, and a dash of currant that rise up out of the glass. I've never been able to dissect scotch like this before. I'd just drink the stuff. Never cared much about all that went into it as long as it did its job and got me sufficiently tossed. But for some reason this time, this time is different.

I should be miserable right now. I should be kicking myself. I just tossed an amazing woman out of my life for reasons I'm still wrestling to understand. But deep down all I feel is relief.

Maybe she's right. Maybe I'm scared of losing someone close to me again. Or maybe, maybe Mom fucked her little boy up just a bit too much for him to ever recover.

Another sip. Just this glass. Just this one glass and then I'm heading over to Goodwin's apartment to find out what the hell she's been up to. But I'm in no rush. There's no Daemons, no intuition, no emergency. Whatever anxiety I felt that drove me to push Carrie out the door left with her.

"It's all in your head, Bill." I peer through the murky glass of scotch. The world is a twisted wonderland. All the patrons are a million miles away, their features disfigured. "Probably how you all really look if we pulled back the curtain," I mutter.

Everyone in here just pretends to go about their conversations, but in reality they're all just waiting to see what I'll do next. At least I provided some entertainment.

Most people in my shoes would do anything in their power to flee the scene after that little circus. But embarrassment doesn't come easy to me. Stubbornness on the other hand, is a good old friend. Still, the tiny amount of disgust I have for myself—for my own cowardice, for whatever insecurity drove me to put on that shit show—it makes it hard to look at them. Instead I turn my attention to the wall to wall windows that run the length of the restaurant and to the dark, empty street and the occasional car that whizzes by. A light rain has begun to fall. The lights of the buildings shimmer off the miniature puddles as they form in the street. Soon a cosmos of neon and fluorescents flicker up off the wet asphalt.

Across the street, everything is closed. A few small department stores and a yogurt shop, all lights out. A single street light—the old fashion kind that looks as though it's lit by flame and oil but is really just another florescent bulb—stands sentry before them. Everything behind it is cast in shadows. The rain picks up and soon it's coming down so hard that even inside the restaurant—all glass and steel—it sounds like we're sitting beneath the tin roof of an old barn.

In the shadows across the street, someone stands up. *Bad night to be homeless.* But the person doesn't run for cover, rather he just stands there in the shadows behind the lamp light—just stands there in the torrential rain. Another sip of scotch and I stand up and slowly walk toward the window. The people I pass are all quite gracious to pull their chairs out of my way.

A man in a trench coat? Jesus, maybe I should buy him an umbrella, I think, then notice the large open-crown cowboy hat atop his head. *Never mind. I guess you got it covered, fella.*

As I approach the window, I take my last sip of scotch and place the empty glass down on someone's table. They don't object. I press my nose against the window and cup my hands around my face for a better view. He's just standing there in the pouring rain. There's an awning a few feet to the left of him, but why bother with shelter when you have a giant hat on? Fricking crazies abound, I guess. But there's something about him… I can't tell if he's staring at me, but I feel uneasy staring at him, that's for sure.

Cars whiz by. The wind whips at his coat. It rains so hard a waterfall sheets down the window and muddles my view. Like the patrons through the glass of scotch, his features seem to morph and melt.

A sudden tap on my shoulder. "Sir? Might I get you something else? The check perhaps? Or call you a taxi? The weather is quite foul tonight." My waiter talks like he's a royal butler.

"I was just leaving," I say, eyes still fixed on the cowboy across the street. Without blinking, I reach into my pocket, pull out my wallet, grab a wad of bills, and pass them to the waiter.

After unrolling the wad and counting the bills, he says, "Sir, this is far too much."

"Nonsense, Wadsworth. Treat yourself to a new pair of turtle cufflinks and an enema." My eyes never break from the distorted figure out the window, but I manage to give my pretentious waiter a pat on the chest and waddle my way past him and six other tables on my way toward the door. The unavoidable collision with a few tables and chairs accompanies my departure from the restaurant, but for some reason I feel compelled to continue my impromptu staring contest with the man over my shoulder—that cowboy standing in the rain across the street.

The lobby of the restaurant is small. A single wooden beam divides the dining area and its enormous bay windows from the glass lobby doors. A split second. That's all it takes to pass through the lobby and push through the glass doors out into the streets. A split second is all. A split second and he's gone. The sidewalk across the street is empty. No man in a trench coat and open-crown cowboy hat. Nothing but the dim glow of the streetlight shining through a wall of rain.

"Jesus," I gasp, with a hand to my chest. My heart is jackhammering my ribs. The sound of the rain grows so freaking loud I might as well be listening to tiny A-bombs detonate all around me. Without thinking I plunge headfirst through the wall of water into the street and nearly get run over by a blue and black Plymouth Sable as it goes speeding by. Its horn blasts a warning, but I care not in the slightest.

"Where the fuck did you go!"

Across the street I scour the storefronts. My busy hands wash the water from the windows so I can peer inside unobstructed. I check the door handles but they're all locked. I spin and spin and spin, looking for an alley or a ladder or somewhere he might've ducked out of sight.

"Come out! Where did you go?"

My face is drenched. It's cold as winter. *How the hell is it not snowing right now?*

Over and over I wipe the rain from my face, frantic to find him, not caring in the least as to the fact I have no rational reason for being so suddenly hell-bent on locating what is most certainly nothing more than a filthy vagrant who was simply catching his death out here moments prior.

And then my phone rings.

Blocked number. I place it to my ear and give my usual greeting, "This is Special Agent Singer."

There's no answer. I can hear breathing, but not a word in response. Again I say, "This is Singer. Who is this?"

Its heavy breathing; calm and deep, rhythmic, almost erotic. A woman, I think.

"Carrie, is that you?" Silence answers. "Carrie, listen, I'm sorry about my, my little explosion at dinner. I don't know what came over me. I think I'm having a panic attack. What the hell does a panic attack feel like?" *Am I having a panic attack?* I've never had one before. But whoever's on the other end of the phone gives me no advice, just more heavy breathing.

An eternity with the phone pressed against my soggy ear, but there's nothing to be heard other than the heavy patter of rain and the whoosh of occasional breaths coming through my phone's speaker. Finally I ask, "Goodwin? Is that you?" Nothing. The breathing stops. "Stay where you are. I'll be there in five minutes. I'm just down the—" Dial tone.

I've seen actual combat. I've heard the zip of bullets as they fly inches above my head. I've seen a man shot to pieces a foot away from me—a death that could've been my own—but for some reason, right now, at this very moment, I'm more scared than I've ever been. I can't stop shaking.

For a time I keep the phone pressed against my ear just listening to the dial tone blare. Then I hold it out and examine it like it's a foreign object. *God I'm lightheaded. What was in that scotch?*

Across the street the restaurant I left is a wall of light on an otherwise dark canvas. Inside, all the patrons' heads are cocked with their eyes on me—on the crazy fool dashing about in the pouring rain talking to an empty phone.

From the Black Book

A wisp of smoke rises from the heart of the wasteland; a sinewy trail that gently dances in defiance of winds that rage, scattering ash and silt and choking dust across this vast plateau. And though the battlefield is centuries cold, ere remains revenants of antiquity still alight with soft gleeds and augural memories.

Crying hark to days of night when the sky filled with flame, and leprous forms carried through the shadows.

Back to a time when man and beast shared skin and a hunger to lay the land desolate.

Now alone upon these hollowed shores, the headland battered by tempest winds and angry seas, a churning fury in effigy of the hatred spent on the long dead. But a visage of those who once stood upon these cliffs, ghosts of yore who bled their brothers in the name of forgotten relics, chasing an impossible dream.

Chapter 23

By the time I arrive at Goodwin's apartment, it's close to nine-thirty. Nine-thirty on a Thursday night, miserable weather outside, where else could she be? Anne Goodwin doesn't exactly strike me as the kind of woman who goes out on a work night. For that matter she doesn't strike me as the kind of woman who goes out on the weekends. No boyfriend, no distractions. Dollars to doughnuts she's sitting on her couch with Doctor Grant's notes strewn about, sucking down an orange soda and masturbating to a lecture on quantum theory on her tablet.

A few knocks and I wait. And I wait. Nothing. So I knock again, louder this time. "Goodwin! Open up! It's Bill. Goodwin!" I peer through the peephole. Not a shadow stirs. So I press my ear to the door and listen, but all I hear is my own breathing and the blood roaring in my ears.

Again I knock, and again there's no reply. The lights are all off. Either she's not here or she's a very sound sleeper. But it's only nine-thirty—too early for bed, too late to be out for someone like Goodwin.

As I stand in the hall outside her apartment, all manner of ridiculous tragedy whirls in my head. I can't help but get the sense something terrible has happened to her. But why? There's no rational explanation for it. Just because she isn't picking up the phone… Just because she isn't home…

I jiggle the door handle. Locked. Then I take a few steps back and ready myself. *I've got to kick it in. She could be in danger. I've got to get in there!*

But as I step towards it, hands at the ready, feet planted, poised to deliver that killer blow to her gray-trimmed door, a sudden burst of sanity strikes. "Jesus Christ, Bill. What the hell are you doing?" *You're gonna kick her door down because she hasn't answered your phone calls? Because she went out for the night? Because you got a wrong number while standing in the rain outside Italiano's?*

I pull out my phone and call her. Ring, ring, ring and then… From inside her apartment I hear the faint sound of her distinctive ringtone—the theme from Star Trek. *She's home. She's gotta be home if her phone is there.* Back to the door for another knock, and then I see a shadow flash past the peephole.

"Goodwin, it's me. Open the door. I know you're in there." And I wait. Another flash past the peephole but no response, no turn of the doorknob.

"Goodwin? Come on. Open up."

I try and peer through the peephole once more, but nothing is visible within. The vague and distant outline of her darkened apartment has vanished, replaced by an empty, black void. And then the void steps away. The form of a man in a long, black trench coat wearing a black, open-crown cowboy hat drifts away from the peephole and melts into darkness. Without thinking I rip my sidearm from its holster, take a step back, and plant my boot directly below the deadbolt. The door flies open with a thwack and I leap into her apartment, gun raised.

"Hands where I can see them!" But I'm yelling into an empty room. There's no one there. Just a dark apartment.

"I know you're in here!" *I know what I saw. That was no figment of my imagination.* "I saw you, you piece of shit! Come out now! Come out or when I find you," I flip on the lights and peer around the corner, "Come out or I'll shoot first and ask your corpse my questions."

Frantically I scour each room, clearing them one after the other as if I'm a Navy Seal infiltrating an Al Qaeda compound. It's a large apartment, but the linear floor plan makes it easy enough to keep my back against the wall. Two halls branch out from either side of the main living area with an open kitchen at the back. He could've ducked down either hall.

I stand still as a statue and listen. Not a sound inside the apartment. And that fear I felt before, that panic—a once foreign emotion—it's gone now. I'm in the moment. I'm back overseas in the sandbox, too pumped up on adrenaline to taste fear or dwell on death. I'm robotic.

As I make my way down one of the halls, I keep the lights off in case he's at my back. Best to conceal myself anyway I can. Room by room I peer inside, the barrel of my .40 caliber pistol leading my eyes from corner to corner. I check the closets, under the beds, in the shower, behind the doors—but nobody's home. All the windows are locked from the inside, not to mention we're ten stories up.

After the apartment is cleared, I holster my sidearm and wipe the sweat from my eyes. "What the hell is going on here?" *I know what I saw. That wasn't some PTSD hallucination.*

Immediately I kick into detective mode. No sign of a struggle, is my first thought. That's reassuring. But her phone is on the coffee table, and it's still on. Her battery indicator is flashing at 4%. It's fingerprint password protected, same as mine, but I can see the last few missed calls on the lock screen. There's my call, of course, and a call from Mom two hours prior, a few others I don't recognize from earlier today, and then several of my calls to her from this morning. Either she's been avoiding the world or this phone has been sitting here abandoned since at least 7:32am this morning. I know how I feel when I don't have my phone. I struggle to even take a shit without bringing it with me. And Goodwin, she's worse than me. There's no way she'd leave it here on purpose. And what's more, her tablet is on the sofa. She may as well have cut her own arm off and left it there. Tech Lupinski can crack her encryption easily enough, so I tuck her electronics away and continue my search of the premises.

God, she's meticulous. Everything in her apartment has its perfect little place. Not an inch of space is wasted. Her flat screen is mounted with all its cords run neatly through the drywall and it's perfectly framed by two bookshelves on either side. Each shelf is a well-orchestrated mix of books and nerd goodies. Things like TV spaceship replicas, a small tesla coil, one of those sand and water alien landscape thingies, along with the occasional geode.

Every corner of the apartment has the well thought-out plant (all fake except for a Venus flytrap on the kitchen counter) atop a hideous art deco side table or console table or the like. As I move into the kitchen, it's more of the same. The counter space, though plentiful, holds just the right amount of appliances and cutlery so as not to appear cluttered, though not look wasted. I never realized she was this caliber of anal. But none of Goodwin's sphincter retentive home décor habits are going to help me. I need to narrow down a window as to when she was last here. The first forty-eight hours are critical when someone goes missing.

On the kitchen table I spot a torn open bag from Chinese takeout. A few Styrofoam containers are open next to it. I dig through the bag until I find a receipt. Date and time of purchase, 7:36pm yesterday. *That's good. At least she was here yesterday.*

I move into the bedroom. The bed's unmade; though I have a sneaking suspicion Goodwin doesn't bother making it up every morning. It smells like her—Dove soap and Lady Speed Stick—but nothing incriminating. No signs of rape or a struggle, no suicide note, nothing out of the ordinary. Under the bed is just dust and lint balls. So I move onto her closet.

I'd glanced inside while clearing the room, but hadn't paid much attention to the contents. Still, I really don't even need my eyes to know what's inside. It's like I have a third eye sometimes. There'll be an assortment of drab business-casual attire on one side, all earth-tones, as Goodwin doesn't have the confidence to choose anything bold of color or style. And then there'll be her very casual attire on the opposing side, and little else. No empty space; that would be wasteful. Clothes will be neatly sorted either by style or color. No jewelry; she doesn't believe in it. No rack upon rack of shoes; she isn't that kind of girl. Goodwin is pragmatic in all regards. It's one of her few redeeming qualities. And as I open the closet, that is exactly what I find inside, except for one small deviation—a large swath of unused space near the back on the floor.

I kneel down to inspect. Four small, evenly spaced divots imprint the carpet. Something heavy was sitting here unmoved for quite a while. A suitcase, perhaps? Suitcase wheels?

Her clothes hamper has a few undergarments in it, but nothing she'd dangle from a closet hanger, and yet there are half a dozen empty coat hangers up above on the *very casual* side of her closet sporadically placed between flannel shirts and eclectic Tees. Everything is color sorted, I notice. And why not? Ensuring her colors match is as deep as Goodwin goes when it comes to fashion. Not that I'm any better. But as grown women are concerned, she's one, "Never Trust an Atom. They Make Up Everything," T-shirt away from working at a comic-book store.

"Packed a few suitcases," I mutter, as I finger through her clothes.

Next it's into her bathroom where I notice her toothbrush is missing. Then room to room in search of any sign of Doctor Grant's files, of which I come up empty handed.

"Where did you go Goodwin? Where did you go? And why? What are you running from?" *Cowboy apparitions?*

Sweat permeates my clothes. My shirt clings to my chest and back. I feel off. But all things considered, right about now any doubts I may have had as to whether something bad had befallen my partner were dead and buried. Something bad had most assuredly befallen my partner. And I need to save her.

From the Journal of Doctor Theodore Grant

Long have dreams been a fascination of mine. When I was a young boy growing up in Arkansas, each winter when the chill built enough to freeze a crust over the stagnant waters of Crane Lake, my brother and I would go ice-skating. For as long as I can remember, every winter all the children in our neck of the woods would take to the ice. From the time I could walk it was a tradition our small town held dear. Even some parents joined in on the revelry; mine included.

One winter, neither an especially cold nor an especially warm one, my mother grabbed my arm as I raced out the door on my way to Crane Lake. She told me, not today Jamie. I don't want you or your brother skating there today. She wouldn't tell us why, not at first anyways. She just insisted we stay home.

I remember pleading with her incessantly. It's plenty cold out, I told her. Tucker and Carlton will be there. We'll only skate near the edge. But no luck. She was adamant. Of course my brother and I were furious. We must have been no older than nine or ten, and we couldn't understand why on Earth our mother would forbid something we loved so much. After all, we hadn't done anything to warrant such prohibition. And the fact that mother refused any explanation only heightened our resentment.

Now my brother and I may have been plucked from the same gene-pool but we were as different as sand and glass. I begged him not to go, even though deep down I thought he had every right to disobey. But of course he didn't listen to me. Why in the world would he obey his little brother if his own mother's words weren't enough to discourage him?

So he went. Paul climbed out the window of our two-story home and snuck off to Crane Lake. He was gone all day. I remember being green with jealousy. And furious; furious he'd left me behind, furious he abandoned me to contend with mother. And when the sun set and we were called down for dinner, I was in tears. He should've been home hours ago. That anger quickly mutated to fear for my brother. We never skated that long. I should've told her. I knew I should've told her sooner but I was afraid I'd get in trouble for letting him go.

But when she asked where he was and I finally did tell her the truth…I'd never seen that kind of horror in someone's eyes before. Horror. Sadness. Terrible sadness.

Paul never made it home. For the first time in fifty-five years, the ice broke and he fell in. God, I miss him.

Years later I asked her how she seemed to know it would happen. After all, like I said, it wasn't particularly warm that year. In fact, we'd skated earlier that winter on even warmer days. But what she told me always stuck with me. It's beyond reason, beyond logic. She said she'd dreamt it. The most vivid dream she'd ever had. She could even smell pine on the wind and feel winter's kiss. And in that sleeping vision she watched Paul fall through the ice and drown. She saw him fall, she saw him struggle, she saw him die… In the end, there was nothing she could do to save him.

Chapter 24

I don't sleep. I don't even go home. It's straight to the office where I fire up my computer and start pulling any and all information I can on Roxanne Margaret Goodwin. First I check her phone records. Only two outgoing calls in the last forty-eight hours; one to the Chinese takeout restaurant across the street from her apartment, and then two days back she made a call to her sister. That was right after we met with Director Kennedy and he pulled us off the case. Her mother and sister both live in Ontario. Maybe she went there?

Several incoming calls; 1-800 numbers, a few calls from her mother and sister following her outbound call to her sister, and of course my calls to her. She answered none of them. Her phone was undoubtedly sitting on her coffee table by then, unattended. Why leave it?

If she traveled far, I should be able to find a record of it. *By plane?* I check her credit card purchases but come up empty handed. No airline tickets purchased, but she did use one of her credit cards at two separate gas stations; Gas-n-Go in Tacoma Park and a Chevron station near the George Washington Cemetery.

"Where are you heading, Goodwin?"

I trace her route from her home to the Gas-n-Go, then to the Chevron. She's heading up 650 toward the I-495 interchange. She could be heading anywhere. *Shit!*

"And why leave your phone?" *Because it's a Bureau issued phone. Because I can easily track it's movements using the GPS logging.*

I flip over to the GPS application on my terminal and review her movements over the past five days. Until two days ago, she'd never been more than twenty feet away from that phone, of that I'm positive. And her movements are completely predictable. To and from the office, gas stations, one trip to the grocery store—the map pattern on my screen looks like a three-year-old tried to scribble the same line again and again and again with a marker. The most perfunctory life I've ever seen. So I trace it back another twenty five days.

The map lights up with even more lines on top of lines. Only a couple of outlier routes, one of which was our trip to the airport and the Ozarks, while the other, the Library of Congress.

"Why would you go to the library? You've got access to the Bureau archives. Why the library? Because you wanted to get online without anyone being able to see what you were doing?"

I check the date. She was there two days after our return from Arkansas. There's not much more for me to go on. It's a little after midnight. I'll head over there as soon as they open, but for now… I pick up my phone and start dialing. A groggy Pollock answers, "Hello? This is, um, this is Lupinski. Who is—"

"Lupinski. Get your Pierogi eatin' ass out of bed. I need you in the office pronto!"

"Singer? Is that you?"

"Who the hell else would it be?"

Still groggy, he replies, "My sister, my brother, my aunt, my uncle, my cousin, Director Kennedy—"

"Don't be a smartass! Do I sound like your sister? This is important."

"What the heck is going on?"

"I'll tell you when you get here. And get here quick!" I hang up the phone. No point in giving him time to ask too many questions. He'll be pissed when he knows all I need him for is to unlock Goodwin's phone, but in the absence of information, a guy like Lupinski will fear the worst and light a fire under his feet.

Next I call Goodwin's sister—the last person she called. Another groggy voice answers, this one bearing a slight French-Canadian accent.

"Is this Claudette Chiffon?" I ask.

"Yes. Who is this?"

"My name is Bill Singer. I work with your sister, Anne."

A brief hesitation and then, "What is it? Is Roxi okay?"

Stay calm. Sound professional. Don't let her panic. "Mrs. Chiffon, I've been unable to reach her for two days now, and though I have no reason to fear anything has happened to her, it isn't like your sister to up and—"

"I just spoke to her? She's missing? Oh Christ, Rox. What the hell happened? Shit, I knew I should've told Mom right away."

"Told her what?"

A deep sigh. "Roxi called me two days ago. She sounded; I don't know… We don't talk much. It's been difficult. We were never that close. She doesn't approve of my lifestyle." I'm dying to ask, but refrain. "When she called, I was, well, I didn't know what to make of it. She just asked me to listen and then went on and on about how sorry she was for everything and how she should've been there for me more. She asked me to tell mom she loved her and that she would be on assignment for a while so we shouldn't try and reach her."

"Did she say anything about the assignment?"

"No. But she sounded really, I don't know, weird. Like, not her usual sickeningly bubbly self. I waited a day before calling my mother about it. I don't know if she ever got ahold of Roxi or not." *She didn't.* "But I'm sure she tried. Rox always was Mom's favorite."

Some heavy breaths. "So there was no assignment? She just ran off? Where's my sister, Bill?"

"I don't know, Claudette. But I'm gonna find her. Is there anything else you can tell me? Any place she might have gone? Anyone she was dating, a distant relative nearby, anything?"

"I'm sorry. I just don't know. Like I said, we don't talk much. But, Agent Singer?"

"Yes."

"She may be a pain in the ass, but she's my sister. Find her, please."

"I will, Claudette. I'll find her."

She starts to cry.

"Claudette, it's likely nothing. She might've just gotten spooked. Our first case together was a strange one. Sometimes agents get the jitters, need time to cool off—time away from it all. I'm sure that's it."

A few more soft goodbyes and finally there's a click, then dial tone. Once a mundane sound, it now riddles me with goose pimples.

Alright, Bill, ask the questions. Why call an estranged sister? What would motivate her to do that yet fail to call her own mother? It's the kind of thing somebody would do if they were a drunk working the twelve steps. That's something I know a little about. Always got hung up on the second step and quit, but I know reconciliation is somewhere on the ladder.

Strange; the thought of alcohol would typically have me reaching for my flask right about now, but there's no desire there—none at all. And no flask, for that matter. Even last night's scotch is some distant, foggy memory; like something from a dream. And the thought of booze usually perks up my olfactory and gets me craving a smoke, but I haven't had one in days, nor do I want one at all. Just the thought of the smell, how they taste—instead of making me salivate it has my stomach turning.

Focus, Singer! Focus. Goodwin. Why the feeble attempt at reconciliation with her sister? Because she's about to do something detrimental, something permanent, something she can't come back from. Maybe something fatal?

Footsteps behind me! I fling about and tear my sidearm from its holster. Tech Lupinski tries to dive out of the way, falls over a chair, and whacks his forehead into the corner of a desk. "Shit! Ouch! It's me, Singer. It's me! What the hell?"

"Sorry. Been a bit jumpy lately." I holster my pistol and help him to his feet.

"You don't say?" He's in his street clothes, unshaved, and his breath still reeks of sleep. My call lit a fire under his ass, alright.

"What did you call me down here for at," he checks his watch, "one o' five in the morning?"

No point in sugar coating it. "Special Agent Goodwin is missing."

"What do you mean, missing?"

I shove her phone and tablet into his hands. "I need access to these. There may be information on them that will help lead me to her."

Lupinski gently sets them down on the desk beside him and rubs his eyes. After a yawn he says, "Seriously, Bill, what's gotten into you?"

"She's gone!" I grab him by the collar and give him a good shake. "This isn't a gag. No one's been able to reach her in days! I went to her apartment where," I stop myself short of saying, "where a phantom cowboy was skulking around," and switch over to, "it looks like she left in a hurry. She made some out of character goodbye phone call to her sister and—"

Tech Lupinski is staring at me like I've lost my mind. A part of me wonders if I have. Am I hearing myself right? I'm doing all of this because Goodwin left her cell phone at home for a few days and went on a trip? Because she tried to make amends with her estranged sister?

Yes! Yes that's exactly why I'm doing this! There's no doubt in mind that something's happened to her. But Lupinski not only looks unconvinced, he looks seconds away from bursting into laughter.

"What? What are you smirking about? This isn't a—"

"Bill, Bill, Bill, calm down. I'm sure she's fine." He brushes my hands off his collar.

"And how can you be so—"

"Because she was here yesterday."

"What? I was here yesterday. She never came in. Did you actually see her?"

"No, but I saw her name on the evidence log. She checked something out."

Do I even have to ask? "What did she check out, Jeff?"

"That um, that thing from the Grant case, I think." *Doctor Grant's contraption. His Daemon fission machine. The pointless science fair project.*

I try and settle myself, more so to keep Lupinski from bugging out. As calm as I'm able, I tell him that I need access to her phone and tablet; that she is missing and in danger and if she comes to harm because he wasted time, then that's on his head. When he again asks for details as to what's going on, I gently let him down with a, "It's above your pay-grade," line.

Eventually he resigns to help. It isn't that difficult to convince him, really. I think he's got a thing for Anne, and the thought—even if he feels it's as remote as the Alaskan tundra—that she could come to harm from his inaction, is enough to make him complicit. The phone takes him no time at all, being Bureau issued and all. But the tablet he tells me will take a while to hack.

"This might take me all morning, Agent. In the meantime, I put a trace-route on her phone. If anyone calls it, you should be able to pinpoint their location." He shows me how to use the application on my terminal and then heads off to his lab to work on the tablet while I tinker with Goodwin's phone.

I haven't the slightest clue what I'm looking for, and frankly, I doubt that if she wanted to hide—which it most certainly appears is the case here—she'd leave any clues on her work phone. But as Goodwin herself once said, if there's even a remote chance of something being a possibility, then exhaust that option before moving on to the next. The Picasso Model. Low hanging fruit. The phone is right here in my hands. It's tangible evidence, even if it's likely a dead end. And after an hour sifting through her notepad application, private emails, search history, contact list, and more, I come up empty handed.

Frustration and worry keep me awake, while mental exhaustion and physical fatigue work their damnedest to put me to sleep. I rub my burning eyes and slurp down a few cups of black sludge coffee, but it just isn't enough. So I slap myself in the face a couple of times. *God, I'm tired.* I can't pull all-nighters like I used to. I'm getting old. My brain doesn't function after twenty hours without rest. Usually it doesn't function after eight hours without a drink and a smoke, but...

A catnap. Just an hour to refresh my batteries, to get me thinking straight. I've hit a wall anyways. And when I wake up, Lupinski should be done with the tablet. Hell, with any luck I might have a sleeping epiphany.

What the hell are you thinking? This is no time to sleep!

And then my phone rings. A recognizable number. It's Carrie, and she sounds like she's seen a ghost.

Chapter 25

"**Y**ou've gotta help me! They're after me! Please, hurry!"

"Slow down, Carrie. Who's after you?"

"I, I don't know. I, I… Ahhhhhh!"

"Carrie! Carrie! What happened? Where are you?" *Jesus Christ! Am I listening to her die?*

"I'm, I'm at…" Every word grows fainter and fainter. It's as if she's running away from the phone. "Help me, Bill! Please help me!" Fainter still. I can barely hear her.

"Where are you? Tell me where you are!"

"I'm at... I'm at, I'm…" The phone's pressed against my ear so hard it stings, and my other ear has my index finger stuffed in it to block out the minuscule amount of ambient noise in the office.

"Carrie? Carrie!" Nothing. Then suddenly I hear it; that methodical breathing. Soft at first, but it intensifies. Soon it's so loud I'm forced to hold the phone away from my ear—so loud it's as if I have my phone on speaker.

And then a migraine strikes. Tremendous pressure behind my eyes. My temples are ready to explode. It's pain unlike anything I've ever experienced before. This is the migraine to end all migraines. It feels like my eyes are bleeding. I can't hear myself scream above the jet engine whine in my ears, but I feel the wind leave my lungs. And the pressure, *Oh God the pressure!* My eyes are going to pop. My optic nerve slowly twists around and around, bunching up on itself.

"Jesus Christ! Stop! Stop! Stop!" I'm down on the floor beneath my desk, hands on my temples, eyes closed, screaming. "No more! No more! Make it stop!"

My phone's on the floor next to me. Carrie's screaming on the other end. "Help me! Help me! Help me! Help all of us!"

The pain is paramount. It's unbearable. It's…

I fling my hand up onto the desk and fumble around for something sharp. Eventually my fingers slide across the familiar shaft of a ballpoint pen. Racked as I am, I can barely hold onto it, but I manage to wrench it down off the desk.

My ears are bleeding, I just know they are. *The pain! Christ, the pain!* My brain feels swollen two sizes too big for my skull. So I plunge the pen into my temple.

There's a loud pop as the pressure releases. Any pain that might have accompanied the act of shoving a ballpoint into my brain is so minor compared to the pain of my migraine it doesn't even register. And then darkness. The whine of the migraine is replaced by the steady wheeze of air inflating and deflating my lungs. There's a gun in my hand. Cold steel pressed against my palm, my finger on the double-action trigger. I don't need eyes to recognize its familiar form. It's my dad's old target pistol. A .22 caliber monstrosity. I only fired it once before I threw it away.

When finally I open my eyes, I'm looking down at a man on his knees with his fingers interlaced behind his head. My twenty-two is trained on him.

"Don't bother with me," he mutters. "Help the rest of them."

"I can protect you," I say. Slowly I circle towards his front so I can see his face. "If you tell me what I need to know."

"But can you protect them? Don't think for a second that Bill Singer is the only person Bill Singer cares about. They can hurt you; hurt you by hurting them. You need to give them what they want. It's the only way."

As I come around the front of the cowed man, a familiar face greets me. "Charles. Always the pragmatist. I've missed you, partner. Everything alright?"

"You shouldn't worry about me. You should worry about them. All of them."

I glance around at the dark, empty warehouse. It's been abandoned for years. In my hand the gun grows heavy. The metal's cold. With it, I scratch my temple; rather I scratch the gaping wound the ballpoint opened. But it's better now, much better. Only a dull throb remains.

I transfer the gun over to my off hand so I can inspect the hole in my head. It's an oozing mess. Fetid smells find my nostrils as I scour the puss covered rim of the hole with my fingers. *Christ, how did it get so wide?* It feels the diameter of a golf ball, not a pen—a massive hole dug right into my skull. *It's large enough, I suppose.* So I shove a few fingers inside.

"You can't pull them out, you know," says Charles. His hands are still up on his head in surrender.

"Well I have to try."

My fingers probe deeper down into the hole. There's no pain, only a slight pressure behind my eyes. I can feel the soft sponge of my brain with the tips of my fingers. The grooves are slick and deep. I pinch one and tug until it releases from the rest, and then carefully pull the long cord of brain matter back out through the hole. Like a sweater, the cord unravels and frees itself from the rest.

"Doctor Grant tried to get them out. Look what happened to him. You should worry more about the rest of them—those you can still help. Otherwise," he glances over at Carrie Dent's lifeless body slumped down on the warehouse floor, "they'll all end up like her."

She's wearing the same dress as the night we met for dinner. But the flush of her skin is gone. Instead of a vibrant primrose complexion, it's tacky and blue. Veins show through translucent skin; various shades of gray. *Oxygen depletion. She'd been dead about a day.*

"Either they all will do it to themselves, or *They* will do it for them."

The bloody cord of brain matter I hold in my hand resembles an umbilical cord. I inspect it for signs of corruption, but find none. So I let it splat onto the floor and plunge my fingers back into the hole in search of another.

"I hope that wasn't something important," says Charles.

"Who are, *They*?" I ask.

Ouch! That one hurt a little, but I manage to get another cord out in one piece.

The man on the floor before me has his head down. His open-crown cowboy hat conceals his identity. He gives no answer.

"Why don't you take that off? A little out of fashion, wouldn't you say? You going for the Lee Van Cleef look? I'd say that style died out with his films." Still no response. Another cord of brain matter slithers from my fingers and splats on the concrete. "Don't feel like talking? Back in the sandbox we had all sorts of clever ways to get the Ali Babas talking. And they always talked. Everyone talks."

With the muzzle of my gun, I flip his hat off his head. "So I'd advise you to just forgo the tough guy routine and tell me what I want to know. Save yourself some pain, Bill."

But Bill isn't having it. His face is still down; so still and lifeless he may already be dead. So I fire off a round right next to his ear.

Bam!

That did the trick! He's down on the ground, hands up over his ears writhing in pain—screaming, "Jesus Christ! Stop! Stop! Stop! No more! No more! Make it stop!"

"Then tell me what I want to know!" I fire off another round next to his left ear this time, then press the hot muzzle of my gun into one of his eyes sockets. "Tell me what I want to know! Come on now. No? You're not gonna talk? You don't want to cooperate? Well, I guess you're no use to me."

I shoot him right in the temple. Just a quick pop and it's over. No more writhing, no more screaming, no more anything. Bill's body is a lump on the floor—a black trench coat running up to a bloody head with a golf ball sized hole in its side.

"You're useless," I say to the corpse.

Over in the darkness where Carrie's corpse is sprawled out, I see Charles climb on top of her. He's naked. So is she. There's a small hole in the side of his skull—the entry wound from a .22 caliber pistol.

I tell him, "What a way to go, huh pal?"

"I'll say," he replies as he enters Carrie. She moans and runs her hands over his back. Her nails dig into his skin and sheer off a few ribbons.

"Hey, pal! That's my girl there!"

"I'm not your girl," replies Charles' wife.

"Oh. Sorry, Marla. I, I thought you were someone else."

She turns her head to look at me. There's no longer enough muscle tissue in her neck to support any grace of movement, so it just kind of flops over and comes to rest with her decayed cheek on the floor. Charles is busy giving it to her good, but Marla seems oblivious to his presence. She just leers at me from beneath him and licks her dry, dirt-caked lips. Her skin is greenish-blue and peeling off in places. Bone gleams through her paper-thin flesh. The skin that wraps her skull is all but gone.

Charles grabs her lifeless face in both hands and turns it back to face him, then thrusts his tongue into her open mouth.

"Charles, pal, you sure you should be—"

"She's my wife! I'll fuck her if I want to."

"But after what she did to you? And I mean, just look at her, man!"

"You always did have a big mouth!" she shouts at me. Then Marla grabs Charles' naked ass with her decrepit hands and pulls him deeper inside her. I hear her hip pop out of its socket.

He always did have a thing for the macabre. And these carnal pleasures wrapped in blood, the mix of love and death, never has anything fit the word better.

Charles' thrusts hasten. Blood pours down his back to cover their entwined bodies. Then he runs his tongue along her cheek, peeling the skin from her jawbone with the motion. He runs it all the way up to her ear then flicks the tip along the rim of the small caliber entry wound on the side of her head—a wound to match his own.

Right where I remember it. The round goes in, rattles around, and doesn't come out. No exit wound, no blood splatter analysis, no mess on your overalls. Right, Charles?

"I hope you took care of that," he mutters to me before jutting his tongue into the bullet hole. The perversion is too much for me to bear, so I look away.

"Took care of what, you sick fuck?"

Where's my gun? It's not in my hand anymore. Something else is in my hands, both of them. Something slimy and wriggling, something alive. Something…

"Took care of that," he replies.

I glance down to find a bloody baby cradled in my arms. It's blue, turning bluer by the second. It struggles to breathe. A few more kicks of its diminutive legs and then it stops moving altogether.

"No, no, no, no, no!" I press my lips to the infant's. They're sticky with blood. A long breath flows through me and into its lungs. Its little chest rises and falls, but still it remains a lifeless husk in my arms.

All around me the drum of automatic gunfire barks. Rounds hit the dirt at my feet, whiz by my head, and ricochet off the mud-brick buildings at my back. Debris rains down on my helmet. My lieutenant screams at me over the radio to just leave the child, pick up my rifle, and fight, but I can't. I can't leave it to die. Not like this!

"No, no, no! Breathe! Please, Kevin, I'm sorry! Please!"

Across the street a small grocer and his family huddle inside their store under the counter. Father in his white and brown turban, mom in her hijab; both of them clutch their two small children to their breasts. They're all just staring at me with the same look in their eyes—pure terror laced with confusion. They wonder why I don't save them, why I'm just standing here in the middle of the street holding a dead baby in my arms instead of coming to their rescue. Then comes the mortar shells. And just like that—father, mother, the two little ones—gone in a flash.

I pull my attention from the ensuing heap of rubble, place my lips to the infant's, and blow once more. An RPG rockets by me and hits an Abrams tank at my six. Again I blow a lungful of air into the child. "Come on, Kevin! Come on! Breathe! Breathe! Breathe! Brea—"

The infant opens its eyes; eyes red as brimstone. Goodwin's voice thunders past its tiny, blue lips. "Don't drink the ambrosia!"

***

"Bill? Bill, wake up! Come on, Agent Singer."

I spin about and grab the hand on my shoulder. There's a pop and a scream and...I'm in my office at my desk with Bryce Coolie's hyperextended wrist in my hand. I let go.

"Fuck, Singer! You nearly broke my wrist." He wrings it out and leaps away. "You were screaming like some deranged lunatic!"

"I, I, I can't breathe," I say. Then I vomit into my garbage can.

From the Black Book

In every drop of crimson that falls from your lance,

You shall find me.

In the eyes of your enemies, in the bleating cries of the fallen,

Look for me.

Jeweled within the crowns which sit upon the heads of kings,

In the cold dark night that precedes the dawn,

When the fire within is benumb of flame and hearts beat not with blood but rage,

When the coffle stretches from downs to dale,

When the last flicker grows faint and thy bones brittle and break,

There you shall find me.

For in despair, there is hope. All love breeds hate. And those brave enough to stand, shall fear the coming tide.

The knell's tongue shall lash as the fires burn low,

When the last breaths run shallow and the earth trembles below,

There you shall find me. There I shall stand.

Come find me.

You need only look.

Chapter 26

"Where are you going?" shouts Bryce at my back. He's still massaging his wrist. I don't bother to answer him.

Shit! What time is it? How long was I asleep? I check my phone. It's nearly 8:30 in the morning.

Bryce chases after me. "Singer, please, what the hell is going on with you? I'm here to help. Let me help you."

Just get rid of him. There's no time for Bryce Coolie! The first forty-eight hours are critical in a missing person's case. "You want to help me?"

"Of course!"

I stop, turn, and mask my true feelings with a serious scowl. "I need you to go to the Library of Congress."

Bryce is stupefied once more. *How hasn't caught on to the fact I'm just throwing him at one wild goose hunt after the next?* "The library, the Library of Congress?"

"Special Agent Goodwin is missing. She went there two days after we returned from Arkansas."

"Goodwin is missing?"

My hand finds his shoulder. Some good eye to eye contact, a little pressure on his clavicle, a calm but stern fatherly tone. "You like Goodwin?" He nods like an idiot. "You want to help Goodwin?" *What an obedient dog.* "You want to help me?" *Of course you do.* "Then find out what she was doing there. Find out and report back to me. This is important." *Not really. It's most certainly a dead-end.*

I leave Bryce in the hall to ponder his new and monumental assignment. Soon I pass Tech Lupinski coming the other way. He tells me he's still working on her tablet. "She's got some pretty tricky AES encryption behind the biometrics. Might take me longer than I thought."

"Keep working on it. I'll be back in a couple of hours."

As I pass Director Kennedy's office, he shouts my name and waves me in.

Damn it! I don't have time for this.

"Special Agent Singer, come in. Sit down."

"I'd prefer to stand."

He looks agitated. I'm sure I look agitated too. Kennedy says, "Were you planning on keeping this a secret from me?"

You don't need to be a mind reader to know he's aware Goodwin's missing. Lupinski likely told him. It's just as well. There's no reason to hide it. "Sir, I've been up all night trying to track her down. I went to her apartment and—"

"Her mother filed a missing person's report with DC metro. Report says you contacted her sister and told her Special Agent Goodwin had gone missing. What the hell is going on, Singer? Who's got her? Does this have anything to do with Farik Al-Shahi?"

"No. What? No, no one's taken her. At least I don't think anyone has. I think..." *Breathe. You remember how to breathe don't you? Why is this so difficult?* "It would appear Anne, I mean, Special Agent Goodwin has, well, if you ask me—"

"I am asking you!"

"...I believe she's gone into hiding." I give it a second to sink in. "I canvassed her apartment. She left her phone behind, packed a couple of suitcases, and has been unreachable for," I check my watch out of compulsion, "nearly forty-eight hours now."

Deputy Assistant Director Kennedy has donned his usual look of smug perplexity. "And why would she go into hiding? Who's after her?"

"That's what I'm trying to figure out, sir. It would appear," *fuck it, just tell him*, "that she may be taking on similar characteristics to those Doctor Grant displayed when he disappeared five years ago."

Kennedy has a finger slung over his upper lip. It's meant to appear he's pondering what I'm telling him, but what he's really doing is trying to hide something from me. He knows something. *What are you hiding, Bennie?*

"How do you know she just didn't get rattled and decided to take some time? I remember my first case—"

I cut him off before he has a chance to go all nostalgic on me. "She wasn't rattled, sir. Intrigued, obsessed maybe, but not rattled. I don't think Goodwin rattles."

He licks his lips and scratches his temple. His eyes dart down to the left. "Okay, well, this is unfortunate news. She's one of us—one of our own. Let's find her. You'll have all the resources of the FBI at your disposal. Local PD is on the lookout for her car. We'll keep eyes on her apartment. Trace her credit cards, scan local video surveillance. We'll find her, Bill. We'll find her."

"Hopefully not like we found Grant."

"Get to it," he replies, and waves me off.

As I rush out of his office, my phone is already in my hand and my fingers are dialing. My first call is to Carrie.

"Come on, come on. Pick up the bloody phone." I have to make sure she's alright. Other than the strangest fucking dream I've ever had, and a suspect blocked call last night, I really have no reason to think she isn't. But there's no answer. So I try her office. Carrie's secretary picks up.

"Hi, this is Bill Singer. I'd like to talk to Doctor Dent, please."

"Doctor Dent is not in right now. Can I take a message?"

"When are you expecting her?"

"I'm sorry, sir, but if you'd like to make an appointment—"

"Pam. It's Pam, right?"

"Yes, sir."

"Pam, this is Special Agent Bill Singer with the FBI. I need to speak to Doctor Dent immediately. Please put me through to her ASAP." *I do love the badge sometimes.*

A moment of silence and then, "Agent Singer, I, she didn't show up at the office this morning. She's usually in before I am, but… I can give you her personal number."

"I've got it, Pam. She's not picking up."

"I tried it as well. Gosh, I hope she's alright, Agent Singer. You don't think she was in a car accident or something?"

"Pam, listen, I need you to call me the minute she gets in, alright." She agrees. I give her my number and hang up the phone. The image from my dream is stuck front and center in my mind; Carrie's cold and lifeless body on a concrete slab.

I rush to my car, fire it up, and light the tires. It's lights and siren time as I speed out of the parking garage. I'm traveling somewhere in the vicinity of Mach twelve, blowing stoplights and intersections. A few horns blast me as I race by, but miraculously I don't cause a single accident.

There are words in my head, words from my dream. Things like; "Either they all will do it to themselves, or *They* will do it for them. You can't pull them out, you know. Don't think for a second that Bill Singer is the only person Bill Singer cares about. Kevin, I'm sorry! They can hurt you; hurt you by hurting them. You need to give them what they want. Don't drink the ambrosia…"

I stomp on the gas. I'm really flying now. "Don't drink the ambrosia?" My siren blares. Blood pounds in my ears. "But can you protect them?"

Right out of Kalorama Heights and over the Mass. Avenue Bridge. A few more miles and I pull down his street. It's been an age since I've driven down this stretch of road. Well before I pull up to the house, I kill the lights and the siren. I pray he's here. He should be. He's in-between jobs—I keep tabs.

As I step out of the car I get this sinking feeling in my stomach. I haven't been back here in years. Even when Charles was still alive I rarely ever went to his home. He rarely did either.

The lawn's in desperate need of a mow. The paint's peeling. There are weeds damn near tall as I am lining the worn-out fence and swallowing up heaps of junk in the yard—car parts, trash, beer cans, and the like. As I plod up to the door I can't help but think how different this place looks in my memories. It was a home once. There were flowers growing along the fence in hanging boxes. Those boxes remain, though they're empty now. There was a small garden on the east side of the home where the rising sun could touch the Earth unobstructed. Nothing remains but motorcycle tire tracks and an old mini-fridge lying on its side. The place was clean and welcoming once. I remember being a bit shocked that he kept his castle so tidy, but then in truth, all that work he left to Marla.

When I reach the front door, I hesitate. *What if he's gone too—gone like Carrie? What if they took him? What if who took him? What are you talking about, Bill? Why the hell am I even here? Jesus, I don't know if I can face him. I can't look into those eyes after what—*

Kevin opens the door before I've mounted sufficient courage to knock. "It's been a long time, Bill. I hope you've come here to tell me you finally caught the son-of-a-bitch that murdered my old man?"

From the Journal of Doctor Theodore Grant

It all stems from predictable end states. If I boil it down to a most rudimentary example; imagine a mouse in a maze. A common experiment, one many utilize in behavioral science, and whenever it is utilized the scientists try their hardest to minimize the effect of chaos on their subject; i.e. they try and reduce as many external variables as possible so the results of the rat's maze experiment do not deviate for reasons outside the bounds of the actual experiment's parameters.

As an example; if you were trying to simply determine if a mouse has the mental capacity to remember through trial and error how to escape the maze, you wouldn't want, say, a gust of wind to deter him from the path he might know to be the correct one, as this would skew your results negatively. Nor would you place a predator such as a scorpion in the maze with the mouse, as the scorpion might deter the mouse from the path it knows to be correct in order to avoid said predator, again skewing the results. You wouldn't run the test outside in the rain one instance, then on a dry and sunny day the next, nor would you place the maze outside at all, as running the test in the dead of night when it is dark would likely yield different results than a daytime test.

You want the maze itself completely isolated and without any outside influences—no matter how small—otherwise you run the risk of polluting the results.

In a perfect world, the maze would be in a completely dust-free, indoor, lighted, sterile environment, inside a vacuum void of air and thusly sound (though the mouse would of course be able to somehow breathe in this vacuum, perhaps through some sort of breathing apparatus). Every wall and every minute detail would be exactly the same. The piece of cheese at the end would be the exact same size and shape and produce the exact same odor of the exact same intensity each time the experiment was run. Point being, the only variable that would change each time the experiment was run would be the mouse itself, or more aptly, the mouse's memory of prior runs through the maze.

But in an effort to explore the bounds of what constitutes freewill, we must start with the fewest number of variables and work our way out. So let's theorize for a moment that you could somehow remove that sole remaining variable—the mouse's memory of prior runs through the maze—by wiping its memory of all previous attempts. If this were possible—perhaps through the use of Cycloheximide—and if the initial state of the experiment was always exactly the same, and there were no external variables to push our furry friend down a different path thereby skewing our results, then theoretically the mouse would run the exact same route every single time it entered the maze. This result is due to the fact that the decision making process used by the mouse—let's call him Steve—would be completely identical every time he attempts the experiment. Without anything to influence his decisions, and since the decision trees constructed by animal brains are not randomized in any way, the end state of his choices would always be the same.

Let's pretend for a moment that on Steve's first run through our maze, whenever given the option to take the path to the right, he exercises it. Even if we run the test a thousand times, as long as we wiped his memory after each attempt he always turns right when given the option. Now the question becomes, why does he make that choice to begin with? Why didn't he choose to turn left each time, or some combination of left and right?

The answer lies with two of the three variables which influence our decision making process. These variables are not unique to *Homo sapiens*, rather all thinking animals rely on these three—I'll call them Prime Variables—when making choices. And that goes for all choices, not just the big ones. When you decide it's time to cut dairy from your diet, that's because your Prime Variables led you to that final decision state. When you decide to butter your toast with almond butter instead of regular butter, that's because your Prime Variables led you to that final decision state. When you decide to butter your toast left to right, top to bottom, that is again because your Prime Variables led you to that final decision state. And when you subconsciously decide to chew that bread a meager three times before swallowing, that is also because your Prime Variables led you to that final decision state.

Regardless of how monumental or inconsequential the decision, the Prime Variables are the reason you chose to make it. And what are the Prime Variables? The first is your genetic predispositions. I, for one, am less predisposed to engage in direct conflict than most people I know. Part of this has to do with my life experience, as fighting was never something that was glorified in my family. But even as a child, long before I had life experience to draw from, I shied away from conflict. The genes of my forbearers lent to passivity. Contrast that with my schoolyard friend descended from Scottish warriors, who as soon as he could walk wanted to hit everyone he came in contact with, and you can see how some of us are simply wired to lean one way or another when it comes to emotional states. And you bet those predispositions play a role in our decision making process.

But our genetic predispositions go far beyond our baseline emotional states and personality traits. There are simple predispositions such as our color preferences, our inclination toward one art form or another, or our dietary palates, or the gait of our walk, all of which we are born with. When you add up the impossibly large number of personality traits and idiosyncrasies passed down from parent to child which impact each and every one of life's decisions, the number of variables is staggering…but not incalculable.

The second Prime Variable and arguably the most impactful to our decision making process is our life experiences. As I'm writing this I can't help but feel a bit silly trying to tie genetic predispositions and quantifiable life experiences to a mouse, but the logic is sound. As easy as it is to see how a mouse in a maze (if we didn't wipe his memory) uses his past experiences to help navigate the maze and make future decisions, it becomes a bit more complex when trying to imagine how this relates to human beings. But know that nearly every decision we make (those not singularly impacted by the first and third Prime Variables) is heavily influenced by prior experiences.

My decision to go into the field of astrophysics, for example, I believe originated from a single influential event—a film I watched with my family as a child—*The War of the Worlds*. I still remember it clear as day; all of us huddled around our black and white television screen in our living room, a blanket draped over my shoulders and the pellet stove roaring. My mother told us that the film originated as a radio broadcast that went out on Halloween. It was delivered via the format of a news broadcast, and was so convincing that many who tuned in thought it was real. Entire communities were thrown into a state of mass pandemonium, thinking aliens had actually invaded America.

Hoax or not, it sparked a thirst deep inside me. For nights after watching the film, my first foray into the possibilities of alien life, I couldn't sleep. My mind was enraptured by the thought that *They* were out there. From that day forth my path was set. Many of the decisions I made throughout my life were based on the chain of events that followed that life experience so many years prior. Had I never watched that film, or done so later in life when perhaps my adolescent mind found less intrigue in the subject matter, perhaps I would have never ventured into this field in the first place.

The third and final Prime Variable is *actus dei*, or acts of God—forgive the parlance. Things like the weather, for example, influence our decisions all the time. Should I go for a jog today? It's raining outside, so I think I'll just stay indoors. These sorts of events are nearly impossible to predict and vary from extreme weather patterns such as hurricanes, tornados, and storms, to more subtle environmental influences like solar flares, the pull of the moon on the Earth, a comet passing overhead, or even something as trivial as a gust of wind. How can a gust of wind influence a decision? Well, what if that gust of wind brought with it a shudder, and that shudder sparked nostalgia, which triggered a memory of an lost love, and that memory prompted you to call that old love, and that call resulted in you reconnecting and someday marrying and having children with this person? A gust of wind just caused a new life to be born. It's Chaos Theory at its finest.

Back to the mind-wiped Steve in the sterile rat's maze. As I said, only the first two Prime Variables are at play here in this example because we've removed actus dei from the equation. In Steve's maze there is no weather or wind or otherwise unaccounted for phenomena that could impact his decision tree. And because of that fact, coupled with the mind erasure proposed prior, Steve will always wind up choosing the exact same path every time we run the experiment.

So how does this relate to freewill in human beings? Well, quite simply, although the number of variables at play which make up even the most rudimentary decision trees of our lives are incredibly complex, our ultimate decisions are still based on the Prime Variables and not some ethereal concept like freewill. The organic computers in our heads calculate every single decision presented to us—even those which we do not realize are decisions, such as how we butter our toast—a trillion times every day, and the method used for concluding each decision is at its very core a highly complex nested Boolean decision tree that takes into consideration the three Prime Variables and nothing else.

We may think we are exercising choice when we decide to return that lost wallet we found rather than keep it, but in reality the choice has already been made for us. It was simply a function of our genetic predisposition towards honesty and integrity, coupled with our life experience and the physical environment which surrounds us.

Now let's pretend for a moment that we created a completely controlled environment—a biosphere in the same vein as Steve's sterile maze—thereby eliminating actus dei. Within that biosphere we placed a group of people, people whom immediately prior to placement inside the biosphere were neural-mapped so we could analyze all their memories and genetic makeup. We know all their genetic predispositions, all their life experiences, and from that point forward we tracked at an incredibly detailed level, every action they made and the chain reaction their actions had on the biosphere's environment, both physically and socially.

The question then becomes, with enough computational power and given a static initial state such as the one described previously, could we with a high degree of certitude, predict their future?

Is it possible that the universe is just one big biosphere and that something with an incredibly vast array of sensors and unparalleled computational power is monitoring us all? Perhaps it's inside us cataloguing everything we do and think and feel and experience? Could it be accurately predicting, or at the least trying to predict our future state at all times? Or perhaps only when we sleep? Could my sleeping mother have somehow tuned in on their prescient divining and became a subconscious viewer? Had some supremely intelligent force analyzed my brother's Prime Variables while simultaneously accessing every living organism on the planet, able to compute the chaos effect of each upon the other, and determined his fate? They would have most certainly arrived at the conclusion that Paul would disobey my mother and head to Crane Lake. They may even have been able to predict the manner in which he would tie his skates that day, the amount of pressure he'd put into each stride, the area of the lake he would skate the most. And should they take into account all the other children skating on the lake that day and all days prior, perhaps seeing his end is not entirely impossible?

Jesus, I know how this sounds. I guess this is why I keep a journal…a private journal.

Chapter 27

We're sitting on his porch watching the morning sun creep over the trees. Kevin reaches down below the bench and slides out a red cooler. Ice and water slosh about inside. From it he plucks a Budweiser, snaps it open, and takes a hearty swallow.

"Little early, wouldn't you say?" *God I'm a fucking hypocrite.*

"God you're a fucking hypocrite," he echoes back. Then he simmers and asks, "Want one?" But as he plunges back down into the icy cooler, I wave him off. "Suit yourself." He leans back, knocks a few empty beer cans off the porch with his feet to clear himself a spot, and kicks his legs out.

"So you're not here about my old man. You found my mom then?"

"I'm not here about your parents, Kevin." My hand starts to quiver. It's a mild shake—likely withdrawals.

"No?"

"No."

"Then why are you sitting on my porch?"

He looks calm and cool as if this is all routine. Kevin always was the collected one. He got that from Charles. His mother, Marla, was the hothead. But beneath his relaxed demeanor there's boiling oil. A few more pounds of pressure and he'll explode. That's the thing about the quiet ones. You never know what's gonna set them off.

"I, I just wanted to check in on you. Make sure you're doing alright."

He smirks, takes another sip of beer, crushes the can and tosses it into the yard. Only nineteen-years-old and already a problem drinker. "What do you care?"

"Your dad was my partner for twenty years. I was there when you were born, Kevin."

"And where were you after the old man croaked? Where were you after mom went missing? Shit, I bet one of your G-men offed 'em both."

Close but no cigar. "It's a cold case, Kevin. I've spent every waking minute trying to—"

"You haven't done shit. A federal agent is murdered, his wife goes missing, and you think it's just, what, just coincidence? That's some government cover-up bullshit if I've ever seen it."

"Why would anyone at the Bureau want to kill your dad?" *Why am I indulging his delusions?*

"You tell me, G-Man."

"They wouldn't." The shake in my hand grows too pronounced to hide any longer. I scoop a beer out of the freezing ice-melt and put it to my lips. It tastes like domestic swill, but it helps calm my shakes a bit.

"Who's this?" comes a young woman's voice from over my shoulder. She's standing in the front door in her panties and a cutoff tank top, looking completely unabashed.

"No one, babe. Just an old friend of my dad's."

"Oh." She yawns and steps out onto the porch to light a joint. She looks young enough to still be in high school.

After a long drag I say, "You do know I'm a federal agent." The girl doesn't even turn to acknowledge me.

"You come here to arrest my girlfriend, Bill?"

She turns, takes a long pull off the joint, and blows the skunky smoke my way. "It's medicinal. I've got, ya know, cataracts."

"Glaucoma, babe."

"Yeah, that too." She shuffles back inside and shouts from halfway down the hall, "You want breakfast."

"I'm good," Kevin shouts back. He gives me a wink.

"Oh, to be young," I grumble.

"So, my mom and dad. What have you—"

"I told you, I didn't come here to talk about Charles and Marla, Kevin. I came here to talk about you."

"Me? I figured you forgot I even existed."

Hardly. I see you every night in my dreams…rather in my nightmares.

"I'm sorry I haven't come around more. I should've been here for you." God it's hard to even look at him. He's got Marla's nose and eyes and Charles hairline. It's like looking at my long lost friend and the bitch that killed him all rolled up into an angry, angst-riddled teenage package.

"Why? You're not family. I'm sure you got more important things to do than listen to my problems. The all-powerful, Special Agent Bill Singer." His expression is half playful, half condescending. "God. The old man never shut up about you; when he was home that is. As rare an event as that was. To hear him talk about you, I thought…I thought you were some sort of god.

"When I was little, mom would get worried sick about him. So then I would worry. I mean, Dad didn't talk much about work—couldn't talk about it, I guess—but we could tell when he had just gotten off some really grizzly case. He'd go all silent treatment on us for days at a time. Wouldn't talk about much of anything. He'd just sit on the sofa and watch some shitty movies. But you… Mom and I worried a lot less once you came along, once we knew you had his back; the all-powerful, bulletproof, genius Bill Singer."

If only a lick of that were true. Some genius I am. I can't even find my own partner. Maybe being Bill Singer's partner is a curse?

"Far from it, Kevin."

He cracks another beer. "I miss them."

"I know you do, son. So do I."

I glance around at the dilapidated house. "I'm surprised you decided to stay here. Don't you have family in Seattle?"

"Seattle's a long way from here. And besides, my girl lives here. She's not about to follow me across the country."

"You alright? You have enough money?"

"Well, lost my job at the auto body. Fucking manager claims I stole some vice grips. Truth is he just wanted to free up the head count so he could hire on his fucktard of a brother. Could've sued, but—"

Kevin notices me glancing around at the state of his home and says, "But I got money! No worries. These checks come in every month from some federal agency—not the Bureau—but some damn place. Severance or life insurance or some shit. Though the old man didn't die on the job, so I'm surprised I get a dime. Maybe I should look into it?"

No, no you definitely shouldn't look into it. "I'd just count your blessings and leave it alone. Maybe somebody made a clerical error. You don't want that money to dry up, do you?"

"Hell no! If you think eleven-forty an hour is enough to pay for this place—to pay for anything—you're nuts."

A few more swallows of beer and he tosses the empty out into the yard. It's hard to watch this kid self-destruct. To watch him treat Charles' home like his personal trash can. But I get it. I really do.

"So you just came over to talk finances?"

"Not exactly." *How do I word this?* "Look, Kevin, you haven't seen, I don't know, anyone snooping around the house? Seen anything strange the past few nights?"

"Saw a chipmunk get the shit kicked out of it by a raccoon. Right over there on the fence. Other than that..." He raises his hands in question.

"Any phone calls? Hang ups? Blocked calls? That sort of thing."

"I don't know. Maybe one. But who doesn't get the occasional wrong number? What's this all about, Bill? You're starting to freak me the fuck out."

What is this all about, Bill? A dream? A goddamn dream?

"I, uh, it's classified. Listen, nothing to worry about, Kevin, nothing really, but since you're not working right now, why don't you take some time? Maybe take that sweet little thing in there on a trip for a few days? Ever been to the South Carolina shore? It's beautiful this time of year."

"You trying to get rid of me?"

"Yeah. Yeah I am." I hand him a wad of hundred dollar bills.

"Okay, now you're really starting to scare me."

Better scared than blue and bloody and asphyxiated in my arms. I don't care how ridiculous this is. There are only three people left on this planet I still give a shit about and two of them are already missing.

"Just do what I tell you. Everything will be fine. Take your girl and head out to the coast. Don't tell anyone. Pay for everything in cash. Don't answer the phone—don't even bring your phone. Just lay low for a few days. It's probably nothing, but better safe than sorry."

"What's going on?" asks his girlfriend. Again the little panty clad ninja somehow snuck into the doorway without me hearing her footsteps. *I wonder how much she heard?*

"Um, babe, go um, go pack a bag. It's about time I took you on a trip."

In a catatonic voice she replies. "We're taking a vacation?"

"Yep. I'm taking you on vacation."

"Okay. Can we go somewhere with mountains? I like mountains. And trees. Trees are nice."

"Sure, I guess." He looks at me to validate the change of plans.

I whisper, "Take her wherever you want, just get out of town for a while. Go hide out in a cabin in the woods for all I care. Hell, ever check out Catoctin Mountain Park? My partner tells me it's—"

Shit… Shit! Shit! Shit! Shit! "I have to go, Kevin. Just, just, I'll be in touch."

Chapter 28

As I race down Kevin's driveway toward my car, I whip out my phone and pull up the maps. Catoctin; it's straight up the 650. It's a straight line from the only two credit card purchases Goodwin made. It's where she was headed—I just know it. If she's following in Grant's footsteps, then she'll have gone somewhere remote, low population density—somewhere like his Ozark compound. But Catoctin; she dripped with nostalgia when she spoke of it in Arkansas. It's a safe place for her, a familiar place, a place that meets Grant's criteria, and most of all, a place no one would think to look…no one but me, that is.

Kevin's standing on his porch with his mouth hung open, just watching me flee. *Sorry about the mind-fuck, kid, but better safe than dead.* I can live with Kevin Moser thinking his Uncle Billy is a lunatic for sending him into hiding because of a bad dream. What I can't live with is a dead Kevin Moser.

As I fly through suburbia with my siren blaring and lights spinning, my phone rings in my pocket. I can't hear it over the sirens, but the vibration clues me in. **Coolie, Bryce**, is on the screen. I kill the siren so I can hear him.

"What is it, Bryce?"

"Well, Singer, you asked me to check out what Special Agent Goodwin was doing at the Library of Congress."

"That I did." *Logging into their public use computers, I'm sure.*

"Well, I found someone there who remembers seeing her."

"Really?"

"I know, right? Sounds unlikely, but one of the supervisory librarians, a Cynthia Cho, had taken a look at something for Goodwin."

"What did Goodwin have her look at?"

"Well, uh, she just said that Goodwin came in with a book she wanted identified. Cho's English was pretty bad, but she gave me a copy of an analysis report she had written up for Special Agent Goodwin."

"And what does it say."

"Um, okay, well it says; Binder: Leather, black. Publisher: Unknown. Publication Date: Unknown. Cardstock Composition: Papyrus—"

"Just give me the highlights, Coolie!"

"Highlights, okay, right. Well, one thing of note here, she says that a wood block printer was used, along with papyrus paper."

"And?"

"And that's a pretty antiquated printing technique?"

"How do you know that?"

"Because it says so right here in Cho's report? I thought you wanted me to summarize this?"

"Right. Sorry. Go on."

"Wood block was primarily used in Asia up until the nineteenth century, Cho says. She also notes that the book looks to be a translated work—though she couldn't tell what the original language was. Though she does note the repeated misuse of a few of the words is a common translation error when converting from Semitic dialects over to Latin based languages.

"Let's see, what else here. Well, she couldn't identify the author or the title or who published the book. Based on the binding material, degradation, cardstock, and wood block print, she placed the age at anywhere from two to five hundred years old. The pre-translated work she estimates was drafted sometime in the fourth century."

"Based on?"

"Certain words and phrases, though she doesn't say which ones."

"Anything else?"

"Yeah. She was, ah, she was frickin' weird, Singer."

"What?"

"Doctor Cho, the librarian. She wasn't normal. She kept shaking like a leaf on a tree and repeating herself over and over. At first I thought it was just a language thing. Ya know, her trying to make sure I caught her meaning. But the more I think of it, the stranger her behavior seemed."

"Why are you telling me this? She's a librarian. It takes a certain breed to do that shit job."

"Don't drink the ambrosia."

My heart stops beating, then races to catch up. "What the hell did you just say?"

"Like I said, she was a weird one. She shouted that at me as I was walking away. I thought it was just some strange Chinese saying she wanted to leave me with, so I didn't ask what it meant. I just waved and said, 'Okay, I won't.'"

A long string of empty air and Bryce says, "Singer? Singer, you still there?"

"I'm still here, Bryce." My skin riddles with gooseflesh.

"Yeah, so... 'Don't drink the ambrosia.' Any idea what that means?"

Anesthetizing Daemons – November 1st, 2018

"It's 1:00PM, November 1st, twenty eighteen AD," says Grant.

"It happened by accident. Like so many breakthroughs, it was completely unplanned. But the ramifications are profound. I figured out a way to put them to sleep." His eyes are wild and searching. He looks feral. "The foil certainly acts as a radiant barrier for EMF, but it does nothing to restrict the Daemons' interbody communications." He scratches the aluminum foil cap on his head and peers around his study at the foil wrapped walls. "I could never be certain if it truly worked, but my theory always maintained that they communicate using some spectrum on the electromagnetic scale. If that's true, then I can minimize or potentially eradicate their ability to communicate outside of this room simply by insulating it, thereby reducing the breadth of what they can manipulate to, well, to just myself and, and, and any organic life within the house.

"You see, the power source has always been a conundrum. Obviously they may very likely be using some form of energy unknown to us—dark energy perhaps—but more likely than not they have at a minimum adapted to absorb photons as a potential energy source, as photons are abundant throughout the universe even in deep space.

Though it's a quandary whether photon radiation alone would be enough to sustain them, or provide sufficient power for long distance communications. And of course, photons, though they may be abundant, are not always available, such as when I'm indoors with the lights off.

"Which is why I surmise their primary energy source likely comes from the organic matter they inhabit. For this reason, I find it highly unlikely they inhabit inorganic matter at all, or at least not for any extended period of time. For just like endoparasites rely on a host for sustenance—absorbing carbohydrates and amino acids for energy—perhaps Daemons do as well. The mechanism, the process by which they absorb human, animal, and plant energy is still an unanswered question. There are a myriad ways they could; thermal transfer, oxidation of the cells, cellular respiration, or perhaps even radioactive decay?

A moment of silence follows. His hands twitch and his eyes flicker. Then he says, "Could it be that the speed at which our cells degrade has a direct correlation to the number of Daemons feeding off them?" Grant is awestruck by his sudden revelation. He tries to scribble a note on a pad of paper but his hands shake so terribly he throws it down in frustration. After composing himself, he looks back at the camera and continues in a monotone, almost beaten voice, "There are numerous accounts—not just biblical, but historical accounts—which indicate that ancient man may have lived on average well over two hundred years. Some claim men survived well into their eight and nine hundredth years of life. This is at a time well before modern medicine and technology, two thousand years before Jesus Christ supposedly walked the Earth.

"I'd always dismissed these claims. Though they were prolific, they also came with too many unknowns for me to ever lend them much credence, but…what if they're true? Perhaps our shortened life spans are a direct result of the Daemons absorbing sustainable energy from our cells? If we could purge them from our—"

Grant glances up at the camera as if he forgot it was still there. His hands are a shaky mess, his teeth yellow and hair long. Barely recognizable anymore. "I'm sorry. I, I went off on a tangent. That is a topic for another day. Let me start over."

He straightens his back and clears his throat. "This is Doctor Theodore James Grant. It is now 1:04PM on November 1st, two thousand eighteen Anno Domini. I have discovered a way to temporarily anesthetize the Daemons living inside me…living inside us all. Through a combination of resonant frequencies and electrical pulses, I have been able to, in essence, put them to sleep. The effects last roughly two and a half hours, after which time their arousal is accompanied by an—" it looks as if the following words bring with them the physical pain they describe, "—excruciating pain in my head right behind my eyes, a temporary loss of vision, and a loud auditory whine. Nausea soon follows, along with debilitating pain in my extremities." Grant whispers, "It's almost as if they're punishing me."

"And it is for that reason that I have now kept them sufficiently anesthetized for seventy-two straight hours. As you can imagine, sleep deprivation has become a problem. I'm forced to wake myself every two hours in order to perform the procedure. But there are notable positive side effects to the anesthetization process as well…"

Chapter 29

Catoctin Mountain Park is a long drive from DC, especially if you're taking I-650. But that's the way I'd go if I wanted to stay hidden. There are no traffic cameras on the 650. Sure I suppose I could've just taken 270 straight there, but if Goodwin took 650 then so shall I. Retrace her steps. I have to put myself in her shoes. What if she saw something on the way to Catoctin that changed her mind? What if her car broke down on the side of the road? What if, what if, what if? There are far too many variables, not to mention I'm not one hundred percent certain she even went to Catoctin.

No, I need to try and follow her trail the best I can. By the numbers, step by step, eyes wide open—there's no room for error.

Well before I reach the halfway mark of my journey, before even crossing into Maryland, the terrain shifts from bone white office buildings and concrete byways, to lush green pastures and rolling hills. Life is sparse out here. Rarely have I ventured beyond the bounds of the city, at least not for recreation. For me, bearing witness to natural beauty doesn't hold the allure it does for most folks. I've seen so much destruction in my days; whenever I come upon an untouched oasis I can't help but think how someday soon mankind will just wipe it off the map. In a few years' time these majestic trees that have grown tall and proud for hundreds, if not thousands of years, will be clear-cut to make room for another strip mall. These grassy hills will be covered in a layer of concrete and the tranquility of this place will be shattered by endless car horns and sirens. And these open plains and fallow pastures, consumed by yet another eighteen lane mega-highway.

I don't know. Maybe I'm just being cynical.

Still, Catoctin isn't without its beauty. It's no wonder Camp David is nearby. To every President since Franklin Roosevelt, it has offered solitude and tranquility. It says so right on the flyers. And driving through these emerald woods with the sun directly overhead, for a moment I forget my worries and just breathe it all in. The haunting smell of pine fills my head and my eyes fall shut.

"I get it, Goodwin. I'd feel safe here too."

A small log cabin greets me as I pull into the main camping area. *Office* is displayed on a handle-chiseled sign that hangs from the lintel. There are various routes out of the parking lot with signs at each. Most have cabin number ranges on them. One points to Camp David, another to a tent camping area, one to Hunting Creek Lake, and another that points to river access.

I park my car and climb the steps up to the office. As I push through the rickety screen door, a bell dings my arrival and I'm assaulted by the reek of cigarettes and wood oil. I haven't had a smoke in days—haven't wanted one either. The smell should send me into a nicotine infused rage. It should have my mouth drooling and mind reeling. I should be down on my knees begging the attendant to bum a stick. But instead all it does is turn my stomach inside out.

Behind the counter sits an old woman. She's got her reading glasses on and nose down in a book; *The Plague of the Pythons*. In the corner, a TV is mounted playing some old rerun of Martha Stewart's cooking show. The woman behind the counter doesn't bother to acknowledge my presence. Or perhaps she didn't hear me come in. I glance back at the bell above the door and then back toward the woman. A clear of my throat and a few taps of my fingers on the counter bring her eyes up to meet mine.

"I'm sorry," she says. "I, I didn't hear you come in." She turns the book in her hands, widens her eyes when she catches sight of the cover, then sets it down. "It's so easy to get lost in a good book. It's almost as if the world just disappears. Has that ever happened to you?"

No, no it hasn't.

Her smile is warm. I find myself suddenly missing my grandmother.

"No problem, ma'am. My name is Special Agent Bill Singer with the FBI." I flip open my badge and receive a look as if she's got a mountain of cocaine hidden behind the desk.

"Oh dear. Is, is there something I can do for you, Agent?"

Her nametag reads; **Mrs. Patty**. I say, "Patty is it? Patty…"

I wait for her to give me her last name but she just replies, "Folks 'round here just call me Mrs. Patty. Now, is there anything I can do for you, Agent?" Her right hand firmly presses down on the book, while her left rests on the counter, fingers nervously tapping. There's a twitch that pulls her left eye shut every few seconds. I try and baseline her behaviors. Not that I have any reason to believe good ole Mrs. Patty—likely retiree, grandmother of two, and longtime employee of the Catoctin Camp Grounds—has anything to hide from me, but…old habit.

"I'm looking for a woman that may have checked in here several days ago. Brunette, early thirties, about this tall, thin, maybe a hundred and ten pounds, probably paid in cash."

Mrs. Patty's twitch doubles up and her fingers stop tapping. "No, I, I don't think we've had anyone like that come through here." She shakes her head and gives me a plastic smile.

"Did anyone else work the desk other than you?"

I hear Martha over in the corner comment, "Now we're going to add some cream and just a pinch of salt."

"Oh no. Just Marshall and I most days, though he's been out on his annual fishing trip since last Wednesday. Won't be back for another week. No, no it's just me here for the time being. Dawn till dusk. I'm sorry, Agent, I wish I could help you. Is this woman in some sort of trouble?"

"No trouble, ma' am. I just need to speak with her. No need to be alarmed."

"Oh, that's good. We, we a, we don't need any trouble up here. This is a trouble-free zone," she forces a chuckle, her eye twitches, and her finger-taps resume.

"That's good to hear, Mrs. Patty. Now if you wouldn't mind telling me which cabin she's in so I don't have to go door to door kicking them all down. Be a shame to bother all your guests like that, when it's only one I aim to bother."

"Agent?"

Martha chimes in—"Mmmm. Now isn't that tasty? A perfect treat for the holidays." *How serendipitous.*

"Mrs. Patty, do you know the penalty for lying to a federal agent?"

"Sir, I'm, I'm not sure what you mean."

"Section one, zero, zero, one of Title 18 of the United States Code, generally prohibits knowingly and willfully making false or fraudulent statements or concealing information in any matter within the jurisdiction of the federal government of the United States, even by mere denial." I point up to Martha. "Even with her top notch lawyers, she spent five months behind bars. Do you have top notch lawyers, Mrs. Patty?"

"It's, it's Grainger. Patty Grainger. And no I—"

"Then you're likely looking at spending the rest of your natural life in a five by five cell for impeding a federal investigation." *Do I feel bad for mercilessly intimidating a senior citizen? Yeah, a little. But then, why is she protecting Goodwin at all?*

"Agent, I, I don't want any trouble—"

"You say that like you mean it," *and she does appear to mean it,* "but then you deliberately lied to me. Just assume I already know she's here. Assume my question is rhetorical. Just answer me truthfully."

"She, she told me her boyfriend would come looking for her."

"Her boyfriend? I'm not her—"

Patty interrupts and confidently declares, "Had quite a shiner when she came in. Said he's a federal agent. Said that he, he beat her and she needed to hide away for a while." *Clever girl, Goodwin.*

"I appreciate your cooperation. And I assure you no harm will come to her. I'm not her boyfriend, I'm her partner."

"She said you'd say that."

A sigh, a plastic smile of my own, and then, "Which cabin is she staying in?"

Mrs. Patty bites her lip in defeat. I'm putting her grandmotherly instincts to the test, but there's no fighting me on it now. I know Goodwin's here. Patty knows I know Goodwin's here. So she says, "Cabin forty."

"And I assume you have a spare key? Wouldn't want me to have to kick down the door, now would you?"

Begrudgingly she wobbles into a back room and soon emerges with the key. As she places it on the counter, she says, "Agent? If anything happens to that sweet, young girl," her lips stiffen, "I may be old, but this granny's got a 12-gauge and she knows how to use it."

Sure I could recite the statute for threatening a federal agent, but instead I just nod in agreement. "I wish there were more people like you in the world, Mrs. Patty."

Anesthetizing Daemons – November 2nd, 2018

"Why didn't they stop me? Why didn't they destroy me upon waking, or force me to destroy the machine and in essence prevent me from administering the procedure again? I wrestled with this question throughout the night, and what I've landed on is this; I am their greatest experiment. After all, their sole purpose is to observe, and through observation expand their knowledge of the universe. And I, I am the only sentient being who is aware of their existence. What a unique and remarkable subject that makes me!

"Sure, there are plenty of people who may feel the Daemons inside them. They've conveniently catalogued this phenomenon as the existence of an immaterial soul. They believe guardian angels and demons tug them to and from danger and temptation. And though their theology might not be far askew of reality, it is shrouded in magic and blind faith and in no way jeopardizes exposure of the real truth. What lives within us, what nudges us towards ruin or guides us towards salvation is not a higher being, an angel, or a metaphysical soul, but rather a parasite of vastly superior intellect.

"Freewill. It's their mandate. They may bend it, they may give us that initial push toward one end or another—perhaps only to bear witness to the aftermath—but they never break our will. No, that goes against their entire purpose for being. As for me, here, trapped, cut off from the world—I'm no threat to them. They can just observe. That's what they long for, after all, to observe. And what better subject than me?"

Chapter 30

Cabin forty. Upon the shoulder of a hill surrounded by a grove of pines and alders; it overlooks the lake, though you wouldn't know it if you were inside seeing as how all the windows have been boarded up. *Not good.*

Goodwin's car is parked alongside the cabin. She's inside and I'm almost certain she's alone, though for some reason I find my hand fidgeting with the buckle of my empty holster as I inch my way up onto the porch. Maybe I shouldn't have left my gun in the car. But if she is here, I need her to trust me. Showing up armed…

I knock, and then I listen. Dead silence within. Nothing stirs. "Goodwin? Goodwin, it's Singer. I'm alone. Open the door? I know you're in there. I just want to talk." My ear's pressed against the door. There's no peephole like at her apartment, just solid oak. I could kick it down easily enough, but Mrs. Patty would consider that "trouble," and the last thing I want to do is cause Mrs. Patty any trouble. Nor do I want to startle the presumably already fragile of mind Roxanne Goodwin. Whatever's taken hold of her and driven her way out here, if it's anything like what happened to Doctor Grant… I recall first stepping foot in his Ozark complex. I had to straddle several evidence markers where Billy Cole had been fried to a crisp thanks to Doctor Grant's booby-trapped front door.

Shared Psychosis—the folly of two. It's rare, but real. A seemingly healthy individual adopts the psychosis of someone suffering from a psychotic break. I once worked a case where a man thought all of his neighbors were aliens hell-bent on world domination. Gary Vallenta; worst case of schizophrenia I'd ever seen up until now. The most destructive force on Earth, I contend, is a mind enthralled by madness.

One by one he picked off his neighbors. A quiet, little, idyllic suburbia rocked by seven murders in five weeks. And he was smart about it too. He'd study their patterns, record their movements to and from work; he knew what kind of cars they drove, when their kids were home alone—he even knew when one of the men that lived nearby was with his mistress. He broke into the mistress's home one afternoon while the two of them were going at it and slit both their throats.

Unlike most serial killers who tend to want to get caught deep down (how else will they ever get their due notoriety?), Gary truly thought he was doing the world a favor. In his mind he was a patriot, a damn smart patriot who covered his tracks well. And what compounded the difficulty in catching him was the inconsistency in evidence. It took me a spell to figure out that he wasn't working alone.

In the end we learned his longtime girlfriend was helping him plan the murders. She wasn't schizophrenic, she wasn't even ADD. There was absolutely nothing psychologically unbalanced about her. Still, she fell into his delusion fully, and before long not only was she a believer, but she claimed she'd witnessed several of their neighbors beam up into spacecraft during the night. She honestly believed it. She'd seen it happen, or more aptly, hallucinated it happening.

God I hope Goodwin isn't seeing aliens. Still, just in case, before trying the door handle I put on some rubber gloves. It's locked.

I make my way around to the back of the cabin. As I clear the woodpile, the trees open up for an unobstructed view of Hunting Creek Lake. About two miles downhill, the glacial blue waters lay nestled in the belly of pine-bearded hills. A susurrant wind stirs; just enough to knock loose a few leaves from the surrounding alders and sprinkle them down around me like fat snowflakes. Down on the water, the wind ripples the surface and sunlight flashes off the peak of every wave. A part of me wishes I could just stay here with Anne and forget about life.

The back door is locked too. "Anne? Come on! I know you're in there?" Nothing. Silence. Not a peep. I'm going to have to kick the door down.

"Anne, if you don't open up I'm just going to kick—" The deadbolt thwacks back into its housing. The handle turns, the door swings inward, and a hand grabs me by the collar and yanks me inside.

Chapter 31

I'm looking at a zombified version of Roxanne Goodwin. Her hair, at least that which is visible from beneath her aluminum foil cap, is greasy and unkempt. She's wearing not a stitch of makeup (not that she wore much to begin with, but the little she apparently did wear hid a plethora of blemishes). There's two-day old bags under her eyes; all puffy and pink. And they're dilated, rheumy, and redder than Kevin Moser's stoned girlfriend's.

"That's ah, that's quite a shiner you got there. Do that to yourself?"

She doesn't answer. Instead she shuffles over to the center of the room and sits cross-legged on the floor with her back to me. All around us whirls a Grant-esque utopia. Foil covers the walls and ceiling. The entire room is strewn with papers covered by indecipherable math equations. And at its beating heart, alone on the floor at the center of the room—Grant's machine.

As Goodwin fusses with the dials, I circle to her front and crouch down to her level. "You've been busy." Her hands shake something awful. "You look tired, Anne. Got any coffee? How about I brew us a pot?"

"Don't drink coffee. Espresso. Not coffee."

"Ah, right. Orange soda then?"

"Not thirsty." She doesn't deign to look at me. Instead she shuffles a few papers around searching for something amongst the illegible scribbles and mind bogglingly complex equations. When it appears she can't find whatever it is she's in search of, Anne pulls herself across the room on her hands and knees to another pile of papers and ruffles through them.

"Anne. I'm here to help. What can I do to help?" *Easy, Bill. Baby steps.*

"You want to help me?" It almost sounds like she's talking in her sleep.

"Of course. You're my partner."

"Set that blue dial to twenty."

"This one here?"

She scans a page and quickly shoves it aside, then picks up another off the floor and mouths something inaudible. "No, wait. Twenty-two. Set it to," she whispers to herself, "one hundred and sixty divided by the vector squared, times the negative difference of mass, adjust for metabolic rate… twenty-two. Yes, twenty-two."

So I set it to twenty-two. Anne scoots her way back over to the device.

"Anne. What are you doing out here?"

She fusses with more dials. "How did you find me?"

"How did I—? It's what I do, Anne. It's what…it's what we do. Or have you forgotten?"

"Didn't want to be found."

"Yeah, I got that impression." I'm at a loss for words. She's gone full *Grant* here. "Sooooo, whatcha workin' on?"

Goodwin stops fiddling with the dials and just stares at the machine for a moment. Her hands quiver. She wrings them out then balls them into fists over and over. Finally she turns to me. "He was right, Bill. Grant was right. Right about all of it. There are," her head twitches and her eyes rapid-fire blink like a camera shutter, "things…living inside us. Intelligent constructs—Daemons, he called them. Nanobots. They feed off us, feed off our cells. They're in everything; the trees and the grass, floating with the pollen on the wind. All organic life is infused with them."

I place a hand on her shoulder. My touch startles her, but she doesn't roll it off. "Goodwin, I, we need to…" *Shit. Baby steps, Bill. Easy. Easy now.* "Even if that's the case—"

"It is the case."

"Then what are you doing here?"

Anne shoots across the floor on hands and knees, scoops up several sheets of paper, and rockets back over to me. She thinks I believe her. There's excitement behind her eyes. "Doctor Grant figured out how to put them to sleep. His formulas were all based off external constants and his own internal dynamics. Every human being is different though. Your resonant frequency is not the same as mine. Well, the Daemon's frequency might be, but your body chemistry, for example, alters your electric current and your resonant vibrations in a slightly different way than mine do. I found it," she holds up a wad of papers, "in his notes. He didn't explicitly state it in his videos, but if I apply these calculations, accounting for my own unique variables… Bill, it works. The machine works. I can put them to sleep. I can turn them off." The lilt of her voice trails off. "I, I, I've never seen the world so clearly before—so unfiltered. It's like there's been a shroud over my eyes. It's like waking from a dream."

She puts a hand to my cheek and looks me in the eyes. Hers are touched by tears. "Would you like to try it? Would you like to see the world for the first time?"

Chapter 32

Even though I watched Ali Nazara use this contraption to no ill avail, a cold sweat racks me as I wrap my fingers around the metal handgrips. Goodwin's busy scribbling away some formula she's apparently deciphered. She takes into account my weight, age, and height, estimates my metabolic rate somehow, and throws in a few more likely useless data points before turning the dials and setting the levels on the machine.

"And this is going to…put the microscopic machines inside me to sleep?" I'm placating her. I know as much. Hell, she probably knows as much. But I need her to trust me. I need her to think I'm above board. It's the only reason I've agreed to this ridiculous experiment.

"That's right. But it won't last. We'll have to rerun the procedure again in approximately two hours."

"And if we don't."

Anne looks grim. "We should rerun it. It's not good to let them wake up after—"

I can't hear her next words. My migraine is back. Shot from a cannon—it came out of nowhere! Bam! Hands up to cover my temples. My brain swells and pushes against the walls of my skull pumping with enough blood to fill this cabin floor to ceiling. *Fuck, fuck, fuck, fuck! Christ, stop! Make it stop!*

She's shouting at me but I can't make out her words. Everything's underwater. Her hands are on my hands. She pulls them over to the machine and wraps my fingers around the cold metal handgrips. I'm screaming and writhing. Anne continually repositions my fingers and holds my hands on the grips.

This is the worst one yet. This is the migraine that finally kills me. My stomach turns inside out. I'm gonna lose it!

And then just as quickly as it came, it's gone.

When I open my eyes, I'm lying prone on the floor with my arms stretched over my head. My hands are on the grips and the machine is humming. There's a dull ache in my head but the worst of it is over. Anne's on her knees next to me with a smile on her face.

"Better?" she asks. She flips off the machine. "It only takes a second or two. Just a quick jolt to open your eyes."

I sit up and rub my aching temples. "Jesus Christ, that was a bad one."

"They saw what you were trying to do. And they tried to stop you."

If a little shock and vibration can cure my migraines, I gotta get me one of these things. "Why don't they just, I don't know, just stop us? Kill us. Explode our hearts in our chests if they don't want us meddling."

"It's like Grant said, freewill. We are their greatest experiment. Grant, now you and I—we're the only people on Earth who know they exist, and we're," she glances around, "trapped here, cut off from the world. We're no threat to them. They can just observe. That's what they long to do, to observe life." She's quoting Grant almost word for word, though I don't think she realizes it. Still, at least my migraine's gone.

There's an old egg timer on the stove in the kitchen. Goodwin winds the dial. "What are you doing?" I ask.

"You'll need to repeat the treatment no less than two hours and twenty minutes from now. I'm setting a timer. If you don't, well, that migraine of yours might come back with a vengeance."

"Anne, we can't just, just live here in this cabin giving ourselves electroshock therapy every two hours until the end of time. What's the play here?"

"Take a look at this." She spreads a long sheet of paper out on the counter. Various equations are scrawled in Grant's unmistakably shaky handwriting.

"What am I looking at? You know I don't understand this shit."

"He was working on a way to purge them without killing the host, but he never finished. I think, I think the months of sleep deprivation, his inability to write with pen and paper any longer, the years of solitude; all of it just wore him down to the nub. His genius just melted away. But he was so close!"

"And you think you can finish his work?"

Goodwin grabs my collar. The shake in her hands is pronounced enough that my shoulders twitch in rhythm with her touch. "Oh yes! I'm close, Bill. I can do this. A few more days, maybe a week and I'll crack it. I know I will. I, I, I just have to work out the formula. He left a trail. It's not easy to follow, but it's there. Deciphering his notes, notes meant only for him, is like solving a codex, a terribly complex code. But with your help, we can—"

"Anne," I step back, "I'm not staying."

"What? But you can't leave. If you leave, how will you perform the procedure? How will you anesthetize them? They'll wake up! You can't let them wake up!"

"Anne, I'll be fine—"

She grabs me and shoves me back against the aluminum foil covered wall. There's a rabid look in her eyes. "You won't be fine," she howls. "If you step out that door, none of this," she looks around at her foil handiwork, "will be there to cutoff their transmissions. They'll try and stop you, try and stop me. They'll, they'll send someone here to stop me. Think about it. You've already seen them at work."

"What?"

"Assistant Deputy Director Kennedy. Didn't it seem odd that he pulled the plug on this case so soon after putting us on it? Something or someone got to him. Or maybe his Daemons just pushed him in that direction."

That or he just came to his senses. "Anne. Freewill, remember?" *Shit, shit, shit. Baby steps ain't working, Bill!*

"People don't even realize they're being influenced. They'll come here to stop me, to, I don't know, but they'll come, and they'll put an end to my work—to Grant's work! There's no way they'll allow me to succeed. It isn't safe out there! Out there they'll know, they'll, they'll, they'll see what I'm planning, they'll organize, they'll fight back! Freewill only goes so far. The experiment can't end. Self-preservation…that trumps all else, Bill. You have to stay right here." Anne releases her hold on me. She's surprisingly strong for such a little thing.

I've got to get her out of here. I've got to bring her back to reality. Whatever this is, whatever she thinks this is, it won't end as long as she remains locked in this madhouse. She'll stay hidden away until she runs out of food and starves to death, or until someone drags her out kicking and screaming.

I don't know what to do. I don't know how to help her without forcing her hand. A fifty-one-fifty would only commit her for seventy-two hours. And I have no doubt that Anne is clever enough to feign recovery and then jump right back into whatever it is this is. I need time to think. I need her to trust me.

Finally I ask, "Where would I sleep?"

Goodwin beams. "You can take the sofa or the bed. It'll be easier with two of us here. We can make sure neither of us oversleeps and misses our window. Remember, we need to anesthetize them every two hours." She yawns. "Best to catch a catnap whenever you can. I've got work to do. Why don't you get some rest, Bill?"

There's no way I can sleep right now. Not to mention I'd be lying if I said I felt safe dozing off while Goodwin is out here in the other room having a mental breakdown. "I'm okay for now. I think I'll just rest my feet."

I plop down on the sofa under a blacked out, foil covered window. Anne nods and gets back to her work. After a few minutes of tapping my feet and silently inspecting her wallpaper job, I say, "Must've spent a fortune on tin foil."

"It's aluminum foil. Helps to restrict communications in and out of the cabin. Grant theorized they—"

"I know, Anne. I know. I was just kidding around."

"Oh. Ha. Yeah, it was quite a project. But it works. I could feel it right away. Do you?"

"Do I what?"

"Do you feel any different? I mean, since you walked in here. Since you put them to sleep?"

Other than my migraine magically subsiding, not a lick. "Yeah. It's like, I don't know, I can't describe it."

"Right! It's incredible isn't it? It's like I'm using my senses for the very first time!"

Shit. She's completely lost it…says the guy that's been chasing imaginary cowboys. "Yeah, something like that."

On the coffee table beside the sofa I notice something that prickles the hairs on my neck. A thousand spiders skitter through my veins. I pick it up and turn it end over end. The black leather of Grant's mysterious, ancient book soaks up the light. Originally I'd taken the book for analysis and given Anne Doctor Grant's journal to review. I'd only read a fraction of the way through it before giving up and turning my attention solely to the notes Grant had slid between some of the pages. The pages where I found a note, I read, though I couldn't find any correlation between them and the content of the pages they marked.

Anne had written a clean summary of all her findings with regards to the journal. For my part, well, I couldn't make heads or tails of the book. In the end she insisted on reading it herself.

"What do you make of this?" I ask her. "Did you read all of it?"

"Yes, and as far as I'm concerned it's unrelated to his research. Just a bunch of bad poetry. Gibberish."

"The librarian you spoke to seemed to think it was quite old…and quite rare."

She glances up at me, surely perturbed I'd tracked her movements. I shrug and ask, "What?"

"Just because something is old doesn't mean it's worth anything. It's nonsense. I thought you read it, Bill?"

I'm far from aesthete, but then, so is a right brained, analytical like Anne Goodwin. She wouldn't know art if it shit on her chest. And poetry?—all poetry has meaning. Even I know that. Sometimes though, that meaning is only obvious to the author. Sometimes that meaning is buried and you have to riddle it out. But what does it matter? From what I can tell, Grant's notes inside the book were the only thing potentially relevant to the case. Even that's a stretch. And from what I could determine they were nothing more than the sporadic ramblings of a man trying to scorn God. Still… I crack it open to a random page and start to read.

> Corporeal in mind and body, when I reach the limit of my ken, the world unravels. A thirst never sated, a hunger that gnaws at my spine.
>
> But before the end, a cup of ambrosia overflows and dashes sweet nectar upon my tongue.
>
> I am reborn!

> Benumb of the manacles birthed by that once unquenchable thirst.
>
> Reborn to a world unbound by the laws of our erudite forerunners. For now, my only desire is to drink endlessly from the cup and let its supernal truths lay waste to all which once plagued me.
>
> Gone is my earthly sight. My third eye opens. It will guide me. Through it I see the universe as it is; so simple, so pure. As am I. As are we all. And soon, we all must drink from the cup, or die by the sword.

Okay. Maybe Goodwin's right. Bad poetry. Nonsense. Still...

I turn the page and continue. Every other sentence I push aside and overlay with scheming thoughts. To her eyes I'm reading an archaic book of ghostly poetry, but what I'm really doing is playing it all out in my head. I'm trying my damnedest to come up with a plan to help her, to get her out of this loony-bin and back to the real world. But I need to be careful how I do it. Traditional psychology, medication, I've got a sneaking suspicion they won't work a lick on Anne Goodwin. This paranoia of hers, it's not a chemical imbalance that can be brought back into check by Thorazine or Loxapine or any of the other 'ines. And mental treatment…maybe, maybe it could help snap her out of this, but I doubt it.

Am I the only one that can help her? Someone she trusts? Someone she respects? I'm someone she looks up to, or at least someone she looked up to before she met me.

But the more I try and ponder our predicament, the more the words on the page slip through and commandeer my attention. The more I try and ignore them, the more I find myself studying the text in my lap.

> I'm afflicted by a new desire.
>
> My heart brims with a passion to appease them.
>
> Those benighted will suffer my wrath.

𝔍 𝔭𝔩𝔞𝔠𝔢 𝔱𝔥𝔢 𝔠𝔲𝔭 𝔱𝔬 𝔱𝔥𝔢𝔦𝔯 𝔩𝔦𝔭𝔰.

𝔗𝔥𝔢𝔶 𝔴𝔦𝔩𝔩 𝔡𝔯𝔦𝔫𝔨 𝔬𝔯 𝔱𝔥𝔢𝔶 𝔴𝔦𝔩𝔩 𝔡𝔯𝔬𝔴𝔫.

...

There's a buzzing from the kitchen. Two hours have somehow flown by while I've been head down in this infernal book. Goodwin readies the device and administers my treatment. It's quick, rather painless. It prickles my fingertips and soon the vibration stems out from my hands to envelope my entire body. Then she administers a treatment for herself. "Might as well get us on the same schedule," she tells me.

Back over on the sofa I pick up the book and try and continue, but my hands shake as if they still cling to the handgrips of Grant's science fair project.

My hands are shaking. My hands are shaking...

The book rattles free of my grasp and splays out on the floor. Goodwin glances over at me but says nothing.

"It's been a day. I could really use a drink." *And I **could** really use a drink.* I ring out my hands. Most likely, it's just withdrawals.

She studies me carefully. "I didn't bring any alcohol."

"You didn't... Why the fuck not!"

That startled her. Startled me too. "I'm sorry, Anne. I...didn't mean to bark. Got anything to eat?"

Head down, scribbling away on a pad of paper with her own palsy riddled hands, she replies, "Help yourself. Brought plenty to keep fed."

As I round the bar that divides the living area from the miniature kitchen, I step right onto a pile of used aluminum foil rolls. Just opening the fridge door shoves a dozen shinny foil cartons aside. Inside is shelf upon shelf of orange soda and bottled water, fruit, salad, and a variety of health foods I wouldn't eat if I were starving to death.

"Is this it?" I ask.

"There's more in the pantry."

Nothing but protein bars and dried pasta, cans of baked beans and soup. I rip into a protein bar and take a bite of what I can only guess is cardboard and sawdust mixed with unsweetened chocolate.

This is how she lives now. This is how we live now.

"So you think you can, ya know, get rid of them? Grant's Daemons, I mean. Isn't that what killed him?"

Goodwin doesn't look up. She's down on her knees in the middle of the room shuffling the order of several papers in front of her so the equations line up, all the while scribbling endless notes of her own. Certain she didn't hear me, I'm about to repeat the question when she responds. "Grant tried to destroy them. This contraption here is a play on Tesla's Earthquake Machine. By doubling the Daemon's resonant frequency, in essence he created total particle fission and... I'm not trying to destroy them. There's no point. They're infinite, self-replicating, unstoppable. But if I can make myself immune, if I can devise a way to alter my resonant frequency so in essence I repel them, then I could be free of them. In time, I could free others too."

"So you're trying to invent nanobot bug spray?" No answer. "And these trans-dimensional tapeworms are just gonna let that happen?"

Silence. A good stretch of silence and then; "I don't know. But I have to try. The world must wake up. Perhaps if enough people join me, the Daemons will just leave us be. But right now, the Earth is just one big rat's maze to them—a global experiment and we're the rats, Singer."

"How can you even be certain they're real. Even Grant admitted he couldn't see them. What if this is all, you know, just in our heads?" *All in your head, at least.*

For the first time since I started probing her, she stops her scribbling, rests back on her heels, and deigns to look at me. "Doctor Theodore James Grant was perhaps the most brilliant mind of the last hundred years. A mind to rival Einstein, to rival Newton!" A deep sigh. "Don't think I don't know how this sounds. If this came from anyone other than Grant, I wouldn't think twice. But then...then I felt them. I felt them behind my eyes looking in on me. I felt them under my skin. Insane, I know. They're too small to stimulate nerve endings, but still...my mind knew they were there. I began to realize that when I had an irrational thought, or a sudden and unexplainable urge, that it wasn't me, but it was them. They were testing me, probing me, nudging me in one direction or another. We call it freewill, but… In Grant's notes he described the decision tree of our lives as a giant Plinko game."

"Plinko?"

"You know, you drop the disc in at the top and it falls down and bounces off wooden pegs until it comes to rest in one of a half-dozen dishes on the bottom. It's an exercise in Chaos Theory. You'd expect that if you always dropped the disc from the same starting point that it would end up in the same dish on the bottom, but it doesn't.

"Anyhow, Grant said to imagine a Plinko game, only there are ramps attached to some of the pegs, ramps controlled by an external force—the Daemons. You're the disc, and each time you strike a peg, you get to decide if you fall to the right or the left. Only now, no matter which way you choose—if the Daemons so desire—they might extend a ramp forcing you back down another path. You might try and deviate again and again, but they'll just keep flipping over ramps to wash you back to their desired end state. You won't realize this is happening, and though you freely made the choice at every crossroad, the roads ultimately lead you to the same endpoint."

"I'm not sure I follow."

"Haven't you ever felt like you missed that stoplight for a reason? It just seemed to turn red a bit too quickly. Or perhaps you always jog the same path every day, but for reasons you just don't understand, one day you decide to take another route home."

"I don't jog, Goodwin."

"The point is, with Chaos Theory, a seemingly insignificant alteration in our chosen path can ultimately result in a radically different outcome. By missing that green light, perhaps you staved off a car accident that would've resulted in a knee injury which would've slowed you down while pursuing a suspect who thusly gets away and winds up murdering someone? Simply by missing that green light, someone in the universe dies prematurely. And that death has its own nearly infinite number of repercussions."

"And you're saying the Daemons can see this future and plan accordingly?"

"Perhaps. It's not as if there are truly an infinite number of possible outcomes to every scenario. An incalculable number for you and I, sure, but the number of outcomes is still finite and has a relative probability of occurring. If a calculating mind were advanced enough, it would be able to see all potential outcomes of any situation and determine a course of action that suited its desires."

I walk back over to the couch and sit down. "Grant said their only desire was expanded knowledge."

Goodwin's back to analyzing the dozen or so sheets of paper scattered around her. "It's just a theory. And it's not like Homo sapiens would be all that fascinating to simply observe, not to the likes of a hyper advanced being. Simple observation only takes you so far. Eventually you need to start adjusting the variables in your experiment. And if you or I or anyone were to try and interfere with their experiment… I fear they might indirectly intercede. They may even put thoughts in your head. Small thoughts, subconscious perhaps. Suggestions. Little tidbits that inadvertently lead you back to their desired path, leaving you none the wiser. A puppet that can't feel the strings, Singer."

"Well I better let you get back to work then."

Anne nods in agreement and I finish the last bite of my sawdust candy bar. My hands are still shaky. Withdrawals, I keep telling myself. *God I want a drink.* I can taste scotch in the back of my throat. But worse than the physical cravings that seem to have returned with a vengeance, I need a drink to stave the boredom—to just clear my head.

And then I'm assaulted by the smell of Virginia tobacco. It fills my nose and dances on my tongue. My skin crawls. *God I want a smoke.* The lack of cravings over the past day or two, however it happened, is long gone—replaced by the strongest pull I've ever felt.

"I picked the wrong week to quit drinking and smoking," I mutter to myself.

"What?" asks Anne.

"Nothing." I crack open Grant's black book and try and ignore the temptations.

From the Journal of Doctor Theodore Grant

Unexplainable phenomena have always fallen into two camps. It is either the handiwork of God or it is magic. More so God than magic nowadays, but everything from the unbelievable effects of magnetized metals to Sir Isaac Newton's failed attempts at quantifying how the various gravity wells in our solar system fail to knock our planets out of orbit and send them spinning off into the sun, have been dubbed either magic or divine will.

Magnets were most certainly magical to those who first discovered them. Though we do not know for certain who first stumbled upon this bizarre phenomenon, a popular theory holds that a Cretan named Magnes was herding sheep when suddenly the nails in his shoes became affixed to a large, black rock on which he was standing. To Magnes, a man who lived nearly four thousand years ago, this was a magical rock. Of course now we know what Magnes thought to be magic or perhaps some heavenly artifact, was likely magnetite—a naturally occurring magnetic material.

As for Newton—perhaps the most brilliant mind in the history of the world—even he gave in to that basest of human desires, an absolute drive to apply an explanation to all phenomena encountered. But when he reached the limits of his abilities and was stumped trying to discern how the planetary orbits worked, he resigned to the old catchall that our solar system's stability must be the result of God's direct intervention and nothing more. Of course Newton was dead wrong.

A century down the road, Pierre-Simon De Laplace pioneered a new form of mathematics to solve the conundrum, and solve it he did. And in the process, he gave us perturbation theory. Had De Laplace given up as Newton had and conceded intelligent design as the answer to this riddle, perhaps we would not have perturbation theory today—a mathematical model which has applications in electronic spectroscopy, iterated fibrations, and more.

The point is, all unexplainable phenomena can be explained. Perhaps we lack the knowledge or technology or mathematical models to divine that explanation today, but that doesn't mean the explanation isn't out there, and it certainly doesn't mean the answer to such questions is sorcery, witchcraft, or the will of a God.

There is nothing in this universe that is not rooted in physical law, and thusly there is no unexplainable phenomena. So imagine the conundrum I faced when trying to theorize how on Earth my mother could possibly have known with such certainty that the ice was going to break beneath my brother's feet and he would drown in Crane Lake that winter so long ago.

For all her strengths, my mother's faith lay not in science and the observable world, but in God. To ask her that question you'd receive a simple answer. God showed her the future. He tried to warn her, but she failed to protect her son.

My mother lived with that regret for the rest of her life. She lived under the false pretense that an all-powerful being gifted her with a vatic dream and she squandered it. In her mind, she should've locked us in a closet until the snows thawed.

Though I certainly do not believe God had anything to do with her premonition, I do believe she was not completely off the mark. Somehow she witnessed a future event through dreams. The question is, how?

Chapter 33

My cell phone is dead. Not that it matters. There's no reception in this aluminum foil prison Anne's built for us. But the clock on my phone is the only one in the cabin. I don't know if Anne threw out whatever wall clocks once hung here or if the campground owners prefer their patrons have no clue what time it is. And with all the windows now blacked out and covered in foil, and the crack under the door stuffed with towels and also covered in foil, after my phone finally shit the bed I completely lost track of time. The routine treatments Anne insists we both endure are perhaps the only indicator of the passing hours, though even those I eventually lose count of and in turn lose all reference as to whether it's day or night or how long I've been awake without sleep.

And it's not just the lack of sleep that plagues me. With the unavoidable malfunction of my internal clock come a whole other slew of issues. For one, I'm certain I've forgotten to eat. I can't tell for sure, but I think it's been about fourteen hours since I last put anything other than water in my stomach, yet somehow I'm not hungry. Hunger, like most human impulses, is heavily dependent on routine and external stimuli. If you don't know its breakfast time because you're trapped in a windowless cell with a psycho FBI agent, chances are you'll forget to eat. Even my bowel movements are off. Usually it's one in the morning an hour after I wake up, and one in the late afternoon after my first drink.

I'm pretty sure I haven't taken a shit in days, if I've even been here that long. Maybe that's because I keep forgetting to eat?

But the worst of it is not the infrequent shits, the lack of sleep, or the out of sync meal plan. The worst of it are the cravings. I've tried to quit drinking many times before, and made it almost of month without a drop once. In the end, a petite redhead with dimples and a perfect ass convinced me to go shot for shot with her. It was the pussy not the booze that broke that alcohol fast. I woke up with my cock in her mouth and defeat on my tongue.

Cigarettes though, I'd never even bothered to try and kick that habit. In fact, this current attempt seemingly happened by accident. *How do you forget to smoke?* But now, as I sit quietly by while Goodwin tries to wrap her sleep-deprived mind around some impossible algorithm, all I want to do is chain-smoke and get shit-faced.

My skin crawls. It itches. My beard's coming in. That itches too. I'm growing a sweater on my teeth. I haven't brushed in God knows how long. And I'm starting to smell my own funk.

"I'm going to take a shower," I tell her.

There's only one bathroom in the small, single floor cabin. It's in the only other room besides the living room-kitchen combo; the bedroom. Goodwin's unopened suitcases are on the bed, and the bed's still made. It appears as though she hasn't slept a wink in over three days.

Once the water hits my cheeks I realize exactly how exhausted I am. Not just physically, but mentally too. How Anne's still awake, and furthermore, how Anne's able to riddle out complex mathematics on a third as much sleep as I, is remarkable. My brain's so spent I've stopped trying to figure out a strategy to coax her out of this place. I've become numb to it all. A part of me—a small and childish microcosm—almost wants to just give her all the time she needs, if only to prove to herself it can't be done. Or even better, perhaps she convinces herself she's done it and leaves with me—leaves of her own accord.

Stupid thoughts. Stupid, sleep-deprived thoughts. The water cascades down my face and washes them away. My eyes are closed, and behind them filling the blackness is Charles and Marla Moser entwined in their sickening, postmortem embrace. Blood spurts from the matching holes in their heads and trickles down their shoulders. Charles caresses her back and smears wide swaths of crimson down to her buttock. When I open my eyes, I'm standing face to face with him.

"Fuck!" I leap back, slip, and land on my ass in the tub. The water sprays right through him and onto my chest. He's naked, bloody; his skin is pale and his eyes are sunken into his skull.

"You know what you need to do," he says to me.

"Fuck! Fuck!"

"What are you waiting for? It's not like you haven't done it before."

"Bill? Bill, are you alright?" Anne's outside hammering the bathroom door. She heard me shouting.

I blink and Charles is gone. I'm alone. And the water is freezing.

From the Journal of Doctor Theodore Grant

If the Daemons are monitoring the Prime Variables of every organic lifeform on the planet while simultaneously evaluating the environmental conditions around us and estimating future states, they could be, with a great degree of accuracy, predicting future events. And if we could somehow tap into their farseeing, then we could, in essence, see these future events. I surmise such occurrences, though rare, have happened without our knowing on many occasions. Furthermore, I believe that some of us are more attuned to such diving than others.

There have been numerous documented accounts of prescient thought, though nearly all of these vatic revelations have been relegated to coincidence or lucky guesswork. Take Robert Heinlein, for example. The famed science fiction author once penned a short story entitled, "Solution Unsatisfactory," where he depicted a future in which the United States developed a nuclear weapon before the rest of the world, and in doing so, spurred an arms race. And as we know, that is exactly what happened.

John Watkins Jr., a civil engineer and curator at the Smithsonian, predicted quite succinctly the rise of the internet and the invention of mobile smart phones back in 1900. He once wrote, "Man will see around the world. Persons and things of all kinds will be brought within focus of cameras connected electrically with screens at opposite ends of circuits, thousands of miles at a span." This may not seem extraordinary, but at the time, to comprehend such a future was rather remarkable.

Raymond Kurzweil, famed technologist, accurately predicted so many future events it baffles the mind. Back in the Sixties he accurately predicted the fall of the Soviet Union by 1991, a computer beating a chess master by the year 2000, wireless internet becoming mainstream in the 21st century, E-books and face recognition software, and much, much more. An evaluation of his prognostications performed in 2012 found he was correct an astounding eighty-six percent of the time!

I fancy myself quite adept at such future predicting, but these men seem to hold an uncanny looking glass into tomorrow. And then of course there's the great auger himself, Nostradamus. His farseeing predictions were so astounding that even today—centuries after his death—his name has become a byword for fortunetelling.

In 1555 he wrote, "The blood of the just will be demanded of London, burnt by the fire in the year 66." Eerily and quite uncannily, in 1666 the Great Fire of London broke out—a conflagration that burned nearly eighty-five percent of the city's homes.

Some even claim he predicted the attack on the World Trade Center in 2011. "Volcanic fire from the center of the Earth will cause trembling around the new city; two great rocks will make war for a long time. Then Arethusa will redden a new river..."

Many believe the "center of the Earth" refers to the center of trade, and the "new city" of course refers to New York City. "Two great rocks" reference both the Twin Towers and the religions of Christianity and Islam. There are additional versus that reference "steel birds," which perhaps is the most eye-opening line of his premonition, for at the time, modern methods of steel production hadn't been invented yet, nor had aircraft.

And perhaps most shocking of all was Abraham Lincoln's confession to his friend Ward Hill Lamon of a dream he had just three days prior to his death; "There seemed to be a death-like stillness about me. Then I heard subdued sobs, as if a number of people were weeping. I thought I left my bed and wandered downstairs. There the silence was broken by the same pitiful sobbing, but the mourners were invisible. Determined to find the cause of a state of things so mysterious and so shocking, I kept on until I arrived at the East Room, which I entered. There I met with a sickening surprise. Before me was a catafalque, on which rested a corpse wrapped in funeral vestments. Around it were stationed soldiers who were acting as guards; and there was a throng of people, gazing mournfully upon the corpse, whose face was covered, others weeping pitifully. 'Who is dead in the White House?' I demanded of one of the soldiers. 'The President,' was his answer; 'He was killed by an assassin.' Then came a loud burst of grief from the crowd, which woke me from my dream."

Chapter 34

She looks beyond tired. Her eyes are completely bloodshot and swollen. And to top it, her behavior grows more erratic by the hour. With the last few applications, she got our calibrations mixed up. And her work; every hour or so she starts to cry, crumples up the paper she'd been scribbling on, and throws it at the wall. There's a healthy pile of failed formulas in the corner of the room now.

Seeing her like this only heightens my own exhaustion. Eventually she'll have to sleep—we'll both have to sleep. My brain went full autopilot some time ago. I'm so tired I'm hallucinating in the shower for Christ's sake! What kinds of angels and demons must Goodwin be wrestling?

"You need some rest, Anne. I haven't the slightest clue how you're even awake right now, but I'm damn sure going days without sleep is only going to make figuring this all out that much more difficult."

She rubs tears from her eyes, crumples up another piece of paper, and tosses it into the pile. Then she dashes her hand into her pocket and pulls out a pill bottle. "There are ways," she says as she tosses it to me.

The label reads; *Lightning Bugs*. They're caffeine pills, strong damn caffeine pills spiked with ephedrine and taurine. Right on the front it claims one pill has the same amount of caffeine as ten cups of coffee. *How is this even legal?*

"What backroads truck-stop did you find this at?"

"It doesn't matter." Anne shakes her head in defeat. "Discovered these little gems back in college."

"This stuff is dangerous. You can't live off caffeine pills. You're gonna start picking at scabs and tearing down the walls." My eyes are bathed in acid. I rub them 'till they tear up and the ache replaces the longing sting of exhaustion. "Why don't you go and get some rest, Goodwin. You're no good to us like this."

She's on her back now silhouetted by piles of white paper staring up at the ceiling. If she flapped her arms and legs she could make paper snow angels on the cabin floor. "I have to figure this out."

A broad yawn follows and I interject, "And you will. But not when you've been up for four days running on nothing but speed. Hell, if I knew it was going to be this kind of party I would've checked a kilo of coke out from evidence."

"I need to get back to work. I need to," her eyes slip shut. She lets out a gaping yawn and over it mutters, "I don't trust myself enough to sleep."

"Do you trust me?"

Anne sits up and looks at me. I must seem as bewildered as she. I rattle the pill bottle next to my head. "Get some sleep. I'll…stand watch. If the buzzer doesn't wake you, then I will. You've got nothing to worry about. Go catch some zees and then you can get back to work."

Just the act of standing is a struggle for her. She's been cross-legged on floor for who knows how long. So I help her to her feet and carry her back to the bedroom. As she crashes down on the bed, she says, "Don't let me oversleep. You can't let them wake up. If you do, we're doomed."

"I won't. You can trust me, Anne. I'm your partner. I've got your back." Before I can get the last of it out, she's snoring on the bed.

Chapter 35

Beyond the fringes of sight, there is nothing. No trees, no hills, no brush or rocks—nothing. It's as if the whole world disappeared. Clouds must've rolled in. The sky is a black slab. Everything is a black slab, everything but that little slice of road visible within the cone of my headlights. That's all I can see. Just gray pavement and the yellow hashed center line racing endlessly by my car. It's all that remains of the world outside. Everything—everything that matters anyways—is right here with me, locked in this steel wagon that races toward a grim finale.

"Would you like some music?" I flip on the radio. A loud buzz rattles the speakers. It's not music, but it's something. "I love this song."

A few minutes with nothing but the static buzz of the radio and I ask, "You understand why I have to do this? No? I know what you're thinking. You think it's all just revenge. You're thinking it's all about an eye for eye, a tooth for a tooth. Am I right? Well, you're only half there. It's more than that. It's bigger than you."

We drive on for a good while with nothing but the buzz of the radio and the methodical thump of the road beneath my tires to keep us company.

"It certainly would be easier to just let you go and let them deal with you. I'm going to a lot of trouble to keep things clean. Not just for my own sake, you understand, but for your son's sake. It's bad enough he lost his dad. If he found out it was his own mother that killed him, well, you understand why I can't let that happen? No, the authorities would make a spectacle of you and your case. And Kevin, Kevin would suffer the most."

Nothing. Silence. "Are you even listening to me, Marla?" I glance back in the rearview. She's looking at me, I think. It's hard to tell if it's even her. Even harder to tell what she's looking at seeing as how her face is a waylaid lump of hamburger meat. It's so swollen I wonder if she can even see me through the slits where her puffed-up purple cheeks meet her puffed-up purple brow.

Eventually she says, "You're doing the right thing, Bill."

"I know, Marla. And sorry about the, ya know, about the face and all. Things got a little carried away. But you really pissed me off." I smile at her. "I'm better now, though. And besides, you know you deserved it, right?"

"Didn't your mother ever tell you it's never okay to hit a woman?"

She sounds playful, so I keep the tone of my response light as well. "No. And really, Marla? You don't think maybe this once, just this one time, it was okay to hit a woman?"

She smiles and says, "You're doing the right thing, Bill."

"For once in my life, I suppose I am."

The road never changes, but the clouds begin to wane and in no time at all they dissipate completely. At the center of the sky amidst a sea of twinkling stars the moon hangs big and bright and full, a cosmic watcher bearing witness to the righteousness I'm about to unleash. And the stars—*my God the stars!* They swirl above us, an infinitely rich vortex of purple, orange, blue, and green specs that pile atop one another until the milky haze of galaxies takes shape. Comets rocket from one horizon to the other and satellites scud north, south, east, and west. I'm awed by it.

"You should probably keep your eyes on the road," she says. "You're doing important work here. Wouldn't want something as simple as a car accident to stop you."

"It is important, isn't it?" Suddenly I'm not so sure. The buzz of the radio intensifies.

"It's the right thing to do, Bill. For once in your life, you're doing the right thing."

"It doesn't feel like the right thing, Anne."

"It's the right thing to do," she says once more.

I give her a sympathetic look in the rearview. Anne's sipping on an orange soda and fiddling with her phone in the backseat.

"I don't know. Maybe I should get you some help. I know a good shrink."

"Carrie's dead, Bill."

"Oh, right. I forgot."

"Just keep your eyes on the road. We're almost there. You need to do this. It's the right thing to do."

"If you say so, partner."

I pull the car off into the industrial park. No one comes here. It's been abandoned for years and will stay that way for at least another hundred and fifty more thanks to the fact that it's been rezoned as a wildlife sanctuary.

"Can you believe it?" I say, as I pull Anne from the car. "An old smelting plant rezoned as a preserve just because some conservationist prick discovered Ivory-billed Woodpeckers nesting nearby. Who gives a shit about woodpeckers? The place is untouchable to developers now. Just a big, ugly, empty, fucking waste of space."

We make our way inside. "I've used it before. It will do just fine for you, partner."

"I know that," Marla replies. She doesn't struggle in my hands. She's totally complicit.

"Of course you do. Silly me."

I take her inside the warehouse. Its stone walls stretch a good eighty feet up. There are scorch marks up and down the sides from when the entire plant and all the surrounding buildings had caught fire back in the early fifties. Nothing remains of whatever held residence within those walls, just a partially decayed concrete floor now covered in an inch or two of dirt and rat feces, and a few old rusted-out containers. Through the broken windows high up on the walls, a willow of moonlight shows us the way. We're heading toward the center of the room; toward the well.

"This is what the world would've looked like," says Anne. "This is what it would all have been reduced to if it wasn't for you, Special Agent Singer. You're doing the right thing."

"I know partner. I know."

I kneel her down next to the well and pull my pistol from its holster. "It will be quick, partner. And then down the well you go. Are you ready?"

"I'm ready, Bill. You're doing the right thing."

I place the cold steel to her temple and gently squeeze the trigger. There's no pop, just a loud buzz—*weeeeeeeeeeeeeeeeeeee*—that carries on long after her body's hit the dirt. Smoke rises from the small crater on the side of her head.

Weeeeeeeeeeeeeeeeeeeee

Where is that coming from? Is that coming from her? It is coming from— I bend down next to Anne's body and roll her over so I can see her face. Her mouth hangs open and from it pours that awful sound.

Weeeeeeeeeeeeeeeeeeeeeee

Her eyes blink and suddenly she's got me in her grasp. Fingernails dig into my collar and she cries, "Wake up, Bill! Wake up, Bill! Wake up!"

I shove her to the floor and erupt up off the sofa. The egg timer in the kitchen blares its wakeup call. Anne's on the floor where I tossed her staring up at me in terror.

"You, you, you slept through it. You fell asleep. How long were you out? How long were you asleep, Bill? How long!"

"I, I don't know. A couple of minutes maybe, a, a, I don't know." In dreams, time is irrelevant. A dream that seems to drag on for hours could span seconds in the waking world, while a few seconds in a dream could span hours. There's no telling.

I check my phone, but it's dead. *Of course it's dead. Old habit. I need to start wearing a wristwatch.*

"I don't have a migraine. I feel fine. We still have time—"

"Oh shit! Oh shit! Oh shit!" Anne leaps over to the machine and starts setting the dials. Soon it's humming and her hands are on the grips. She shimmies about as the handles vibrate and deliver their current. I reset the egg timer in the kitchen.

"Quick, Bill, you have to do it. You have to—"

"Shhhh," I say. "Did you hear that?"

"Hear, hear what? What are you talking about? You need to do this! Get over here!"

"Quiet, Goodwin. I thought I… Yeah, I definitely heard something."

I'm standing next to the kitchen window. It's shut, covered by a bedsheet and sealed with aluminum foil, but it's far from sound proof.

"Outside the window. Quiet, Anne, quiet. I can hear someone traipsing around out there." I start to peel back the foil.

In an instant Anne's up off the floor racing to stop me. "No, you can't! Not a crack. It has to stay sealed. What are you thinking?"

"Anne, relax. I'm just gonna take a peek."

She tears me away. "Are you nuts! You can't break the seal. Not a crack or they can get in! They can try and communicate. And you, you, you're not anesthetized. You need to—"

Crack, thump, crack. Someone's right outside the window.

"There. Did you hear that? You had to have heard that!"

"Heard what? Bill, there's nothing there. It's the Daemons. They're messing with your—"

I shove her back away from me—just enough space to buy me time to tear a swath of foil off from the window—and peek outside. Anne screams in protest but she's too late. I've opened a tiny portal to the world outside, a glimpse into the dark, empty void beyond our foil wrapped prison cell. It's nighttime. I can't see much beyond the first set of trees. There's no one out there but—

"Wait. There. There's someone out—" He comes into view for only a second as he moves between a stand of trees twenty paces from the window. A dark, ghostly figure wrapped in a trench coat, head down, face concealed beneath the brim of an open-crown cowboy hat. Shocked, I lunge back away from the window and trip over the garbage festooned about the kitchen floor. I land on my back at Goodwin's feet, slamming my head into the linoleum. For a second all I see is stars, and then my eyes meet hers. She looks more terrified than I am.

And then I notice the gun in her hand.

Chapter 36

Once again I find my fingers wrapped around the machine's metal handgrips. The shock that follows isn't any more severe than placing your tongue to a nine volt battery, but I've quickly grown to loathe the idea of electricity permeating my body. It's a circuit, Anne tells me, and when both hands are on the grips my entire body completes it and I fill up with electrons. She's calmly explaining this to me with her Bureau issued forty caliber pistol snubbed up against the back of my head.

"There," she says with a sigh. "That's better. Do you feel better?"

I play along. "Yeah. That's much better. I, I'm sorry. I don't know what came over me." I turn to face her. She looks relieved, though that relief doesn't result in her lowering the firearm stuck in my face. And her finger is on the trigger; her shaky finger.

"If you're going to keep that thing trained on me do you mind at least taking your finger off the trigger?" There's a strange look in her eyes. I don't like it one bit. *What are you thinking, Goodwin? Are you seriously contemplating killing me right now?*

"Anne. Anne, it's me, you're partner. Can you put the gun down? I did the procedure. All is well. No Daemons at our door." No response. Her handshakes intensify. Tears glimmer in her eyes. "Anne. Anne, listen to me. I can leave if you want—leave you to your work. Even bring you back some supplies. Is there anything you need? I'm here to help, Anne."

"No," she says. "No you're not." She starts to cry. "Why did you do that? Why, why, why, why! You shouldn't have done that! They know now. They'll try and stop me. You can't leave, you can't. But…but you can't stay here."

Shit, shit, shit! Why the hell did you have to peel away her safety blanket?

"Anne, listen to me." I slowly rise to my feet, hands in the air. "I'm unarmed. I came here to find my partner—to help my partner no matter what. I'm unarmed. Unarmed because I trust you." *You're doing the right thing.* Words in my head. "Anne, this isn't you." Seemingly out of place words. *You're doing important work here.* "Look at what you're doing." *You've done this before.* "Anne, it's me, Bill Singer. I'm not your enemy." *You need to do this. It's the right thing to do.*

I'm standing face to face with my own end. My partner, Roxanne Goodwin, is a lost cause. She's gone completely over the edge. There's no doubt in my mind that any second now she'll pull that trigger and end me. And it won't be clean like Charles and Marla. That's a big damn gun she's got there. No, my brains will be splattered all over the wall behind me. And Anne, poor Anne Goodwin will be left here to continue her crazy work beneath her own tapestry of death while my corpse slowly rots in the other room. She won't go outside; she won't dispose of the body. There's no leaving this place for her. It will be dead Bill Singer and brain dead Roxanne Goodwin locked in this hell until the bitter end.

There's only one sensible thing I can do here. And it's the right thing to do. Not the easy path, that's for sure, but the righteous one.

I jerk to the side and snatch her wrist with my left hand. The gun goes off. A feel a twinge of pressure and pain in my right shoulder, but I hang onto her. Then I pivot and smash my hip into her stomach while I wrench her wrist back over on itself. Another shot rings out and tears into the sofa. Her wrist hyperextends and she loses her grip. The gun thuds on the floor.

Goodwin and I dance about for a second or two. She's surprisingly strong for a woman of her size. But in no time my military training kicks in and I have my arm around her neck and my legs wrapped tightly about her waist. We're down on the floor rolling about while I squeeze the life out her. My shoulder's on fire, likely broken, but still I squeeze with all I can. With my good arm, I press the back of her head forward further constricting the blood flow to her brain. A gurgle is all I get in response. Anne goes limp in my arms.

I kick her unconscious body off me, try to catch my breath, and pick up the gun.

Chapter 37

The whole ride back to DC I can't help but think about cowboy stalkers and dead friends in the shower. Just Daemons messing with my head or hallucinations brought on by sleep deprivation and insurmountable stress levels. In the end, does it really matter?

I slip my hand under my coat and check for dampness. The makeshift bandage I wrapped about the wound is dry; the bleeding's finally stopped. The round grazed my shoulder. Tore a nice swath of flesh across my collarbone. I'd tried to hastily stitch it up with the twenty-year old first aid kit I keep in my car, but the stitches kept busting. Still, I got lucky. Really lucky. The pain though, the chasm in my deltoid that used to be muscle and sinew, now burns like its full of hydrochloric acid and aches like I just walked up the Empire State Building on my hands. Luckily I have just the thing for the pain. Four caps of Dilaudid, twenty-six milligrams—*that should do the trick*. And boy does it. I'm floating down the highway now, riding atop a black cloud with the words Lincoln Town Car etched on the back.

"You understand why I have to do this, Anne?" As I check her state in the rearview, I'm struck by déjà vu. I've got her tied up good and tight in the backseat. I had to gag her because the minute she woke up she started screaming about being outside the cabin, out where they could get to her. And she didn't stop screaming for a good ten minutes no matter how hard I tried to talk her off that ledge.

"There's no other way, Anne. There's only one viable option here."

She's staring out the window as the dark world whizzes by. God I wish I knew what she was thinking. She looks calmer now. And when I catch her trying to mumble something through the gag in her mouth, I reach back and pull it out so she can talk.

"It doesn't matter anymore," she mutters. "It's too late now, anyways. I'm out in the open; exposed. I should've killed you the minute you arrived at my door. Now…now they've got a hold on you. I'm finished no matter what you do."

"No one's got a hold on me, Anne. This is Bill Singer talking, Bill Singer driving the car, Bill Singer calling the shots."

"I'm sorry you can't see the truth, Bill. It's only going to make living with yourself that much harder when this is all over." She shakes her head and with a surprisingly calm candor, says, "Yes, it's Bill Singer talking right now. Yes, it's Bill Singer driving this car. But Bill Singer is definitely not calling the shots."

"It's my choice, Anne, not microscopic robots in my brain. Do you even hear yourself? I can take you in, have you committed, and watch you rot away in a psychiatric facility until you're ninety years old. But meds won't cure you, I don't think anything will. Or I could just pull over here and let you out of the car. Watch you scamper away into the woods and go into hiding. Live like a mad hermit for the rest of your days? You'd just drive yourself further down the rabbit hole.

"You're a good person, Anne. You don't deserve this, any of it. But you'd end up hurting someone." I scratch the stitches where the bullet ripped through my shoulder. The wound has gone completely numb. "Most definitely hurt yourself," I whisper.

"What choice would I have?" Anne nudges Grant's contraption that's in the seat next to her. All his files and her notes are stacked in boxes in the car's front seat, remaining back seats, and trunk. "*They* wouldn't let me get far, anyways."

"Which leads us to option three... I'm going with option three. I don't like it, it's the hardest option available to me, but it's the right thing to do."

Am I really going to do this? Can I do this? But I've done it before. It wasn't easy, even with Marla, but it was the right thing to do—the only time in my life I did the right thing when it would've been easier to do the wrong. But every time I look at Anne's face all I see is that excited young agent thrilled to actually get a chance to work with Bill Singer; the same agent whose excitement turned to disappointment when that dream actually came true. I see the hidden beauty beneath the surface; this incredibly gifted, intelligent woman wasted on the world, torn asunder by unrelenting madness. I see a gift given to me by fate; my compass toward a moral and meaningful life about to be shattered by my own hand.

I pull the car over on the side of the road just outside the city limits. It's nearly ten o'clock. No one stirs out here. She asks what I'm doing, but I don't respond. I can't look at her right now—can't talk to her. I just need to prepare myself.

One by one I pull the boxes out of the trunk. The brilliant and insane Doctor Theodore Grant's life's work on the side of a highway. Then I grab Anne by the arm and pull her out of the backseat. Before she can object, I cram the gag back in her mouth and motion for her to get into the trunk. It shouldn't be easy, what with only one good arm and all, but surprisingly she doesn't put up much of a fight and climbs in on her own. The few boxes I can fit, I toss in with her. Sitting on top of one box is Grant's black book of bad antiquated poetry. For a second my eyes linger on it, but then I snap out of it and shut the trunk. I never make eye contact with Goodwin. I can't.

This is going to be hard—very hard. I'm gonna need some help.

After I load up the backseat with the boxes from the trunk, I pop another Dilaudid and pull back out onto the road. I drive the speed limit, use my blinkers, and try to stay calm. The radio helps a little. I turn it to a cool jazz station. I don't even like cool jazz, but right now I want nothing in my ears but soothing melodies. I don't want to think, not about anything. Even the occasional words of the station's disc jockey put me on edge.

I'm nauseous for reasons beyond count. "This is going to be hard, but it's the right thing to do," I reassure myself. "But I'm gonna to need some help. It's not like with Marla." From the glovebox I pull out an old pack of smokes and fire one up. I notice the shake in my hand is gone. That's a step in the right direction. My stomach settles a bit with each drag, but still my nerves are unravelling. I'm going to need some help to get through this night. I'm gonna need a lot of help.

"My old friend…" I can almost taste that sweet burn in the back of my throat. "It feels like it's been years. It's time I paid you a visit."

Darkness dwells at my back. The bright lights of the city lie ahead. And soon, this will all be behind me.

Chapter 38

I leave the bar with a half bottle of scotch and five Dilaudid in my belly. Couple that with little more than an hour of sleep in the last two days and my nerves pounded to dust, it's some kind of miracle I can even stay on the road. I guess I have that amazing hormone adrenaline to thank. But the booze, the drugs, they're not just to numb me up. There's a battle raging inside me. The entire time I sat in that bar I prayed someone would hear Anne moaning and kicking in the trunk of my car out in the parking lot. Imagine my surprise when I emerged to find no network of police surrounding my Lincoln sedan.

Even now, deep in my heart I pray for a wreck. I pray I get pulled over and a cop finds Anne in the trunk. I pray something guides me away from this path I've chosen, this terribly difficult, terribly gruesome path—*the right path*. Let someone else deal with her. Let me sleep soundly knowing at least I tried to do the right thing. But no such luck.

I arrive at the warehouse without issue. Of course if you asked Anne, I'm sure she'd say the Daemons saw to it that nothing stood in my way. Fate, some people call it, but to her there's no such thing. To her, it's all part of their experiment, part of their intelligent design. But the truth is so much simpler. I got lucky…or unlucky I guess, depending on your perspective.

Just as I remember it. A vacant lot on the shore of the Georgetown Channel. Across the river the lights of DC burn, but over here in this desolate park it's as if the world's been blasted away by a neutron bomb. All the surrounding buildings are crumbled and vacant. Every window is broken out, and every door kicked in or boarded up. There are no streetlights out here, no homes, and no businesses surround the old, abandoned smelting plant. Even the road leading to the twelve acre lot the plant rests on is in disrepair. It's almost like this place was put on the map just to play host to junkies, mob executions, and corpse disposal.

I haven't been back here since, well, since Marla Moser. That macabre nostalgia has me riddled with spiders. I've tried so hard to forget her, but the more I try the more the awful memory bubbles back up. And soon, soon I'll have a new awful memory to drown in a sea of scotch each night before bed.

The main building on the campus is the largest of the five. It resembles an airplane hangar in size and shape, with two smoke stacks rising from the west end. I park just outside and open the massive sliding doors which once allowed forklifts to easily move to and from the facility. But before I pull my car in, I do a quick survey of the premises. Junkies flock to places like this, and though I found it deserted last time I was here, you can never be too careful.

Inside, the floor-space is open enough to play a game of football. Whatever machinery they were able to salvage before shutting the plant down, they took with them. All that remains is rusted out storage containers, a few furnaces, and pile upon pile of debris. Scorched concrete walls are covered in graffiti and ivy. Weeds sprout like grass all over. Nature is slowly taking it back.

Nothing stirs, but with my flashlight in hand I make my way across to the far side of the building, wary to check every alcove, every nook and cranny for signs of life. The deeper I delve, the more my skin crawls. I can't see it yet, but I know it's there hiding in the shadows, boarded up and covered…a pit that leads straight to hell.

My flashlight catches the off-orange hue of its particleboard cover. As I draw near, all manner of insects wriggle in my guts. Just seeing it again puts me on the verge of emptying my stomach. It's fenced off by a weak, rusted chain I could snap with my teeth, covered by a rotting, makeshift particleboard slab that couldn't support the weight of a child. If I didn't know any better I'd say whoever sealed this place up wanted someone to fall in this freaking well.

They used to bring groundwater up from the river to cool the metal here. At one time, when the plant was operational, a giant pump was sealed over this hole with pipes running all over the plant to the various furnaces and smelters. Now there's just a hole with a slight lip where the pump was once bolted down.

I peel back the particleboard cover and shine my light down the well. Only darkness. It's so deep and black I can't see the bottom. But I don't have to see the bottom to know what's down there. Beneath the skin of that icy groundwater, anchored to the murky depths with a length of chain and a cinderblock, rests Marla Moser's bloated corpse. And soon…soon she'll have company.

Chapter 39

I left my gun in the car. No need to use my own when I have hers. And right now the muzzle of her gun prods her forward with pokes to the spine. As she crosses the threshold into the warehouse, she asks, "What is this place?" and I tell her. Not its storied history as a smelting plant or about the genesis of its now deplorable and useless state as a woodpecker sanctuary, but the truth.

"This is where I brought Marla Moser, my old partner's wife." As we near the well, Anne cuts her steps in half then tries to turn and flee, but I press the gun to her chest and push her onward. "Right there is where I knelt her down, let her say her peace, and put a .22 caliber round through her skull. Her body is at the bottom of that well."

"Why…why are you, why are you telling me this?"

"I'm not trying to scare you, Anne. I just…I've never told anyone. I couldn't tell anyone. But I needed to."

Anne peers down into the abyss. "Why did you do it?"

"She murdered my partner. It was never proven. Forensics cleared her and she had an airtight alibi. She even volunteered for a polygraph. I've gotta hand it to Marla, she was a smart one. She beat that machine without breaking a sweat, but she couldn't beat The Human Squawk Box. No, she couldn't fool me.

"Even after they cleared her as a person of interest, I continued my investigation into Marla Moser. And once I was certain she'd done it…"

"You just wanted revenge?"

"At first, yeah. At first I wanted her to suffer. But in the end…in the end I did it for Charles' son. I couldn't let him grow up knowing his mother killed his father. Better to leave that mystery unsolved, Goodwin. Sometimes ignorance is bliss."

She turns to me. "You did the right thing, Bill."
Somehow…somehow she looks unafraid.

The shake is back in my hand. I grab hold of my wrist and try and calm it. Anne dons a perplexed look, slowly raises her hand to my face, and wipes away a tear. She says, "I forgive you, Bill Singer. I forgive you for this. It's not you holding that gun. It's not you."

I back away from her and shout, "Who the hell else is it, Anne? Grant was insane! This whole bloody world is insane!" As I raise up the pistol, Anne closes her eyes. "Why can't you see it? You say I did the right thing killing Marla Moser, but why can't you see this? This is no different! If you're right, if Grant is right, then what good could possibly come of exposing that truth to the world?"

I point at the lights of DC across the river. "Those people over there, all the Kevin Mosers of the world… If you're right, Anne, if you're right…what good will come of it? Nothing! There's no way this plays out where you're a hero—"

"I don't want to be a hero. But the world has a right to know."

"No, Anne, they don't. They have a right to live and be happy and die in blissful ignorance just like Kevin Moser. They have a right to live protected from the wrath of whatever it is you believe hibernates inside us. Sometimes the right thing to do is to do nothing at all. Sometimes the people need to be shielded from the truth."

"Spoken like a true G-Man, Special Agent Singer."

Now she's pissing me off. I step to her with the gun inches from her nose.

"Tell me, Bill. Does Marla Moser haunt you?" *Every minute of my life.* "How do you live with that decision? Do you find peace at the bottom of a bottle, Bill?"

"I never look back. It was the right thing to do. I know it was. And I'm content with it. No ghosts haunt me, Goodwin. And when you're gone down that hole, you won't haunt me either." The greatest lie I've ever told, but somehow I say it convincingly.

I now know why Charles loved his slasher movies. They desensitized him. They numbed him to this violent world we live in. He wouldn't even hesitate were he in my shoes. But me, I'm trying with every ounce of willpower I have left to pull that fucking trigger…and I'm failing.

"Anne, please. Please! Listen to me. You have to let this go." Tears come pouring. My hands rattle like they're still hooked up to Grant's contraption.

"I'm sorry, Bill, but I can't. I know the truth. I can't unknow it."

"Just…just look away then. Turn around."

But she doesn't turn. Her contentment is almost as unsettling as what I am about to do. "Turn around!" A lake of tears pool in my eyes and the world melts into a dark, underwater cave.

She steps to me and whispers, "Promise me something."

God, let this be over with. Just let this be over. Turn around. Stop talking. Just let me do what I have to do. "It's the right thing to do!"

My sudden outburst doesn't deter her in the least. "Will you promise me something, Bill?"

I'm shaking. I'm weeping like a little girl. "I have to do this," I try to remind her. "There's no other way."

"Promise me, Bill."

"Promise you? Promise you what?"

She's a breath away from me now. Suddenly her lips are caressing mine and before I know it her tongue is in my mouth wrestling mine into submission. All the pain washes away in that momentary embrace. The burn in my shoulder depressed by booze and painkillers evaporates completely. That dreary longing from all those sleepless nights, the never ending ache in my bones, the chill in my heart, gone, replaced with warmth and contentment.

My eyes close. Her hands find my hips and pull me in. With a head full of booze and pills, my balance is off. I have to grab onto her to steady myself. And as I reach around behind her, a sudden strike of pain floods my groin and bursts in my abdomen. Anne retreats as I hunch over in anguish. Then her knee catches me just under the chin. The gun goes off, not once but three times, but her hand is on my wrist wrestling it away. When I don't release, she lodges her fist in my sternum, then gives me another knee to the groin. A fourth shot rings out, then a fifth, then my grasp releases and the gun falls to the ground. It's the same dance we did at the cabin, only now I'm half a fifth of scotch and five Dilaudid drunker—and on the losing end.

A part of me just lets it happen. A part of me is glad it's happening.

Anne thrusts her hip into my groin and pivots. Booze and pills—two things diametrically opposed to balance—have completely sapped all that I have. With ease, she flings me over her hip. I come to rest with her hand firmly around my outstretched wrist, the rest of me dangling precariously out over the rim of the well. The world spins.

"Promise me," she says as I hang on the cusp of oblivion.

"Promise?—"

Goodwin looks stricken, afraid even. As reluctant as I was to pull the trigger she seems equally abashed at letting me go. *She won't do it. She wouldn't do it.*

Then she says, "Promise me, Bill. Promise me you won't drink the ambrosia."

Before her words even register, she lets go of my wrist. My stomach rockets up to my throat and the world tumbles away.

Then it's down.

So far down.

Down, down, down.

Down into darkness.

Down into a pit of nightmares.

Down into the abyss.

Down into hell…

Chapter 40

"Goodwin!" My first gasp is accompanied by a mouthful of rancid water. "Good—" Another gulp of putrid soup—a cocktail of death and decay in my mouth. Other than the corpse I put here, what other diseased-riddled bodies decompose down in this pit? Rat's, dead birds, insects, feces?

"Good—Goodwi—Goodwin!"

It's so cold. So bloody cold! My arms flap spastically about and my legs run at a sprint beneath the water. Every few kicks I feel something brush my feet.

"Anne! Please!" *Why do I even bother? Why would she help me when I was about to do the same to her?*

Up above, the little dusking light that remains does little to illuminate anything. I can't see my own hand in front of my face. For all I know Marla Moser is floating on the surface right next to me. And the thought, it keeps my arms flapping and my legs kicking in exactly the same space—too timid to reach out beyond the tiny swathe of stagnant water I know to be corpse-free.

"P-please," I mutter.

How pathetic I've become. This is how I die? After being shot at God knows how many times? After two tours in the deadliest geo on Earth? I've lived near cities where every damn person wanted you dead. I'd walk down the streets of Fallujah and I could see it in their eyes. Even the children wanted to shove an RPG up my ass.

"H-h-help me. Anne, p-please. Help-he-help me." My pleas are but a whisper now. I resign to silence. It's too much energy to scream.

It's so quiet down here. My only senses—touch and smell—are assaulted by the charnel reek of decay and the gelid touch of death itself. I'm quickly going hypo. Soon my muscles will seize and I'll sink like a rock to the bottom of this pit.

Bill Singer's final resting place; right beside your old lady, Charles. Right beside, *her.* I can look my victim in the eyes for all eternity.

But it was the right thing to do. It was the right thing! Wasn't it?

I can feel her in here with me. She's just beneath my toes; reaching, stretching out her grotesque, bloated arms. Her peeled skin is all around me floating on the surface of the water, I just know it. It's in my hair, it's in my mouth, mixed in and dissolved into the surrounding putrescence. She's reaching for my heels. Her waterlogged fingers grope and try to pull me down so I can slumber beside her in hell forever.

Another brush upon my thigh and I fling myself to the side and into the wall of the well. I claw at it, desperate for a finger hold, for anything—any means to climb out of this deathtrap. The scrape of my nails on the concrete and the splash of the age-old stagnant water—these two sounds are the last I will ever hear. My nails tear off right to the cuticle, but I don't care. *God, just get me out of here! Not like this. Not like this!*

Something splashes down in the water beside me! It scares me so bad I leap away and knock the back of my head against the side of the well. A ringing builds in my ears. *What the hell is down here with me!* Again I claw at the smooth concrete walls, but there's no chance of climbing out. As I flail about in the freezing water my hand brushes something fibrous, something thin, something…a rope.

Far above, the little ambient light that peters over the rim of the well—that which originated from my car's headlights—vanishes. The rumble of the engine grows faint and then it's no more. Goodwin is gone.

A few tugs on the rope. It's secured to something up top. My muscles quiver and tighten. I'm transforming into a block of ice. If I don't climb out now, I'll never climb out. So I grab hold of the rope and start my ascent.

This is my rope, I realize. The very one I planned to tie around my dead partner to anchor her to the bottom. But there's no time to dwell on the irony. I must climb. I have to climb. Climb or die.

God I'm out of shape. In the pitch of the well, I can't tell distance. I can't see the top. For all I know it could be ten feet above my head or sixty. Each pull with my right arm sends a shockwave through my shoulder and down to my toes. I can't put any weight on my right shoulder for more than a microsecond before I'm sapped of the strength needed to carry on. And my grip is slipping. The sludge that filled the bottom of the well feels more like oil than water now that I'm out of it. Combined with the shiver that still racks me and the torpor in my bones, I wonder if I'll—

I fall. I'm in the air for only a second before I splash back down into the murk. Something wraps my leg, another rope below the water. *Marla!*

I kick and kick and kick and when finally I break free, I'm back scaling the walls as if sharks circle below. After a few feet my adrenaline purges and exhaustion sets in. My shoulder throbs with pain and my grip weakens once more. I'm going to fall again. I'm going to die down here.

"Anne! Anne!" Nothing. Of course nothing. She's gone. And I let her go.

Calm down, Bill. "Calm the hell down! Relax, buddy. Relax. Just breathe. Breathe. There's nothing down here but old bones. You have to use your head. You have to breathe. Calm down. In through your nose, out through your mouth."

My old sergeant always told us that whenever things got hairy he'd just close his eyes, count to ten, breathe in through his nose and out through his mouth, and think about nothing but the problem at hand and the first step to solving it. Usually the first step was to open your eyes and get the hell out of the line of fire. Outside of direct contact, the method was reasonably sound.

I slide back down the rope and come to rest in the water. I can't see my skin but I'm fairly certain it's the color of glacial ice right about now. I've got two, maybe three more minutes before I'm hypo, and then, then there's no getting out of here. And I can't bear to think of the putrescence seeping into the open wound in my shoulder.

"Relax. Jesus, man, you were military. Don't you remember how to climb a damn rope?" *Yes. Yes I do remember how to climb a rope, though usually there isn't a corpse in a pool of viscera at the bottom waiting for me to fail, nor had a round from a .40 cal just cut a trail through my anterior deltoid.*

I let the rope fall to my left side, hook my right foot under it, and prop myself up on the formed loop with my left foot. They call it the break-and-squat technique. Every soldier learns it in boot camp. You use the rope as a step, locking it between your feet so you can rest as you ascend.

"You're getting out of here. You're not dying down in this goddamn hole, Bill Singer."

With my good arm I pull myself up a few inches and relock the rope with my feet. Then another pull and another step up the makeshift rope ladder. Even with one arm I can make this climb. But that doesn't mean it's easy. The torpor in my good arm brought on by the myriad combatting factors makes every push up the rope a struggle. And in the darkness I can't see the rope beneath me. On several occasions I kick up only to lose the feel of the rope beneath my boots and struggle to hang on with one arm as I reposition it below me so I can stand and rest.

But slowly, very slowly, the abounding darkness begins to ebb. Soon I spot the rim of the well a dozen feet above. The miniscule amount of starlight that breathes color into this world shows me the slick gray stone I've yet to climb. Just a few more feet and I'll be out. Another step. Then another pull. *Step and lock. Step and lock. Deep breaths. Stay calm. Rest as long as you need to.*

My right arm steadies the rope below me but it's more or less useless now. The chill of that freezing well water is gone and the adrenaline's purged the booze and painkillers. My body's racked by pain and fatigue. This exertion has me sweating buckets.

I'm signing up for a gym membership first thing tomorrow. I'm going to live! "I'm getting out of this goddamn well!"

When finally I reach the top I barely have enough strength left to pull myself over the lip. And when I manage to break the cusp; the rat feces, mildew, and decay covered earth that coats the floor of the once factory is so welcomed I just lay face down in it for a time and laugh. With each breath I suck in ordure. But I don't care what's beneath my nose as long as it's not the fetid water my victim's corpse has been decaying in.

I roll onto my back and inhale the stagnant air like I'm nose down in a fine wine. Big, deep breaths fill my lungs. I'm alive. I'm still here. "Fuck your nine lives, Cat. That's number ten."

The rope; it's tied to a pylon not far from the well. That's all she left me. My car's gone, all of Grant's work is gone, his device is gone, everything's gone. Everything except...

After long last I retake my feet. Now I know how a newborn calf feels, all wobbly legged and awkward. But I stumble my way over to it, over to the only thing Goodwin left behind.

I pick it up. Then I start the long walk home.

Chapter 41

She's really toned it down. I don't think I've ever seen her in a pantsuit before. And it's loose, poor fitting. *Is she trying to look like shit because I'm here?*

"You were telling me about your dreams," she says. "Or lack thereof. Why do you think you haven't been dreaming lately?"

The Daemons in my head are done tinkering with me. Such a thought makes me chuckle a little, which of course she notices and has to comment on.

"I'm sorry, I must've missed something. What's so funny?"

"Nothing, Doc. Nothing. And I don't know why I haven't been dreaming. But I've been making a lot of changes lately. Took a leave of absence from the Bureau—a much needed vacation—and I've spent it working on myself." I pat my stomach. "Started here." No more mini-gut. "And I quit the booze…again."

"That's excellent. It shows. Do you still smoke?"

"Hey, one fatal vice at a time, Doc." I've been fiddling with the Zippo lighter in my pocket this entire session. And now, thanks to her pointing it out, I'm having a full blown nic-fit.

"So what initiated such a bold transformation, Bill?"

That's a good question. That's a damn good question. "I guess I was just ready for a change. I didn't like what I saw in the mirror anymore."

She looks unconvinced. "Bill, like I told you at the start today, this will be our last session together. So don't be shy about coming clean with yourself…or with me. No more hiding the truth, no more trying to convince me—trying to convince yourself of any untruths, okay?"

"If you think you know something, Doc, then why don't you just tell me and stop playing shrink?"

"That's not how this works. And I am a shrink, Bill."

"Hey, like you said. You refuse to see me anymore—"

"There's a conflict of interest here. I, I did something completely out of character when I got intimate with you. It's regrettable."

"Your time with me is regrettable, Carrie?"

"You know what I mean."

"No. No I don't think that I do. We made love right there on that desk. And…and sure I wasn't, I probably wasn't ready for a relationship then, but now—"

"Control," she blurts out. It shuts me up midsentence.

"What?"

"Control, Bill. That's why the changes. That's why you quit drinking…again. That's why you've changed your diet and your demeanor. You want to prove to yourself that you are in control of Bill Singer. Whatever demons you were wrestling, it was blatantly apparent you felt you weren't in control of your life. Your mother, your ex-wives, your partner, your director, all of them. You weren't the one pulling Bill Singer's strings, and now, now you want that control back. And what better way to prove to yourself that you're in control?"

A moment of silence between us. She's probably right but I'm not about to dwell on it. No, I'm still trying to figure out how to get her back. But there's no getting her back. I know that now. I blew it. And now that she's made up her mind, to her I'm just another asshole ex. Women like Carrie Dent don't give assholes second chances. Nor should she.

"Where did you go?" I suddenly ask.

"What?"

"After our dinner that night. I tried calling you the next day, I left messages—"

"Bill, we're diving into some seriously deep water here. Let's stay on point."

"I don't want to stay on point. I want to know what happened to you after you left the restaurant."

"Bill." She says my name the same way a mother says her son's name before launching into a life lesson.

I return it in spades. "Carrie. Answer me."

A deep sigh and then, "Did it ever occur to you that maybe I didn't want to talk to you?"

"It did. But your secretary, she didn't know where you were either. Did you not want to talk to her too?"

"My personal life is just that, personal."

"Where did you go, Carrie?"

"Bill—"

"Carrie! Just, please, I need to know. Just tell me what happened and I promise you I'll leave you alone. I need," *what do the shrinks call it? Oh yeah,* "closure."

She crosses her arms and her face hardens to granite. But only for a moment. Not a second later she softens and demurely says, "I got a call. My mother. She had a…she had a stroke. They didn't know if she was going to pull through. I was on a flight to Arizona that same night. Didn't even bother to pack. My phone died. No charger. I didn't care. I didn't even notice. She's my mother, Bill." There's a long empty stare between us before she concludes with, "Happy?"

No I'm not happy. Then I accidentally mutter aloud, "How convenient."

"Excuse me!"

"That's not, I didn't mean it like that, I just—"

"You think my mother nearly dying is convenient? What, you think I'm lying to you? That I'd need this sick excuse to break it off with the enigmatic Bill Singer?"

"Carrie, calm down."

"You don't get to tell me to calm down!" *The psychologist has left the building.* "I can't believe I'm telling you this, but thanks to you I'm seeing a shrink of my own."

I guess I drive all the women in my life crazy, I think to myself—thankfully only to myself this time.

"Convenient? Get out of my office, Bill. Get out."

Not a convenient excuse. I know it's not an excuse. I know she's telling me the truth. I'm a human lie detector, after all. No, no it's convenient that right then, right at that moment of all moments in time, something occurred to pull Carrie Dent off the face of the Earth for a spell. An impossible coincidence. Goodwin would be laughing her head off and chirping, "Told ya so," like a schoolgirl if she were here right now.

I make for the door to her office. There's nothing left for me here. Before I walk out I tell her I'm sorry; sorry she fell for a piece of shit like me, sorry she compromised her integrity for me, sorry for everything.

Once the door slams shut and that chapter in my life is officially closed, clarity strikes. In hindsight, she was a shit therapist.

Chapter 42

Sleep deprivation. It has got to be one of the all-time greatest torture mechanisms. And as torture techniques go, it's a classic. Up until recently it was even standard practice for the US military. They said it was humane. I suppose since nobody lost a drop of blood in the process it makes sense they would spin it that way, but I can tell you flat out, it's far from humane.

The sessions would go on for weeks sometimes. They'd starve the prisoners so hunger pangs would build and their stomachs would bloat. Chained up by the wrists and ankles wearing nothing but a diaper, they'd force them to listen to the theme song from Barney or Sesame Street or some equally sadistic children's show at a deafening volume.

If I had a choice I'd rather they put the thumb screws to me or yank out my toenails, because this…this staring at the ceiling all night, this watching the blue neon of my bedside clock endlessly flip the minutes by, this dull headache that builds with every hour I fail to doze off, this fog brought on by the overdose quantity of sleeping pills I've been taking (which have been completely ineffective), the ants under my skin; all of it is driving me nuts. I can't help but think about her. I'm plagued by regret, regret for what I was prepared to do, and perhaps regret for not doing it.

Was it the right thing to do? The less I sleep, the harder it becomes to reason it out in my head and the more I just want to find Anne Goodwin and save her from herself.

I roll onto my side and return to the staring contest I'd been engaged in with my alarm clock for the past three nights. Time heals all wounds, they say. *They* are some dumb sons of bitches. Time just mutates wounds. Time twists memories until what you once thought was righteous you now question, and tomorrow, you condemn.

But I have to sleep. *Can lack of sleep kill you?* If I wasn't so goddamn tired I'd get out of bed and look it up.

My eyes burn from refusing to blink. I wipe away the tears and shift my gaze to the book on my bedside table. The only thing Anne Goodwin left me. If I'm not going to sleep, I may as well read.

I sit up, pick up the book, and turn on my bedside lamp. Its black leather jacket is scabrous. Not exactly comfortable in one's hands. Why would anyone choose to bind a book like this? Still, there's an allure to the whole package—the age-old bindings, the antiquated print, the ancient language, the nonsensical enumerations…

Grant's black book. When I found it by the well I initially considered tossing it in. Why I'd kept it, I can't say.

The page is still dog-eared where I left off.

A wisp of smoke rises from the heart of the wasteland; a sinewy trail that dances in defiance of the winds that rage, scattering ash and silt and choking dust across this vast plateau.

And though the battlefield is centuries cold, ere remains revenants of antiquity, still alight with soft gleeds and augural memories, crying hark to days of night when the sky filled with flame and leprous forms carried through the shadows.

Back to a time when man and beast shared skin and a hunger to lay the land desolate.

Now alone upon these hollowed shores, the headland battered by tempest winds and angry seas, a churning fury in effigy of the hatred spent on the long dead. But a visage of those who once stood upon these cliffs, ghosts of yore who bled their brothers in the name of forgotten relics, chasing an impossible dream.

For now no mark of man remains; just blasted, havocked, razed lands. My feet fall upon ash and ebon sands. Yet still I know what meets my steps—a million final breaths. And with each step a hunger swells, a hunger to hold that which burnt these lands.

Upon the tumulus mound, suddenly it's there at my feet, then in my hands, now held high before my very eyes. No breaths pass through me, I am in awe of its magnificence, and though its once brilliant form is long disfigured, beneath its blackened husk I know its true splendor beats at its dark heart.

Cold are its remains. My prize holds no value amongst the dead. It holds no power over these razed lands—not any longer.

Still, it is my prize and mine alone.

Its jagged husk cuts deep into my fingertips. My blood is lost to its charred skin. So thirsty, it steals away a part of me, and though heavy and burdened, twisted and cursed, I cannot resist feeling its weight upon my brow.

I place it upon my head.

The world takes its final breath.

Special Thanks

I'd like to give a special thanks to E.G Sergoyan, author of *The Gathering Place, Stories from the Armenian Social Club in Old Shanghai*, and Robert Holt, author of *A Plea in the Darkness*, for their help in making this book a reality. Their scientific insights as well as their critiques were invaluable in ensuring the accuracy of the technical content and the quality of writing.

Made in the USA
Charleston, SC
08 December 2015